A CHANGE IN DESTINY
DARK CHOICES

JANET K. SHAWGO

Black Rose Writing | Texas

©2023 by Janet K. Shawgo
All rights reserved. No part of this book may be reproduced, stored in a retrieval system or transmitted in any form or by any means without the prior written permission of the publishers, except by a reviewer who may quote brief passages in a review to be printed in a newspaper, magazine or journal.

The author grants the final approval for this literary material.

First printing

This is a work of fiction. Names, characters, businesses, places, events, and incidents are either the products of the author's imagination or used in a fictitious manner. Any resemblance to actual persons, living or dead, or actual events is purely coincidental.

ISBN: 978-1-68513-335-1
PUBLISHED BY BLACK ROSE WRITING
www.blackrosewriting.com

Printed in the United States of America
Suggested Retail Price (SRP) $21.95

A Change in Destiny, Dark Choices is printed in Minion Pro

*As a planet-friendly publisher, Black Rose Writing does its best to eliminate unnecessary waste to reduce paper usage and energy costs, while never compromising the reading experience. As a result, the final word count vs. page count may not meet common expectations.

Author photograph by Heather Eubanks-Westerfield, Sweet Jeans Photography

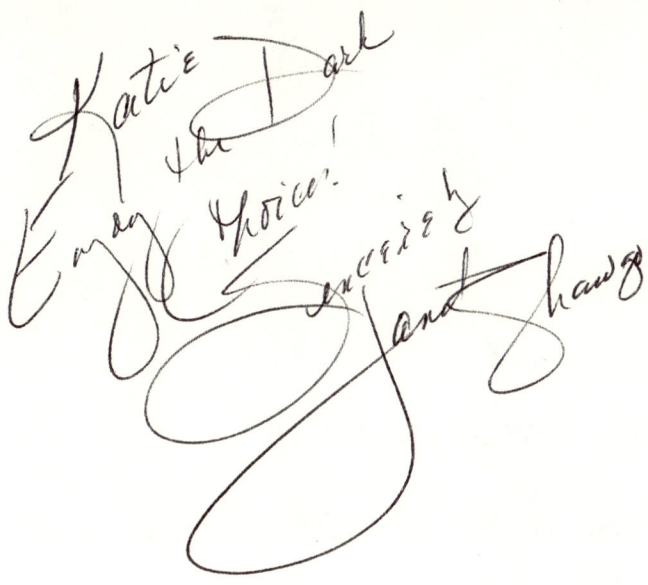

To those who dream, never give up on what you desire.
It's out there waiting for you.

ACKNOWLEDGEMENTS

On the road as an author, I have been fortunate to have the best family and friends to travel with me.

I want to thank my twin sister Joan Acklin, who never gives up on me and never stops torturing me on edits and rewrites, every last one of them.

Authors Michelle Rene and J.L. Yarrow, who have stood beside me with constant encouragement, raising me up and pushing me forward when I started to waver.

To Rosemarie Masetta, who has seen this novel go through multiple transitions to its final form, reminding me each time not to give up because it's a good story.

Reagan Rothe and his staff, who believed in this book, and gave me the opportunity to be part of Black Rose Writing, thank you.

My gratitude to the beta readers, my word keeper, Diane Garland and many followers who have supported me toward this moment.

A CHANGE IN DESTINY
DARK CHOICES

CHAPTER ONE

Pig Farm
Wyoming
November

Darkness can seep into the mind and soul of a person at any time and change them forever. Charlene (Charlie) Edwards couldn't remember which psychology book she had read that statement from, but it couldn't be any more poignant than at this moment. She never would have believed love could turn this black and bond family in its transgression.

She pushed away the grim thoughts tromping through the mud and muck towards the last pig pen. A breeding sow named Blossum rooted in the empty feeding trough. Her twin sister, Dani, warned this particular animal could be aggressive when it came to food and to be cautious. Charlie thought the name of the animal seemed odd and the spelling incorrect until her sister explained the sow had been named after the owner's mother. They spent all morning feeding what seemed like hundreds of pigs for Dani's friends. After this experience, pork would no longer be on her diet forever. She poured a bucket of slop over the fence, backing away from the splatter.

The sound of a truck made her turn around as it pulled up to the outhouse. Her sister advised the outdoor toilet was a temporary situation due to a financial misunderstanding between the brothers and the plumbing company.

Dani walked around to the tailgate, pointing. "Do you need to go in here before I start this?"

"No!"

Charlie leaned against the wooden fence and watched her sister pour bucket after bucket of thick ooze down the hole. She turned around and looked at the hog gobbling down the food.

"Blossum, can you tell me how my once perfect life came to this?"

The sow didn't answer, but the memory of the past year replayed in her mind like an old black-and-white movie from the 1940s.

The one where the young couple contemplates a life of happiness, but somewhere along the way tragedy strikes and dreams fade. She smiled, remembering those movies usually had a decent ending. It was probably because the women never murdered their husbands.

• • •

May
Six Months Earlier
The Woodlands, Texas

Charlie cringed at the sight of the Mercedes still sitting in the garage. She glanced at the bloody scrubs and decided to disrobe before entering the house. Last night had been a long and violent one in the city of Houston, especially for her as an investigator for the medical examiner's office. Jon disliked her coming home in work clothes, and she didn't wish to argue with him this morning. She pulled a pair of sweats from the trunk and quickly changed before entering the house.

"Charlie!"

She bit her lip. "Yes."

"Are you in your work clothes?"

"No."

"Come upstairs," he told her.

She walked up the stairs to their bedroom. "What is all this?"

Jon exited his bathroom, placing a gold Rolex on his wrist. "Charlie, why must I continue to explain how my shirts are to be hung?"

The twenty shirts she picked up yesterday from the cleaners had been pulled from the plastic bags and thrown across the bed and floor.

She glanced towards him. "I was in a hurry and it slipped my mind."

He reached out pulling her into his arms in a tight embrace, kissing the top of her head. "We've been married long enough for you to know that I won't accept those types of excuses."

"Jon, you're hurting me," she said, and stepped away from him. "You aren't the only person in this house who works. If you're unhappy, maybe you should drop your clothes off at the cleaners to make sure they're done to your specifications."

He smiled. "Maybe I should, since my wife can't seem to do something so simple. Why don't you try once more and see if the cleaners can get it right this time?"

"Not this time, you do it." She started towards the bathroom when he grabbed her arm and shoved her hard against the bedroom wall, slapping her.

"Why do you make me do these things, Charlie? You will take the shirts back to the cleaners and have them laundered properly. Do it today," he said, then picked up his jacket, and left the bedroom.

She leaned against the bed, waiting until the door to the garage slammed before moving to the window. A drop of blood fell on her hand as the white Mercedes backed out stopping long enough for Jon to glance up at the window. As the car disappeared, she closed both eyes and remembered the warning her mother once gave.

"Charlene Leanne Parks, never let a man hit you. Once you allow it, he will never stop."

She looked at the clear blue sky. "I'm sorry, mama. I should've listened."

Charlie wiped away the blood and walked into the bathroom to assess the damage. The cut on her lip appeared small this time and would be an easy fix. She pulled up the sleeves of the sweatshirt and looked at the yellow bruises on her arms. Anger replaced feelings of hurt and disappointment for allowing this situation to escalate. Her parents raised strong women, who accomplished their goals even when the odds were against them. The mental and physical abuse Jon inflicted continued to increase with even the slightest resistance.

She once suggested they separate and quietly divorce. His response to this was a weekend of social engagements showering her with gifts in front of his parents and business associates, assuring everyone of a solid marriage. When they were alone, his physical actions became a constant reminder divorce would never be an option. Her confidential conversations with lawyers confirmed any proceedings would be costly and lengthy, with the outcome not in her favor. The publicity of a divorce in the "Edwards Banking" family would be unrelenting in every Houston newspaper, something his family would not accept or tolerate. She knew this situation would not improve, only deteriorate, which gave her few choices.

She walked downstairs to make a cold pack for her lip, discovering her work bag had been thrown on the floor with the contents scattered. Charlie found her cell phone and called the one person who would help at any cost. Her hands shook as the number rang over and over before someone answered.

"Charlie?"

"I have to see you," she said, choking back the tears.

"I'll be there tomorrow."

CHAPTER TWO

Estes Park, Colorado
Danielle (Dani) Emory Parks, thirty-two, walked out into the Colorado morning light, filling her lungs with the fresh smell of pine. She enjoyed the peace and quiet, waiting for her foreman to arrive at the farm. The hardest decision today was which smelled better, pine trees or coffee? The final answer is both. Over the last five years, she had built a good life in the Estes Park area after leaving Texas for Colorado. Her move to the mountains proved to be the correct choice, although it kept her and her sister Charlie apart. Until her sister's marriage, they were inseparable.

She thought back on their lives and parents who provided a home, food on the table, and clothes to wear. Their father worked long hours as a mechanic in the local garage in town, making a livable wage. They had a mother who stayed home taking care of the family, occasionally taking in clothes for alterations. Dani remembered her mother's skill with just a portable Singer sewing machine on the kitchen table. The money she earned helped to supplement a tight and sometimes stretched home budget.

They knew any college aspirations would be through hard work and good grades. Their model builds of five-foot-seven and one-hundred and thirty-five pounds gave them an edge. They had beautiful long auburn hair and amber colored eyes, with a cat like glow. Their mirror image and unique attributes were noticed by an agent from a well know modeling agency in Houston. They were offered a contract with the possibility of international travel. Though their parents knew this would be an exceptional opportunity, they objected because of their age and naivety.

Dani took a job at the local meat market, where she became a skilled butcher. Charlie opted for a job in the town's only bakery. Her sister's cake decorating skills brought orders from Galveston to The Woodlands, giving their little town some notoriety. Even working part-time during high school, they maintained high-grade averages, helping them procure grants and loans. In order to save money and continue working, they attended a junior college, moving on to Sam Houston State University.

Dani shook her head, thinking of how much both accomplished on little money and long nights of study. Their respective degrees made it possible to achieve good-paying jobs and Dani to move forward with a Master's Degree in chemical engineering.

She walked back into the house to refill her coffee cup and glanced at the photograph of her parents. It was taken the Christmas before their accident, the last one of them as a family. Dani remembers their father tearing up the day they handed them the keys to the rented motor home for a well-deserved vacation. Dani told Charlie this was the least they could do for all they'd sacrificed for them. What should have been a fun, relaxing trip ended in death and grief. The final report from the insurance investigator advised a manufacturing flaw had been responsible for the accident. Dani contacted a good friend to represent them in the lawsuit. She remembered the day they were taken into a large conference room where the company's corporate attorneys waited.

"We are very sorry for your loss," the spokesman for the company said, pushing an envelope across the table.

Their attorney opened it, taking a few moments to observe the amount on the check. She turned towards them and nodded.

Dani regretted not saying something, though it would not have brought their parents back. The same year, her sister's fiancé broke off their engagement. A short time later, Charlie became engaged to Jonathan Edwards. His proposal seemed a little quick, in her opinion, but it seemed to fill an empty place in Charlie's heart. Dani never felt comfortable around him, and after more than one argument with him in the first year of their marriage, she moved to Colorado for her sister's sake.

She spent months researching the area for the best location and crop that would flourish and withstand the weather. Hemp ended as her top choice, with its ability to produce well and multiple applications. Dani discovered this product could be sold to companies making foods, medicines, clothing, and more.

Her realtor discovered a small farm outside of Estes Park and when she made an offer, the owner quickly accepted. The rest, as they say, is history. Dani became successful with the hemp crop and developed a personal line of products for men and women, from hair care to face creams. The income from these sales and her side butchering jobs helped during the early years between growing seasons. What started in her tiny kitchen progressed to the garage because of the needed space for the increasing orders for products. The hair colors were so popular she had a problem keeping up with demand in town.

Dani could have used the money from the lawsuit and made life easier, but that wasn't her way. The sound of a horn brought her back to focus as José Herrera drove his older blue Chevy pickup through the front gate. She walked back outside and remembered how he helped plant the first acre of hemp. A knowledgeable man, a hard worker, and a good friend. The pickup rattled as he pulled up in front of the house. She laughed as he exited, turning back and cursing in Spanish.

"Good morning, Miss Dani," José said.

"Morning José, coffee?"

"Sí, please," he said.

Dani disappeared for a few moments before returning with his coffee and her cell phone. She could smell the scent of breakfast burritos before getting into the truck.

She settled in the front passenger seat, smiling at José. "Chorizo this morning?"

"Sí, and bacon. Where's Koda?" José asked.

"I'll have one of each," she told him, then rolled down the window and whistled. Dani pointed out the front window. "He's coming."

"Did you get the report on what type of dog he is?" José asked.

She nodded. "The lab report said he is half pit bull, a fourth Labrador, and some shepherd, hence the longer snout."

José reached into the small cooler, removing two burritos as the dog jumped in the back of the truck, shaking it. "My wife is a very good cook."

Dani unwrapped one, opening the window in the cab, allowing Koda to stick his head through. "I love these," she said, biting into the first one.

"I think Koda wants one," he said, and patted the dog's head before starting the engine.

"He's already been fed, so the answer is no."

Koda whined at her.

"Go," she told him and closed the window.

"He is such a big, mean-looking animal, no one would believe he runs from the cats in the garage," he said, laughing as they drove towards the fields.

"I run from the cats in the garage. The only person he has ever growled or snarled at is my sister's husband," she said, and opened another burrito.

José raised his eyebrows. "You know, dogs have a sense of people."

"So I've been told." Dani remembered the morning she found Koda sleeping on her porch. People dumped animals all the time outside the city and she felt that was how he ended up on her door. He was just a puppy, skinny and in terrible condition. A fast trip to the vet in town saved him. She knew he would never be a lap dog, but proved to be a gentle giant and fierce protector. This earned him the name Koda, which meant friend.

"What's on your mind, Miss Dani?"

She held up the burrito. "You know, I've tried to make these burritos, but they never turn out like your wife's. I can't replicate the smokey flavor or spices."

He smiled. "Family secret. Miss Dani, my brother wants to know if you would process a deer for him?"

"Is his wife making tamales this year?" she asked.

"Sí, Sí, every year."

"Tell him fifty dollars and five dozen tamales," she said.

"Thank you, Miss Dani," he said.

When she first moved to Colorado, Dani knew it would take time before she would see profits. She diversified the money from the lawsuit and received an occasional dividend check, saving it for retirement or future land acquisition. The small building at the edge of her property provided an area for her to butcher meat with the few upgrades she'd added. The last two years of processing had been for herself and friends. The building showed wear because of the harsh weather and she felt this would be its last year. The feel and smell of earth in her hands was preferable, compared to the stench of slaughtered animals.

"Miss Dani, why are you not married?" José asked.

She smiled because this conversation always came up around this time of the year. "I've been a little busy, so not a lot of time to check the dating websites."

He looked at her and laughed. "You should go out, and have some fun, the work is getting harder for you."

She opened another burrito. "I'll think about it."

As they pulled up to the fields, Dani's phone began to play *Bella Donna* by Stevie Nicks, Dani frowned. "Well, this is interesting."

"Problem, Miss Dani?"

"I'm not sure, it's my sister."

"I'll wait in the fields for you, Miss Dani." He stepped out shutting the door. "Come, Koda."

She nodded, watching him and the dog walk away. It had been almost two years since they'd seen or spoken, other than an occasional text. Jonathan began his disdain for her when she insisted Charlie have him sign the prenup. What belonged to Charlie financially from their parent's death was hers, and no reason for him to claim any of it.

Dani remembered how agitated he became over signing the papers, but agreed because of his love for Charlie. She found it suspicious he didn't require Charlie to sign one because of the Edwards' vast fortune from a long family lineage in Houston. Her visits deteriorated as following his instructions or demands, like a lap dog was not within her makeup. Dani's last trip to see Charlie ended badly when she noticed his increasing verbal abuse to her sister. Their last conversation flashed forward.

"Danielle, in this house you speak when spoken to," Jonathan told her.

"Outside this house, Smith and Wesson will do my talking. You would do well to remember that, Jon," Dani responded.

The sound of her sister's voice and a simple request were all the detail Dani needed to know a bigger problem existed. She would go without hesitation.

"I'll be there tomorrow." Dani ended the call and walked out to join José, her boots sinking slightly into the mud. The fields look good, and hopefully, the farm would have another good harvest.

"Miss Dani, if the weather is good this summer, we might get eight feet on growth this year."

"I would go for that height since I'm considering a contract with a food company."

"It might be tight with two company orders to fill, but we'll make it work for you," he said.

"We'll need to make every plant count this year, more work for everyone."

"I'll see it's done right," he said and smiled.

Her farm hadn't progressed to the point of needing equipment, so the fields were harvested by hand. A tedious process, and one which provided jobs in the area. "José, I need to be gone for a few days. I'd appreciate it if you'd check the house, feed Koda, and handle any business until I return."

"Is everything okay? Nothing serious, is it, Miss Dani?"

She smiled again, thankful for his friendship. "No. It's personal business."

"I'll take care of everything for you. Maybe Koda can come home with me."

The dog barked and wagged his tail in approval.

"Give me a few moments and then meet me at the truck." She walked away, making a reservation on a flight out of Boulder arriving in Houston the next day for breakfast.

CHAPTER THREE

Status

Jonathan Styles Edwards III, thirty-four, drove out of the exclusive neighborhood in The Woodlands entering the I-45 ramp heading towards downtown Houston. He glanced at his right hand at the blood, then reached for a Kleenex to wipe it off. A moment later, he squeezed the steering wheel with both hands until his knuckles turned white.

"Why can't she just do what I ask and not question me? Jesus Christ, we've been married long enough for her to figure it out. I'm in charge of our lives, not her," he shouted.

These situations wouldn't be happening if he wasn't married. Jonathan longed to be single, enjoying the life he had before Charlie. The never-ending parties, drinking, drugs, and a different woman every night are a constant reminder of the prison he endures daily. If it had not been for a few indiscretions which ended in the newspaper, he might still be single. His father could no longer hide his philandering ways and gave him two options.

"You have embarrassed the family and bank for the final time. You will find and marry a decent woman, maintain a stable home life or live as a penniless playboy. The decision is yours."

In the beginning, Jonathan thought of defying his father, but knew no other job would pay the salary he received from Edwards Bank and Trust. Unfortunately, the women he associated with were not the quality his father would accept. His fortune changed when Charlie called him one day crying on his shoulder about the breakup between Brian and her. The three were close during college, although she was definitely not his type. He agreed to meet with her and talk. Jonathan realized she would be the perfect answer to his problem. Within six months he proposed and laughed, remembering Brian's face when Charlie announced their engagement. Jonathan added to the insult and asked Brian to be his best man.

Married life for him wasn't easy in the beginning, though over time he went back to the old habits. Charlie became the acceptable wife his father required. In the beginning, she seemed awkward at large social engagements, but with his guidance adjusted properly. Jonathan hadn't planned on her having a strong work ethic or money. He needed a wife to be completely dependent on him for control and manipulation. The inheritance from her parent's death was signed away in a prenup, something he regretted at this moment. He knew she would never willingly give him the money, and only her death would allow him to control it.

Jonathan weaved in and out of traffic, ignoring the honking of horns by other drivers. Slow drivers and the incident at the house delayed his usual early arrival at work. This concerned him with the constant scrutiny he'd been under since requesting to be considered for promotion and transfer to the bank's recent acquisition in California. An advancement like this would assist with the little side venture in Las Vegas.

He smiled as the phone rang. "Lon, give me good news. I need to be uplifted this morning."

The voice on the other end laughed. "Wife or girlfriend giving you problems?"

He ignored the comment. "Did they accept the offer?"

Silence. "We need more capital."

"Send me the amount. I'll do what is necessary."

"We don't have a lot of time. They aren't willing to wait much longer."

"See if they will give us six months."

"You're pushing it, and them. The money we've given isn't refundable," Lon reminded him.

"Just get them to agree to the extra time. I'll take care of the rest."

The call ended as he drove into the underground garage, parking in his reserved spot. He took a deep breath and leaned back in the seat thinking about the conversation. Everything that mattered to him depended on this promotion and transfer. He stepped out and locked his car before entering the elevator. When he reached the sixth floor a young woman looked up and smiled as the door opened.

"Good morning, Mr. Edwards."

He stopped at the desk. "Good morning, Jordan. Will you please find me another shirt and go downstairs for my usual from Starbucks?"

"Right away," she said, handing him several envelopes and messages.

Jonathan entered his office, removing the tie and unbuttoning the Armani shirt.

The door to his office opened. "I see the cleaners failed to press your shirts correctly," Styles said.

Jonathan turned, facing the man who expected him to carry the Edwards legacy into the future. Three generations of the Edwards family guided the bank to where it stood today, they were leaders, politicians, and ruthless financiers. He and his father stood six-foot-three, giving them a commanding presence when entering any room. His father's hair had faded from their dark brown to gray, but the eyes, still a deep brown. Jonathan's opulent lifestyle increased his weight to almost two-hundred pounds a decent twenty pounds heavier than Styles.

"No, father, they didn't, but it isn't completely their fault. My wife cannot keep her work and married life responsibilities straight."

Jordan entered with a fresh shirt on a hanger and his coffee.

"Can Jordan get you something to drink, father?"

"No, thank you." Styles waited until the secretary left, then sat down in one of the leather chairs. "Is she new?"

"She's been here six or seven months. My last secretary left when her husband transferred to Florida. Is there a problem?" he asked, changing shirts.

Styles leaned back in the chair. "No, not with your choice of employees. I am disappointed your home situation isn't stronger at this point."

Jonathan knew where this conversation intended to go and needed to stop further criticism. "I'm working on the problem you seemed to be concerned about."

"You never should have allowed her to continue working after you were married. It seems to be an obstacle and gives Charlene too much freedom from your necessary directions."

He finished knotting the tie, sitting down at the desk. "There is a plan in motion."

"What seems to be the issue? She doesn't need the money."

Jonathan leaned back in the chair. "No, it isn't money. I offered a proper and generous allowance to run the house if she would stay home and not work. She doesn't want my money."

"I have another question."

"About Charlie?"

"Yes. Can you explain why she has an account at one of our competitors?"

"The bank is one her parents used for years. I didn't see the harm and allowed it. I doubt there's enough money in it to drive across town."

"And the money from the lawsuit?"

"To my knowledge, it has been invested. The prenup I signed keeps me from inquiring."

Styles intertwined his hands. "The prenup you signed, on her terms, was a mistake. Your assumption she doesn't have money is another issue."

"Her paycheck from the city goes to that account. I am aware of what she deposits, and it isn't enough to be concerned over."

"How are you dealing with her job at the medical examiner's?"

He shook his head. "Distasteful. I have stopped any discussion of it in my presence or social gatherings."

"Our friend in the district attorney's office praises her work. He said she is an invaluable employee of the city. Abe always asks about you and it's important to keep our powerful friends close. I'd like for you to join me on my visits to his office."

"Agreed."

"I appreciate your immediate intervention in her appearance and clothing choices, averting further embarrassment to the bank. Being contacted by a board member's wife advising of her inappropriate and unkept appearance in public was unnecessary. If you had been doing your job as a husband, the incident would never have happened. I would have thought Charlene knew as your wife, she represents you and this bank."

"Charlie would be happy wearing jeans, a t-shirt, and tennis shoes every day. The personal stylist I hired chose a line of designer clothing from lingerie to footwear. All of her previous personal clothing has been removed from the house. A photograph is text to me before she goes out in public for approval, except for work. The dead do not care about proper makeup or hairstyles."

Styles nodded. "Stay on top of this situation. We can't afford any further incidents." He stood up and looked down at his son.

"Is there something else bothering you, father?"

"You understand the importance of how a man runs his home. It speaks to his ability of how he handles his employees and business."

"I assure you every facet of my work and home life is being properly attended to. A horse will eventually break and allow a rider to mount it. Charlie is heading in the right direction."

Styles nodded. "Good. It would disappoint me to know a simple domestic issue prevented further advancement with the bank. Your mother had a strong will at the beginning of our marriage. I took the time to guide her in the proper direction. At the end of our first year together she understood her place in public and the home. You seem to be taking an unusual amount of time to correct a simple issue."

"Unfortunately, times have changed since you and mother married. Law enforcement and the media were easier to control. If not handled in a slower, methodical manner, a slight indiscretion could become front-page news. The issue will be corrected."

Styles nodded. "Agreed. Progress has not been kind to those of us who hold to a harsher form of instruction and compliance. I look forward to the adjustments you've set forth."

"You understand the most important priority to me is the future of this bank."

"I'll see you in my office at eleven. We have a meeting with the mayor at noon, then drinks and dinner with him and the district attorney at six."

"No wives tonight?"

Styles shook his head. "Business."

Jonathan stood as Styles left the office. This day had gone from annoying to disastrous with the context of his father's visit. The message was clear control your wife or lose the promotion. His father's subtle threats were not to be taken lightly. In the past, Styles purposely denied him a promotion. This action was to prove who had compete and total control over every facet of the bank and his life.

He thought about the Nevada project, hoping there would still be time to meet the financial demands. When the cell phone on his desk vibrated, Jonathan smiled at the text Lon sent advising he would meet with the parties involved to discuss the extension.

He stepped out to Jordan's desk. "Please contact the Golden Nugget in Lake Charles and reserve my usual suite for the weekend."

Jordan nodded, never raising her head. "Right away. Your wife is a lucky lady."

"She works hard for the city, and it's always a pleasure to surprise her with these little unexpected weekend trips." He returned to his desk, pressing an icon on the cell phone.

"Happy Companions, this is Laney. How can we help you today?"

"I have a standing request associated with this number. Three nights at the Golden Nugget starting tomorrow evening, six-thirty," he said.

"Yes, sir. Red will be available for you. Are there any changes to the card we have on file?"

"No." He turned around, leaning against the credenza and closed both eyes. "Someone who listens obeys and is totally submissive, everything my wife isn't."

CHAPTER FOUR

Friday
The Plan
Charlie locked herself in the downstairs bedrooms and parked her car in front of the neighbor's house after work. It had been a light night at work and returned home around eleven p.m. She knew Jon would be out late after the text stating his meeting at the club turned to business and wives weren't invited. The last thing she wanted from him was drunk sex or being abused because of his inability to perform after indulging in alcohol with his father at the club. When the kitchen door opened at two in the morning, she prayed he would remember the comment about going into work. The fact he didn't call out or search for her meant he was too drunk to care.

The sound of him moving around the house this morning woke her. She lay in the bed, waiting until he left the house before opening the door. Charlie went upstairs to dress, picking up his clothes thrown on the floor before making the bed. As she began to leave the bedroom she stopped and turned around, leaning on the wall. How had Jon conditioned her so easily? Why did she allow this subservient situation to persist? It had to stop.

She went downstairs, made coffee and baked so Dani would have something to eat after a night flight. The first text from Dani indicated the plane landed, the second displayed a mad emoji. The next message

          Hertz due to a shortage of cars.

        a pan of scones from the oven as a horn honked in front
       Charlie laughed knowing the neighbors would complain

to Jon later. She opened the door to the sight of a small red sports car at the curb and ran out the door, embracing her sister. Charlie tried not to cry, but the tears came anyway.

"I didn't think you were the sports car type."

"Damn rental companies never get anything right."

"You must have hustled to get a flight," Charlie said.

"I could tell it was important. Charlie, it's been too long." Dani released her sister and stepped back. "Jesus, sis, you're pale as a ghost."

Charlie laughed. "Not a lot of sunshine in the morgue. I've missed you."

"Ditto."

"Who's watching Koda?"

She laughed. "José took him home. I hope he still has a wife when I get back."

"Come inside so we can discuss my problem."

Dani dropped a small bag at the entry. "It's taken you long enough to realize, **He** is the problem."

"My life has changed so much over the last two years and not for the better," Charlie said.

"I can tell by your statement my opinion of Jon as a decent human being is not going to change from zero."

Charlie poured cups of coffee for them and pushed a plate of warm blueberry scones in front of her sister.

Dani raised her eyebrows. "This must be serious if you made me scones."

"I never have the chance to cook or bake like I once did."

"Doesn't Jon eat?"

"My schedule and his don't always allow for dinners at home very often. He doesn't seem to think I can cook, and most of what I bake is taken to work or thrown out."

Dani took a bite of the scone and closed her eyes. "You haven't lost your touch. You were Mason's best baker at the Morning Glory."

Charlie leaned against the back counter. "I loved it there, except having to show up at four-thirty in the morning on the weekends."

"If you get tired of dead bodies, Estes Park needs another bakery." She finished the scone and reached for another. "Do you want to tell me what caused the phone call?"

She opened the cabinet, pulling out a bottle of Bailey's and placed it in front of Dani. "I know you didn't want me to marry Jon."

Dani opened the bottle, pouring a healthy amount into her coffee cup. "Why are you stating the obvious? He proposes to you after only six months of dating was my first concern."

"It wasn't as if we didn't know one another. We'd all been friends for some time."

"I remember the type of women he went out with, and you weren't his type back then. What changed?"

"Age, maturity, I can't answer your question," Charlie told her.

"The money from the lawsuit seemed to be a good incentive to me. It's the reason I insisted you get the prenup, more coffee, please."

"That money is a fraction of his family's worth."

"Ah, true, but he doesn't control his family's wealth, does he?" Dani asked.

"No. You're correct."

"Charlie, stop stalling. You didn't have me fly out here for scones."

She nodded and walked over to the refrigerator, opening the bottom freezer drawer, removing a padded envelope. "I have been collecting information over the last two years."

"I assume a lock box in the attic wasn't an option?"

Charlie frowned. "I've been moving it from one part of the house to another, concerned he might find it. I need you to take it back to Colorado with you."

Dani emptied the contents on the breakfast bar, scanning the photographs and reports from the private investigator. "I'm surprised you found someone brave enough to do this."

"I hired someone from New York, expensive, productive, and didn't give a damn about Jon's status in Houston."

"I see he has a taste for redheads and long weekends in Lake Charles. You realize this doesn't mean much in his circle," Dani told her.

"True, but his new secretary seems to believe he is taking me on all those trips. Jordan and I have become good friends over the last few months having a couple of Saturday lunches at the club. She is happy to talk about being his secretary."

"I hope this is going somewhere."

"It is, just give me a little leeway here. I've discovered through these lunches Jonathan has asked to be considered for a promotion which will include a transfer to California."

"He hasn't mentioned this to you?"

"No."

"What else?" Dani asked.

"Two years ago, Jon began to make little comments regarding my job taking too much time away from him. He complained about my appearance and choice of clothes. I ignored him in the beginning."

"But."

"One morning I came in from work to find all my clothes gone."

"What do you mean gone?" Dani asked.

"Gone, as nothing except scrubs for work in my closet. Everything down to my lingerie had been replaced with expensive designer labels."

"His explanation for this invasive act?"

"It seems someone of importance at the bank observed me out in distressed jeans, an inappropriate t-shirt, a messy bun, and no makeup. Someone made a complaint directly to Styles. Apparently, Jon was given a directive to change my embarrassing appearance."

"And does the fashion police have a name?"

Charlie shrugged her shoulders. "I don't have a clue and Jon didn't tell me. I have been instructed not to leave the house without being presentable."

"What the hell does that mean?"

"It means no more ragged jeans or messy buns, and a full face of makeup anytime I leave the house except for work. A photograph must be sent for approval before leaving the house."

Dani rubbed her face. "You aren't serious?"

"He insisted on a reduction of my work hours in order to be seen with him at all official matters. As the wife of a bank's Chief Financial Officer, I needed to be at his side."

"I can guess what caused the call yesterday." She pointed to Charlie's lip.

Charlie pulled up the sleeves of her sweater, revealing the yellow bruises. "These are from me questioning his work trips. Yesterday's argument happened over his shirts not being pressed correctly by the cleaners. It isn't just the physical abuse, the mental stress is becoming unbearable."

"Did you tell him to complain to the cleaners?" Dani asked.

"I did. Then explained if he didn't like the way the cleaners pressed them go and tell them himself," Charlie said.

"What did he say?" Dani asked.

"You see what he said, with his hand," Charlie said.

The silence in the kitchen was deafening. She watched Dani refill her coffee cup. Charlie knew what her sister would say next.

"You remember what mother always told us."

"Yes, the reason for my call," Charlie said.

"What else has happened?" Dani asked.

Charlie pulled out several pages of text messages. "Do you remember Lonnie Walker?"

"How did you get those?"

Charlie held up a hand. "Don't ask."

"Okay, yes, I remember him, Ray Walker's son. His father spent more time in the county jail for being the town bookie and drunk than at home. I felt bad for him, terrible home life, the other kids at school making fun of his clothes because they were old or hand-me-downs."

"I remember Dad buying him a new pair of shoes. He couldn't stop smiling when we gave them to him."

Dani smiled. "What's the interest in him?"

"It appears Jon and he are involved in some kind of deal in Las Vegas. The best I can figure is they are trying to buy a casino."

"Jesus, how are they financing something like that? And how in the world is your husband and him mixed up together? They aren't on the same social scale."

Charlie shrugged her shoulders. "I have no idea. Did you know Lonnie became a big-time gambler apparently making enough money to survive?"

"News to me, I figured he ended up like his dad. I know one thing Styles will not involve himself or the bank in something like a casino. What about your joint accounts?"

"Jon handles our major finances, house payment, and bills. Until now, there has been no reason to be concerned. I checked the joint account and found no irregularities. Thankful, he has no access to my personal account at our old bank," Charlie told her.

"Any inquiries about your inheritance?"

"No."

"The prenup is solid. There are only a couple of stipulations that allow him to access the money," Dani said.

"I cannot and will not be involved in his deals or continue to be abused," she said.

"You could divorce him," Dani said.

"I threatened to leave him a few months ago."

"What did the bastard say?" Dani asked.

"I am his property and would remain so, there would never be a divorce."

"He called you property."

"Just like a car or piece of furniture. It took a while to find an attorney I could trust about a divorce," Charlie said.

"Were they any help?"

"She listened to me and said a divorce would be lengthy and expensive. The plethora of attorneys his family has on retainer would make sure I lost everything. If the wrong judge presided over the case, the prenup might become an issue. I could lose part of the inheritance," Charlie said.

Dani stared at her sister. "You're holding something back what is it?"

The two stipulations on the prenup for him to get the money."

"You either give it to him, or you die," Dani said.

"I think he is going to kill me or have me killed," Charlie told her.

"Did your investigator find any proof or is this one of your feelings?"

"Common sense, if he receives this promotion we will be moving. He will cloister me away from my friends, and you. I doubt he will allow me to work, which means I become a full- time trophy wife. I believe he will show me off for a few months then I will suddenly become ill and be sent somewhere to convalesce."

"Then I will hear of your sudden death."

Charlie nodded her head. "All nice and neat, with a quick burial or cremation."

"I've heard enough. You need to just fucking kill him."

"I intend to, but need your help," Charlie said.

"You're serious."

"I am. Dani, I will not become a submissive trophy wife living on booze and pills like his mother."

Dani turned on her cell phone checking the calendar. "Do you have a timeline?"

"When is harvest?"

"Fall."

"It will need to be after your workers are gone. Do you still have your meat processor?" Charlie asked.

"Yes, but building needs repair. This will be my last fall to butcher and process deer for my friends. I'm too busy with the farm."

"You know what I have in mind?" Charlie asked.

Dani held up a hand. "Is that the garage door?"

Charlie looked at the clock on the stove. "I guess he's leaving town early."

Dani shoved all the papers and photographs back into the envelope. "Good, it will give us all weekend to plan his demise."

Charlie replaced it in the freezer. They watched the door open and Jon entered stopping as his eyes landed on Dani.

"It's been a while, Jon. What no hug for your sister-in-law?" Dani asked, holding out her arms.

Jon smiled, looking pensive at Charlie. "I wish you had called sooner to let us know you were coming. I'm afraid I cannot entertain you this weekend, bank business in Lake Charles. Charlie can take you to the club for dinner, I assume you brought something appropriate to wear."

Dani smirked at him. "I'm sure my sister and I will be fine without your wit and charm to entertain us. No need for an expensive meal at your club when a Sonic is a couple of blocks away."

"Sweetheart, could I speak with you for a moment?"

"In just a minute," Charlie said.

"I'm afraid it can't wait. You understand Danielle being a businesswoman," he said.

"Of course, Jon, and that would be a successful businesswoman."

"My mistake."

"I'm right behind you, Jon."

Dani waited until he left the kitchen. "He will not abuse you while I'm in this house. If he touches you, there will be no need for a plan. I will kill him."

"He won't as long as you are here, can't afford to have a witness."

Dani nodded.

He called out again. "Charlie, I need your opinion."

She returned a few moments later. "He wanted to know how long you would be staying?"

"Did you tell him as long as I damn well please?"

Charlie smiled and moved closer. "I told him you didn't say for positive how many days. His business trip will be all weekend which means he won't be back until Monday."

"He's being extremely accommodating."

"This works to my advantage as I go back to work Monday night." Charlie placed a finger over her lips as the steps on the stairs announced his return.

"I'll be home Monday after work." He kissed Charlie on the forehead. "Dani, enjoy the weekend."

"Why, that's almost human of you, Jon. I hoped we might continue our in-depth discussion from the last time I visited," Dani said.

"You have me at some disadvantage since it has been a few years. What discussion would you be referencing, we've had so many memorable ones?" he asked.

"The discussion of how women are inept and incapable of survival without a man to manage their lives," Dani said.

Jonathan straightened his posture. "A discussion for another time."

Charlie locked the kitchen door behind him as he left and snickered. "I will hear about your comment for weeks."

Dani waved a hand toward her sister. "Good riddance."

Charlie refilled their coffee cups. "Now, sit down and let me tell you, what I have in mind."

CHAPTER FIVE

Decisions
Monday
Jonathan opened his eyes and stared at the ceiling shortly before the alarm on his cell phone buzzed. He reached over, turned it off then lay back facing the ceiling thinking of the past few days. Surprises and disappointments of any kind had always been things he detested. The sight of his sister-in-law standing in his home compared to discovering dog crap on new shoes. He tolerated her most of the time and happy she moved away to the farm. Dani's last visit almost two years ago ended in an unpleasant confrontation between them.

"Danielle, if you will just see this from my side. A farm like yours is a large project and you should have a man overseeing the day-to-day business," he told her.

Dani stood up facing him. "I find that comment strange coming from a pansy-ass playboy, who has never worked a day in his life except to lift a pen."

"Charlie, I believe your sister doesn't respect my experience in such manners as business," he said.

"I don't respect you at all, and before you say another word, there is a gun in my truck."

The woman threatened him on more than one occasion with bodily harm and that time he requested she not return. Thankfully, he had kept their disagreements within his house. The one thing Jonathan didn't need was his father discovering he couldn't control two women. He knew the only reason Dani would return would be if Charlie invited her. Any discovery of an invitation without his approval would mean Charlie will wear long sleeves all summer.

Jonathan moved up in the bed realizing Dani's appearance wasn't the only issue he needed to deal with this weekend. He stood up and walked into the center room where the naked body of a tall redhead lay across the murphy bed. His sexual expectations were high when it came to spending money on escorts. He would demand full reimbursement for her failure to service him due to an overconsumption of liquor and cocaine. His body reacted with her movement on the bed and if time had allowed would have taken what was owed to him. Jonathan turned away knowing this would be his last encounter with Red. He picked up his clothes and walked into the bathroom splashing cold water on his face.

He needed to put any thoughts of Dani or Red out of his mind. The casino needed to be his foremost priority.

"Damn bitch, if she would just give me the money," he whispered.

"What's wrong, baby?" Red asked, entering the bathroom.

He looked into the mirror at her naked body standing next to him. "Nothing you would have the intelligence to understand."

She shrugged, sliding away to turn on the shower. A moment later she wrapped her bruised arms around his chest. "A quick shower with me this morning?"

He ignored her offer and dressed. "I'll pass on the last-minute offer."

"Your loss," she said, walking into the shower.

He waited until the steam covered the shower door. "No, your loss permanently."

Jonathan did not leave his usual tip for acceptable service. She needed to understand failure had consequences. He called the valet for his car then picked up the Armani jacket and left. Normally he didn't stop at the front desk, but the clerk motioned to him.

"Good morning Mr. Edwards was your stay satisfactory?" the desk clerk asked.

"Is my car waiting?" he asked.

"I believe it's being brought to the entry, now. How would you like to handle the bill?" the clerk asked, pushing a piece of paper across the desk.

"Bill?" Jonathan asked, surprised at this statement. "This casino has never presented me with a bill."

The clerk took a moment before speaking carefully. "Unfortunately, Mr. Edwards, you did not meet the minimum in the casino this visit. I'll be happy to call the manager if you wish to speak to him."

"No, that will not be necessary. I just need to check the charges," he said, then removed six one-hundred-dollar bills from his wallet and threw them on the desk.

"Thank you, enjoy your day, Mr. Edwards."

Jonathan walked away leaving the twenty dollars owed to him. This was a small reminder to spend less time in the room on his next trip.

"Good morning, sir. Your car is a beauty," the young man opened the door holding out the keys.

"Yes, it is, a piece of machinery you'll never have the opportunity of owning," Jonathan said, palming the valet a five-dollar bill. He placed the Mercedes in gear, driving away.

"You rich asshole," the valet said, flipping him off.

Jonathan ignored him and headed toward the expressway, thinking about his present circumstances. He needed more money, the appropriation of funds at the bank could not be hidden forever. Charlie's inheritance would be helpful, and the one way to get it would be if she died. He picked up the Ray-Ban sunglasses and the right lens fell out in his lap.

"Damn it," he said, throwing them out the window and then screaming at the car call system. "Call Charlie!"

"Hello."

"I hope you had a pleasant weekend?"

"Actually, it was, Dani left this morning."

"I'm on my way back to Houston and have dinner plans with father at the club. I suppose you're working when you should be at my side."

"They're short-staffed tonight and I've been asked to work. I'm not interested in another dinner and night of boredom listening to your father," she said.

"We'll discuss your comment about my father another time. Do not come home again without showering," he told her disconnecting.

He knew Charlie's attitude and response were connected to Dani's visit, a problem to be corrected later. The phone rang, showing Lon as the caller.

"Jonathan, we might have a break here."

"Tell me, because my weekend has been a total waste of time and money."

"They've agreed to an extension."

"How long?"

"The money must be in their hands by January first. Failure to do so will forfeit all funds and no further transactions will be accepted."

"I'll have it," Jonathan said, disconnecting.

He knew the promotion and transfer to California would only be one part of succeeding with the Nevada project. In order for him to meet the demand for full payment, his beautiful wife would need to meet with an unfortunate, fatal accident. Such an incident needed to be public or the involvement of a third party to keep his hands clean.

He smiled at the thought of her falling off a mountain on a ski trip or being kidnapped due to his family's wealth, tragically being killed before the money could be delivered. Maybe a small town out of state where the local law enforcement is poorly equipped for a kidnapping, but perfect for an obvious accident. Both scenarios would need a ploy one he could easily arrange like a trip to celebrate his good fortune. This would be exactly what they needed to rekindle and soften their strained relationship as of late. The perfect plan is to become the grieving widower and slip back to his playboy life after the funeral.

• • •

Las Vegas
Lonnie Walker walked out into the sunlight searching for a place to sit down and smoke. His hands trembling as he lit the cigarette. Jonathan was placing him in a bad position with the hierarchy of Vegas and this experience would not be repeated. He replayed the scene over in his mind once more to make sure he understood what they were now committed to finishing.

When Lonnie entered the casino on the strip, he moved to the first elevator where a guard stood and presented a passcode allowing him to enter. The floor number was pressed by the guard and a keycard was inserted before the doors closed. On the way to the floor, he thought about the opportunity to be part owner in a casino. It seemed a good investment at the time. As a partner, Jonathan appeared to be the perfect man to make it happen. Lonnie had always been in good standing but asking for extensions on a contract could be dangerous with these individuals.

When he walked off the elevator another guard direct him to a room down the hallway. Lonnie hesitated then knocked.

A man opened the door and smiled. "Come in Lonnie, I thought a more casual setting would be appropriate."

"Thank you, Mr. Caccia" he said entering the room looking for more bodyguards.

"Drink?"

Lonnie cleared his throat. "Whiskey, please."

"Max, call me Max. We've known each other long enough for you to call me by my first name."

Lonnie took the drink. "Cheers."

"Salute," Max responded. "Sit so we can talk."

"Have you considered the request?"

"I have, though my associates are not inclined to give you more time. Do you believe your friend will have the money?"

"Yes."

"Then I will put my name on this extension. You understand this is the final exception on payment to this contract. There will not be another if you miss the deadline. Everything promised will be forfeited."

"I understand, we understand," Lonnie said.

"Call your partner and let him know. Put it on speaker."

Lonnie nodded and gave Jonathan the good news about the extension then hung up. "Problem, Max?"

"Not at all I like to know how my words are explained. You're blunt and to the point. I like that about you, always have."

"I won't take up any more of your time," Lonnie said and stood up to leave.

Max walked him to the door and shook hands. "It's just bad business to allow anyone to back out of a contract."

Lonnie finished the cigarette and closed his eyes knowing exactly what forfeit meant. He had always loved everything about Vegas never regretting his decision to move there and make gambling his profession. Until the money was ready to be delivered, he needed to leave and stay out of sight. Maybe a trip home and renew old friendships, find someone who will let him hang out for a few weeks maybe more.

He looked at the phone. "Time to get rid of this."

CHAPTER SIX

The Perfect Job

Their weekend had been too short, and the goodbye bittersweet this morning when Dani left, but they knew it would not be forever. Charlie's plan would be risky and a lot of work for both over the next few months. In order for this to succeed each step was crucial. She spent the rest of the morning cleaning the house before leaving for work, so Jon would not have any complaints. As she left, the new organic cleaner filled the air with the scent of frankincense and myrrh, giving a peaceful feeling.

The drive into work felt lighter for the first time in a year and she smiled as the doors to the locker room opened. Charlie listened to the Stevie Nicks station on Pandora through the new wireless earbuds a gift from Dani. The whiteboard in the hallway overflowed with the names of bodies waiting to be autopsied, including several John Does. She made note of her assignment, which autopsy room, and grabbed personal protective equipment.

The forensic investigator's job for the Houston medical examiner's office meant everything to her. The feeling of accomplishment and recognition of her work was something Jon could never understand. He had been given his job, where she fought to get hers. Charlie entered the examination room to a cool blast of air and bright lights gleaming off the metal table. The body of a well-built middle-aged man lay naked, gray, and mottled. She picked up the file from the counter, quickly reading over the report from Houston Police Department. The body had been discovered early this morning in one of the canals. She moved to the table taking time to distinguish the brown water from dark blood around his mouth and nose. The smell of alcohol appeared to be present, though not overwhelming. She completed pre-autopsy photographs and fingerprints, taking time to look at the man's clothing. Everything was wet and needed to dry before a detailed check for trace evidence. She jumped when someone touched her on the shoulder, turning to see Dr. Ginger Harrison pointing to her ears. Charlie turned off her phone, placing the wireless earbuds in the pocket of her lab coat.

"Sorry about that lost in the music," Charlie said.

Dr. Ginger Harrison was one of the newer Medical Examiners with two years of experience in Houston. She had been born in Ireland, raised by an Irish mother and an American father. They moved to the States so she could attend college and go to medical school. She decided to become a medical examiner and eventually found her way to Houston. Her small build, green eyes, and fiery red hair made her a formidable opponent in court and a stickler for the proper procedures at crime scenes.

Ginger smiled. "Not a problem. Who do we have the honor of autopsying today?"

"Meet John Doe #35."

"Thirty-five, you say. I think we are lower this year than last of John Doe's."

Charlie couldn't believe this woman could remember last year's numbers. "I can't say for sure, but can check the computer for you."

"That isn't necessary, I just know the numbers are down this year. Would you be kind and collect the vitreous fluid for me?"

She laughed and took the syringe, placing a large-bore needle on the end. "Still can't do it. What did you do in medical school?"

"I had a friend like you who helped me out," Ginger said and winked.

"How nice."

"Of all the things I do, this one minor procedure makes me want to run screaming out of the morgue. At least I have you."

Charlie changed positions to the victim's head, opened his eyelid, and slowly inserted the needle. She placed the fluid in the proper container and correctly identified it for the lab.

"Anything else I can do for you, Dr. Harrison?"

"It's Ginger. We've worked together long enough that I believe first names are appropriate."

Charlie smiled at her. "I'll do it when we're alone, but not around official ears. My mother wouldn't approve, she always said to give respect when it's due. The MD and ME behind your name demand that."

"Thank you, but please, call me, Ginger. Let's get busy with John. Did you and Jonathan do anything fun over the weekend?"

"He went out of town, bank business."

"I wish we'd known you were free. We had a busy weekend in the city, any chance you might work a few extra shifts this week?"

"I'll make it happen for you," Charlie answered.

"Are you sure? The newspaper's social page said your calendar might be full," Ginger said.

Charlie lowered her head pretending to be interested in the body on the table. "Jonathan never misses an opportunity to be in the spotlight."

"You looked lovely in Sunday's society section of the newspaper, dinner with the mayor, money for the new cancer wing at Children's Hospital, and opening night at the theater. I don't know how you do it."

"I would trade it all to be back in the field," she said sadly, then looked at Ginger.

"You will always be my favorite here and I miss your thoroughness at crime scenes. I've never seen an investigator who has a gift for discovering evidence."

Charlie waved a gloved hand at her. "Stop, you're making me blush."

"It's true and you know it. I'm not observing any external indications for his untimely demise. If I'm unable to find anything on physical examination, toxicology may give us the answers. Charlie, pass me a scalpel."

She took a position across from Ginger as the Y incision was made causing her nose to wrinkle beneath the mask.

"Goodness, the alcohol is stronger now that you've opened him up," Charlie said.

"We'll check the blood level." She took a moment and checked the man's throat. "This is interesting, there is swelling here," Ginger said.

"I don't see any bruising."

"It could be due to some type of anaphylaxis then he slipped and fell into the canal."

"Ginger, aren't some reactions immediate, causing death?"

"Yes, although I don't believe this is what may have happened in this case."

"But we can't make assumptions," Charlie said.

"Correct, this could have been an accident as I said earlier or someone helped him."

"In my forensic classes the instructor kept reminding everyone there is no perfect crime," Charlie told her.

"It's funny how people think they can commit the perfect crime, especially now with all the techniques for discovering evidence. Science has and will continue to change the way we deal with crimes."

"Criminals forget there is always something left behind."

Ginger laughed. "And they can't keep their mouth shut."

CHAPTER SEVEN

Family Disappointment
Tuesday

Jonathan watched the traffic on I-45 from his office window drinking an afternoon latte. The deadline on the casino seemed to be always on his mind, along with keeping the bank transactions hidden. The board had been meeting all morning making the final decision on who would be promoted. He couldn't believe his future hinged on a handful of old men and a wife who couldn't adjust to his needs. Maybe his father was right, he'd been too lenient with her training.

The door opened behind him. "Mr. Edwards," Jordon said.

He didn't turn around. "What is it, Jordon?"

"Your father is asking for you to join him upstairs."

"When?"

"He said now," she answered.

He nodded. "Thank you, please inform him I'm on my way."

"Yes, sir."

He took a deep breath. The excitement he should feel didn't seem to be there, just dread. A question of whether he would be honored or disappointed lay in the hands of his father. He threw the latte in the trash and replaced it with a glass of Scotch, quickly drinking the amber courage. Jonathan placed his jacket on, smoothed, and buttoned it.

"Best face forward."

Jonathan left the bank driving toward The Woodlands after being given the rest of the day off by his father. The scene about to take place at the house played over in his mind. He entered the silent house frowning as it meant she was still sleeping. A smile crept across his face as he walked into the bedroom standing over her. He would finally have the upper hand and complete control over his fate and her. The next moment he threw open all the curtains allowing the sun to fill the room.

He turned to face the bed. "Charlie! Wake up."

She sat straight up in bed blinking both eyes. "Jon, is something wrong? What time is it?"

He ignored the questions. "Are you working tonight?"

"No."

"I would like for you to get up and come downstairs with me."

"Why?" she asked, frowning at him.

"I will not ask you again," he said, leaving the room.

"I'll be down in a few minutes," she said.

He walked downstairs and into the family room, opening the doors to the bar. He poured a drink as she entered the kitchen in a long robe.

"You couldn't bother to dress?"

She walked to the Keurig and started a cup of coffee. "You didn't give me much time. Isn't it a little early for Scotch?" she asked, turning back toward him.

He downed the drink and could feel the heat rising in his face. "I have some news for you, but there are a few things we need to discuss first."

"What is so important we need to do this now?"

He crossed the room and grabbed her by the arms, shaking her. "Why do you always have to question everything I say?"

"Stop! Jon, let go of me. What the hell is wrong with you?"

He let go of her and stepped back. "Why was Dani here? Did you invite her?"

Charlie rubbed both arms staring at him. "Dani surprised me. Jesus, Jonathan! I haven't seen my sister in nearly two years."

"Whose fault is that?"

"Yours and Dani's, damn it. Neither of you can be civil to the other. I have a right to see her."

"I hope you two enjoyed yourselves."

"We did, not that you care." She turned around and walked away, to put distance between them. "Why are you home this early?"

"The bank recently acquired another property. The opportunity for promotion was presented to four individuals. You are looking at the new bank president of that acquisition. A unanimous decision among the board members according to my father."

She turned away picking up the cup of coffee. "Jon, this is wonderful news. Is the bank local or in another large city, Austin or Dallas?"

He smirked. "No, this bank is in California. I take full management of the facility the first of the year."

Charlie turned around. "California?"

"San Francisco to be exact, a beautiful city. You'll love it there."

She walked to the island putting down the cup. "I do not understand why you would consider an out-of-state promotion without discussing it with me. This affects me, too."

He struggled to keep his emotions under control. "I would have thought by now you'd realize it is my profession, not yours, that is our future. We will go where the money and advancements are best for me." He walked over to the island preparing for her next statement.

"I'll check with the medical examiner's office—"

"No!" He slammed his hand on the marble top.

Charlie backed away. "Why can't I have a job?"

Jonathan pointed a finger at her. "No, you will no longer stink of the dead. Your one and only job will be to dress appropriately, entertain my guests, and pleasure me."

"Where will we live? There is so much to do, our home."

He closed his eyes. "Charlie, please stop talking. Father and I will fly the company jet to see our new acquisition in two weeks. He is arranging for us to meet with a realtor and look for houses. We will be there two maybe three weeks."

"I'll go with—"

Jonathan laughed interrupting her and shook his head. "I do not need you to do anything except follow my orders from this point forward. I'll decide what will be acceptable for a new home. Father has agreed to sell the house after we move."

"Then the decision is made," she said.

"Yes, and you will accept it without question. Any comment coming from you will be positive."

"I think there is a bottle of champagne in the refrigerator, we should—"

He held up a hand. "We are expected at five-thirty for drinks, and dinner with father. The board members and their wives will be attending. Charlie, I do not want to hear one damn word about your disgusting job."

"What if someone asks?"

He shook his head. "Not one word, do you understand?"

She nodded.

Jon walked back to the bar pouring another drink. "Go shower and dress, I want you to wear the red Armani dress and shoes that match."

He turned around watching her walk away. A moment later he headed towards the stairs.

"Sweetheart don't shower just yet. I have something to give you."

CHAPTER EIGHT

Colorado
June
Monday

Dani leaned against the porch railing listening to her dog snore, concerned with all the things to accomplish besides the fields and harvest. The hair product orders increased substantially from the two shops in town, selling faster than she could produce without help. She stepped off the small wooden porch, turning back to view the house. Koda raised his head for a moment then laid it back down.

The small dwelling was originally built as a hunter's cabin according to the realtor five years before she bought it. The owner had taken great pride in building a sturdy structure to withstand the winters. Though perfect for one person to live in, she outgrew it rapidly. For now, it would be fine and most of all the haven Charlie would need.

She received a card from her sister with children's stickers inside nothing more. They used to do these types of messages as kids to avoid parental scrutiny. A plane, the number eight and three. Today was the eighth, so Charlie would be in sometime after three today. She replaced the card in the envelope striking a match, burning it just as José pulled up to the house. He held up a white sack from one of the local bakeries, smiling.

She walked to the truck opened the door and smiled. "Is your wife mad at you? No burritos this morning?"

"She went to see her sister in Denver. No luck with your lottery tickets?"

She laughed. "You mean the usual burning of the losers? One day I won't burn them. Is your wife's family good?"

"Sí, no problem. She went to visit and will be home in a couple of days."

"José, tell your brother I need the deer early if he can get one. I don't want to be processing late this year."

"I will, Miss Dani. Your building does not look good."

"It may be my last year to butcher and process."

"My brother will be sad to hear this. You do the best job and the others don't barter for tamales," he said, laughing.

"The farm is doing well and my hair products are becoming popular at the local shops. I don't see how it's possible to continue processing. I'll speak to Walter, the butcher in town to see if he will give your family a discount next year."

"Thank you, Miss Dani."

"I want to check the fields and stop by the processor. If it needs some repairs, I'd like to get them done before September."

They drove out, taking time to check the growth and well-being of the plants. Her order for new saws and blades, including the motor for the pulley system would arrive soon. She'd been out twice since returning home, checking on all the machinery inside. They walked through the building, making note of several missing boards and two holes in the roof. The permits were still hanging on the wall though she didn't know how. Hopefully, there wouldn't be a surprise visit from an inspector before repairs were made.

"Miss Dani, you need some work done out here pretty soon. I have a cousin who can make these repairs."

She looked at the roof. "José, bring him out here this weekend and make a list of supplies. I'll contact the hardware store to let them know he'll be in and to charge my account."

"I don't think it will take him long to fix all of this," José said.

"It just needs to stand up long enough to get through this season. If I had used metal instead of wood or located it closer to the tree line, it might have weathered the winters better," Dani looked at her watch.

"We need to head back in, my company should be there. You'll have to do without me until next Monday."

Dani noticed him smiling as they drove up to the house. She didn't want to disappoint him, and the charade would serve a purpose.

· · ·

Charlie walked into her sister's house after kneeling down and allowing Koda to smell and lick her several times. She immediately made a pot of coffee and changed into a pair of Dani's jeans and a T-shirt. She opened her suitcase removing a new pair of Skechers smiling as her feet slid into them. As the front door opened, she spooned a dollop of whip cream on top of the coffee handing it to Dani.

Dani coughed slightly. "I see you found the Jameson, but where did you get whip cream?"

"I stopped in town and would have been here sooner, but everyone kept asking about the farm and my clothes. I said everything is wonderful at the moment," Charlie told her and laughed.

"It's a good thing you'll be here a few days. I don't want to explain the huge diamond you're wearing. How was your flight?"

Charlie reached into her purse and pulled out an envelope. "Good. Thanks for purchasing the ticket and rental car."

Dani shrugged her shoulders opening the envelope with repayment in cash. "What choice did we have? Besides, I knew you were good for the money."

"What did you tell your foreman?"

"He thinks I have a man here. It's best if he doesn't see you until later."

"I agree."

Dani added more coffee to the Jameson. "Nice tan."

Charlie rubbed her arm, holding it next to Dani's. "Not too bad for just three weeks of tanning. I'm using a tanning accelerator to catch up with you."

"Do it soon, wearing long sleeves in the summer is going to kill me. Did you get the hair products?"

"Yes. I love them."

Dani leaned against the counter. "I assume there's an issue or you wouldn't be here. You haven't changed your mind, have you?"

Charlie gave her a no chance in hell look, which Dani knew well. "I need to catch you up on a few things since your visit."

"The floor is yours."

"We didn't see each other for a couple of days. Apparently, the woman in Lake Charles is a scratcher, this is the first time I've noticed marks."

"I'm surprised he allowed evidence. Do you think it's the same woman?" Dani asked.

Charlie shrugged. "It's the same cheap cologne."

"Bastard," Dani said, moving to the couch.

Charlie took the hint and followed her. Koda took his place at the end of the couch. "Two days after you left, he came home early one afternoon and woke me after a dreadful night of work, with important news that couldn't wait."

"He's giving you a divorce?"

"A divorce would be nice, but no. As I expected he received the promotion and we are being transferred to California after the first of the year," Charlie said.

Dani leaned back into the couch, sipping coffee. "I see a problem with that decision as he will be dead."

Charlie laughed. "It's been difficult to play along since I already knew. He couldn't wait to tell me all about my new job as the trophy wife. His father has finally given him the praise and acknowledgment he always wanted. The two of them have been in San Francisco for over two weeks. I was able to make the trip because he sent a text, saying they would be delayed another two weeks."

"He seems to be accommodating us nicely to complete his murder. You called all of it."

"He knows I will comply at first but eventually rebel, the abuse will escalate."

Dani rubbed her forehead. "We'll need to rearrange a few things, but I think we can still make it work."

"Dani, we have to make this work. I refuse to be a prisoner and end up like his mother."

"I've got a lot to do before you arrive with him. The processor needs some repairs, thankfully José has family who is happy to help. If I can make it through one deer and Jon, then the weather can have it."

"I'm afraid much of this plan is falling on your shoulders, I'm sorry," Charlie said.

"It will get done one way or another. The good thing is harvest will be over and the workers will be gone until next year. I usually take a fishing trip so a visit from family will not seem suspicious."

"Did you buy the equipment we talk about?" Charlie asked.

"No, our initial conversation and plan sounded good, but I realized explaining a large purchase for bone disposal would be questioned especially if I stopped butchering meat."

"Since you don't seem worried, I presume you've discovered another way to get rid of his body," Charlie told her.

"I have been researching another option with less problem and easier disposal."

"Do you want to elaborate?"

"Not at the moment. I'm still working on the details," Dani answered.

"What did you do with the package I gave you?"

"I mailed it to a friend of mine for safekeeping," Dani told her.

Charlie looked shocked. "Aren't you worried they might open it?"

"No, attorney, client privilege. I promise you it is in safe hands and locked away."

"Okay, I trust you and whoever this person is. Do you want to tell me anything more?"

"No."

She frowned at Dani.

"Let it go, Charlie."

"You aren't going to tell me, are you?"

"No."

"Alright then, were you able to find a suitable house for me to rent? No one would ever believe the three of us stayed here for over a week," Charlie said.

Dani nodded. "I found three. We'll run out tomorrow and look at them. You need to decide soon because the company requires a deposit with the reservation. They provide everything including bathroom amenities. These places are huge, like his ego."

Charlie nodded looking down into the coffee cup. "I worried you wouldn't help me. If this goes wrong, we're both going to jail for life."

"I've wanted to kill him several times since you married him. Love is blind, which never allowed you to see him for the complete narcissistic asshole he's always been. You're my sister and I care about your happiness. It's the reason I have stayed away. Charlie if we don't do this, he will kill you."

"I regret the last two years. It has been miserable, but no more," Charlie said.

"How do you intend to get him to the farm? He will never come on his own accord."

"I've spoken to Styles about a huge celebratory party for him at the club and we agreed on a Halloween date. It will be a grand affair, one for the society page. Jon will become his usual obnoxious drunk self, requiring help to the car. Once he passes out, with a little help from Ambien, I'll drive to Colorado," Charlie said.

"Basically, you're going to drug and kidnap him. Does his family know about the disagreements between Jon and me?" Dani asked.

"Oh no, he could never admit his inability to control you. The Parks' family is not a topic of interest to the Edwards' and I've never mentioned any of these issues with anyone."

"Good to know. One less worry about your trip out here."

"It will not be an issue," Charlie said.

"What's your story for his family?" Dani asked.

"Over the next few months, I will become the submissive and demure wife. Once we leave, there will be some texts sent. I'll use his computer to email information to his secretary. These notifications will say he's decided to take a couple of weeks off with his beloved wife," Charlie said.

Dani held up a hand. "Stop, I may vomit."

"If there are unanswered phone calls, I'll blame it on the spotty coverage in the mountains," Charlie said.

"How will you explain his absence when you return?" Dani asked.

"I haven't made a decision, still working on two options."

"You need to remember the GPS will be checked," Dani said.

"Cell phones can be traced," Charlie said.

"Not if you don't turn them on. I'm working on a few things for sisters to do the first week you are here. We'll mention Jon when we go into town, buying presents for him and to-go meals. He must have the appearance of presence," Dani said.

"There is a possibility the SUV will need to be detailed after I arrive."

"We can't clean it up too much, it needs to show you two were active in the car afterward. I suggest spilled foods and liquids, including liquor," Dani said.

"I'm positive the SUV will be impounded and processed when I return. It might as well be interesting. A clean, detailed vehicle will be a huge red flag," Charlie said.

"Sis, I'm going to change the subject for a minute. Why do you and Jon have two completely separate bathrooms? Most couples share one."

"The house was built to his specific design to include the two separate bathrooms in the main suite. When I questioned him about it, he said sharing a bathroom in college had been a disgusting experience and swore he would never share one again."

"So, no showers or long baths together?"

"Oh yeah, all done in my bathroom, never his."

Dani grimaced. "Who cleans the damn thing?"

"He does."

Dani laughed and shook her head no. "I don't believe you. The great Jonathan Styles Edwards III lowering himself to scrub a toilet or clean the shower."

"Well, he does. I made the mistake of entering one day to clean it. He went into a rage, forbidding me to enter his private bathroom again."

Dani didn't speak for a moment. "He's hiding something."

Charlie shrugged her shoulders. "Whatever it is, someone else will have to find it."

"We should have done some snooping when I was there."

Charlie shook her head. "I prefer not to know, especially now. The police can open Pandora's box."

"One more question," Dani said.

"How am I going to kill him?" Charlie asked.

"Yes."

"I'm going to put him into anaphylactic shock."

"Jon has allergies?" Dani asked.

"Just one," Charlie said.

"What?"

"Vodka."

"Does he wear a necklace with a tag on it? I've never seen an alert bracelet."

Charlie shook her head no. "There is no tag or bracelet and never will be any type of alert."

"That isn't very smart, since you aren't with him twenty-four hours a day."

Charlie nodded in agreement. "I begged him to buy something or have it made the first year of our marriage in case I wasn't with him."

"What were his reasons?"

"According to him, any type of imperfection is a sign of weakness and now his obstinance is to our advantage."

"Why?" Dani asked.

She smiled at her sister. "We are the only two who know. What smells so good?"

"Roast. It should be about ready. I don't know about you, but all this talk of murder has made me hungry."

"Did I see fresh bread rising?"

"Mom's recipe."

Charlie stepped over to the refrigerator tapping the door. "I see you're still wasting money on these silly scratch tickets."

"You'll change your mind when I hit a big one."

CHAPTER NINE

Acceptance
September
Friday

Summers will fade away in most places, except in Houston. Since Jonathan's announcement, he spent more time in California and less at home. She and Styles spent a great deal of time together planning the perfect farewell celebration. Thanks to Jon's father the entertainment and media attention would be the best Houston could offer. With a little over seven weeks left it was time to reveal their plans and secure his approval. Charlie knew with his father's involvement he would accept the celebration, giving his blessing.

She walked to the staircase, and took a breath, calling out to him. "Jon, I need to speak with you downstairs."

"In a moment."

"I'll be in the kitchen."

She placed several items he would consider important considering his ego and allure toward gaudiness. His acceptance and input were key to her success with the party. He entered the kitchen with his suitcase, moving to the island.

He picked up the invitation. "What's all this?"

"Your father and I know how much you hate surprises. I spoke with Styles regarding a celebration honoring your promotion and transfer to California."

"When?"

"Your father reserved the club for Halloween," she said and held her breath.

"Why in God's name on Halloween and a Friday?" he asked.

"If we wait, the holidays will be upon us. Your father thought you would be pleased to have your friends available to congratulate and wish you well," Charlie said.

"He believes there will not be an issue with it being on a Friday night?"

"In regard to having an outstanding response?"

"Yes."

"In his opinion, day or date will not matter when it is to praise his son's accomplishments," she said.

He picked up the invitation. "And you are sure father approved all of this?"

She smiled. "He's been on board since I first suggested it."

"Then you can proceed, but I want to see more gold on the invitations."

"Of course, anything else you'd like to add?"

"Make sure you run everything through father. He is to have the final say, understood?"

"Not a problem," she said, gathering up the invitations.

"Charlie, it's time for you to give your notice."

"I wrote my resignation this morning, and discarded my scrubs, shoes, and anything associated with my old job." She could see he seemed surprised.

"Excellent. I'll be back in a week," he said, picking up a suitcase and walking past her to the garage.

She smiled as the door shut and for once agreed with him. It would be necessary for her to be at home working on the party and his death. Charlie moved to the bar and pulled a book out on making cocktails. This evening she would test her bartending skills with the only friends Jon allowed her to have. She needed a cocktail made with vodka and a second liquor to cover the chance he might smell or taste it. To her surprise there seemed to be a large combination of mixtures that would work.

At six o'clock, Charlie smiled at the image reflecting back at her in the mirror. A happier, confident, and nicely tanned individual smiled back. There were no bruises, scars, or missing patches of hair to cover tonight. The front doorbell rang as she placed the diamond Rolex on her wrist.

She took one last look. "Showtime."

The door opened to her friends and colleagues bearing gifts and dressed to the nines. She invited them a week ago to a lady's night out hoping this would soften the news of her departure. Donna Green nurtured and mentored her as an investigator from the first day she stepped into the morgue. Throughout her preceptorship, Donna's guidance made Charlie one of the top investigators at the medical examiner's office. Her promotion to head of the department did not surprise anyone and was well deserved.

Namisha Johnson was one of the best Assistant District Attorneys in Houston's history. The first African American to hold her position and one who rarely lost a case. Namisha is responsible for Charlie's testifying abilities to handle the harshest cross-examinations. Charlie holds her in the highest respect for her position and as a friend.

She held back a tear as Dr. Ginger Harrison smiled at her. She would miss her most of all with that feisty attitude and supportive manner when they worked the worst of cases together. Over the last year, their friendship grew at work through mutual respect. Jon's control and abuse decreased her circle of friends over the last few years, but these women never wavered. They included Charlie in their social activities, keeping her from being totally isolated by Jon.

"Come in, my friends. Let's have a quick drink before we leave," she told them.

They followed her into the family room. She realized how much time had passed since any visitors, besides Dani were inside the house. Charlie pushed back the tears and anger knowing this was another way

Jon controlled every aspect of her life. She couldn't understand how she simply accepted it without question.

"Charlie, your home is stunning. How much square footage do you have?" Namisha asked.

"It's just under thirty-five hundred," Charlie answered.

"Do you have a cleaning service or someone regular you use?" Donna asked, wandering around the kitchen.

"Charlie cleans her own home," Ginger answered.

The room grew silent.

"You do all this yourself?" Namisha asked.

"Since I cut back on my hours, you know idle hands. We rarely use the two bedrooms downstairs. The family room and kitchen are basically what is lived in and the master bedroom upstairs."

"It's beautiful," Donna said.

"It appears you've taken some time to relax in the sun. You look good with a tan," Ginger said.

"At least I don't look like one of the bodies in the morgue anymore. Anyway, I didn't ask all of you here tonight to showcase my cleaning skills or discuss my tan. I have an announcement."

"I think we have some idea of what you are going to say," Namisha said.

Charlie frowned. "I should have known the news would slip out some way. How did you find out?"

"I inadvertently stepped into the district attorney's office one afternoon and overheard Styles discussing it with him. They swore me to secrecy until the announcement is official in what, two weeks." Namisha said.

"Since you know, this explains the rush to make sure my open cases are ready for court. I can fly back anytime you need me," Charlie said, smiling.

Ginger walked over, placing an arm around her. "We are worried about you."

She took a moment to look into each of her friends' faces.

"The scarves, long sleeves in the summer, heavier than usual make-up. We've all seen it before," Donna said.

"I tried, guess it wasn't good enough."

"Why didn't you say something to us?" Ginger asked.

"The situation here is complicated and it's difficult to discuss with your best friends," Charlie told them.

"Then let us help you. Leave him," Namisha said.

Charlie wiped a tear away. "I can't, and please don't ask me any more questions. This is a huge promotion for him, we have to make it work. I do love him."

Donna walked overtaking Charlie's hand. "I want you to file a leave of absence and not resign."

"Donna, that's sweet of you," Charlie said.

"I don't want you to make anything permanent for now," Donna said.

"When will you be leaving?" Ginger asked.

"The plan is to leave after the first of the year. Styles will sell the house."

Namisha turned towards Ginger and Donna, who were wiping tears away. "It appears we will be making some trips to San Francisco."

"You will be welcome anytime. I haven't seen the house though Jon said it's magnificent."

"He bought a house without you?" Ginger asked.

Charlie nodded then proceeded to the bar pouring four glasses from a metal shaker. "No more tears, it's our night out. Tell me what you think of this?"

"A toast first," Donna said.

The four women raised their glasses.

"To friends," Donna said.

They all touched glasses. "To friends."

"This is refreshing," Namisha said.

"I can taste the bourbon, there's something else. What is it?" Ginger asked.

"Vodka," Charlie answered.

"You can't taste it," Namisha said.

"I found the recipe in *Mix-drinks for Dummies*," Charlie told them.

"I like it," Donna said.

"Ladies, we have a seven-thirty reservation at the club. We should go," Charlie announced filling everyone's glass again. "One for the road."

She joined Ginger in the back seat of Namisha's BMW thinking about the mixture of the drink as they drove into town. If Ginger could taste the vodka, it needed a little more bourbon or maybe Scotch. With the severity of his allergy, it would not take much for the reaction she needed. The other option will be to overdose him with Ambien and Xanax. Thankfully, his mother wouldn't miss the bottles she'd taken the last time they visited.

"Charlie, it's a shame you're leaving. I hear someone you know is coming back to Houston?" Donna said.

"Who would that be?"

"Brian Deeds. He is being transferred from Florida back to Texas."

"How do you know him?" Ginger asked.

"Brian was Jon's best man." She turned to look out the side window. "We were all extremely close at one time."

CHAPTER TEN

Uneasy Feelings
A Week Later

Namisha leaned against her hands thinking about Charlie being alone in a new town miles away from anyone who actually cared about her. The early knowledge of Jonathan Edwards' promotion made her uneasy. The moment she shook hands with Styles Edwards in the district attorney's office, her skin crawled. Edwards Bank and Trust held the old money of Houston along with high social status. The power and money Styles waved around appealed to those vying for his favor, but there would be a price to pay. His pompous attitude reminded her of a time when women weren't allowed in private men's clubs. The days of smoke-filled rooms with men playing poker and drinking Brandy, thankfully, no longer existed.

She shivered, remembering the day she met Styles' wife, cowering with each glance or harsh glare, unable to voice or have an opinion. She couldn't stand to see this happen to a friend though it appears Jonathan was following down the same dirt road as his father. He managed to keep his abuse away from the eyes of social media only because of Charlie. Namisha couldn't understand why a bright intelligent woman would accept such torment.

The glass walls of her office allowed her to observe the work floor and avoid surprises. She caught a glimpse of Donna and Ginger waving to her which meant she'd been daydreaming too long. It had been two weeks since the girls' night out, and time for them to help Charlie. She wasn't exactly sure how they planned to do it but felt they must try.

"You were in some serious thought," Donna said, entering the office.

"I hope it's similar to ours," Ginger added.

Namisha nodded. "Give me a moment." She walked past them, leaning over to speak with her assistant who nodded.

"Where are we going?" Donna asked as Namisha returned.

"The Capital Grille on Sam Houston Parkway."

"Why there?" Ginger asked.

"We need privacy, where our presence and conversation aren't circumspect."

"Ginger and I will meet you there," Donna said.

The three left the office together going separate ways to their cars. Namisha made reservations yesterday for them requesting a booth in a back area. She arrived first and waited outside.

Ginger walked up frowning at Namisha. "Isn't Donna here?"

"No. I thought you two were together."

"We took separate cars in case one of us needs to leave. I bet she's caught in traffic," Ginger said, looking around. "There she is."

"Sorry, I had a call that couldn't wait," Donna told them.

The hostess seated them leaving lunch menus on the table. A young woman appeared, introducing herself as Bea.

"Bea, a bottle of the house red wine, three glasses, and three shrimp cocktails. We'll order afterward."

"Right away," she said and left.

"I apologize for ordering, but it will keep her away from the table."

"Works for me," Donna said.

"I love shrimp," Ginger added.

Bea brought the wine, showing it to Namisha who nodded, waiting for a small amount to taste. Smiling, she acknowledged, waiting for her to fill everyone's glass.

"I'll be back with your cocktails in a moment."

Namisha held up her glass. Donna and Ginger raised theirs, meeting in the middle of the table. "Friends."

Bea appeared with appetizers. "Do you wish to wait on ordering?"

"Yes. Would you check back with us in thirty minutes?" Namisha glanced towards her friends who agreed.

The young waitress nodded, leaving them.

"I appreciate both of you taking off this afternoon to join me for lunch."

"It's my day off anyway and nice to be with friends," Ginger said.

"When I asked you to come to the office it was to give the appearance of an official meeting. We know the reason we're here, Charlie."

"Did everyone receive an invitation to the gala?" Donna asked.

"I wasn't going at first, then realized it would be the last time to see her," Ginger answered.

"We all need to be there for her. God knows the man will push her to the side to be front and center all night," Donna said.

"I miss the old Charlie," Namisha said, smiling.

"The one before Jonathan's abuse?" Donna asked.

"She was always so bright and bubbly then slowly it changed. I couldn't understand the reasons until I noticed the bruises on her arms one morning in the locker room. When I touched her shoulder, she jumped away covering her face with both hands," Ginger said.

"We've all seen it too many times. She didn't seem the type to allow his abuse," Donna said.

"Donna, no one wants to be abused. She never would have married an abuser. He's handsome, wealthy, and chose her. The honeymoon period seemed to last longer than most," Namisha told them.

"Jonathan Edwards is like his father. The apple just took a little longer to fall from the tree," Donna said.

"I've been privy to more than one conversation between Styles and my boss."

Donna seemed surprised at the comment. "I didn't think Abe was close to him."

"My boss is a politician."

"Of course, he is," Ginger said, pouring more wine into her glass and emptying the bottle.

"Namisha, I think this may be a two-bottle lunch," Donna said, then waved to Bea.

"Are you ready to order?"

The three ladies nodded, giving their requests to her, including another bottle of wine.

"Any elected official needs financial support. I've never known their relationship to be anything except business. One afternoon three or four years ago Abe divulged Styles once withheld a promotion from Jonathan while still single. It seems his playboy lifestyle wasn't the image Edwards Bank and Trust wished to have in upper management."

Donna ceased eating, placing her fork on the table. "He married Charlie out of necessity, not love."

"It appears he did," Namisha said.

"Who are these horrible people?" Ginger asked.

"Individuals with a lot of power and influential friends," Namisha answered.

"Charlie lives in a prison with her husband as the jailer," Ginger added.

"The day she requested less work time because of Jonathan needing her socially I knew. Control and isolate, one and two of an abuser's play cards," Donna said.

"We've all seen Styles' wife. She is a shell, beaten down," Namisha said, then held her finger up when the server headed towards the table with a tray.

Bea opened the second bottle of wine, filling their empty glasses. "Shall I check back on you for dessert?"

Donna and Ginger shook their heads no to Namisha. "I believe this will be fine. I'll find you when we are ready to leave."

"One check or three?"

"One, my treat today," she said, smiling.

The food at the Capital did not disappoint. Their conversation ceased long enough for the food to be consumed. Bea appeared once more to remove dishes.

Ginger leaned back in the booth shaking her head. "I can't imagine what will happen when she is no longer close to anyone. We're the closest thing Charlie has to a family."

Donna turned to Ginger. "Charlie has family."

Ginger sat up shocked, looking at Namisha who nodded yes. "What family? She told me her parents were deceased."

"They are, but she has a sister," Namisha said.

"Not just a sister, an identical twin named Danielle, or Dani. She lives in Estes Park, Colorado," Donna said.

"She runs a successful hemp farm," Namisha said.

"I didn't see any photographs of her at the house. Thinking back to our visit, I didn't see photographs of anyone," Ginger said.

"The house is a showcase, sterile, complete control of all aspects of her life, including family," Namisha said.

Donna took a moment to search Namisha's face. "You know something else."

"You do?" Ginger asked.

The information she intended to share caused several sleepless nights since receiving the package. They needed to know what she felt Jonathan might be planning for his wife. Namisha reached into her bag pulled out three files pushing them across the table. Donna and Ginger each took one carefully reading the contents. Their expressions were the same as hers the first time she read through them.

"Who gave this to you?" Donna asked.

Namisha shook her head. "I can't say."

Donna raised her eyebrows, studying her friend. "Can't or won't?"

"You didn't pay them, did you?" Ginger asked.

Namisha laughed. "No. Let me say this individual felt obligated to see this information end up in trustworthy hands."

"We need to do something. Can't you do something about this?" Ginger asked almost crying.

"Namisha, what are you planning to do with this?" Donna asked.

She took the files and replaced them in her bag. "According to the law, unless I receive additional evidence or information these are just additional insurance policies."

"There's something else you're not telling us," Ginger told her.

"You think he is going to kill her," Donna said.

Namisha leaned back in the booth, looking out at the bright Texas day. She never turned back, speaking into the clear glass. "It's highly probable."

"Ladies, we cannot just sit here and do nothing," Ginger told them.

"This is the reason you mentioned frequent trips to see her, isn't it?" Donna asked.

Namisha nodded and turned back to face them. "I'm hoping and praying a steady presence around her will deter any plans he might have."

"We can only do that for so long," Ginger told her.

"Then what? Just wait until she disappears?" Donna asked.

"We can't force her to leave him," Ginger added.

Namisha turned back to face them. "Ladies, we, unfortunately, will have to let this play out."

CHAPTER ELEVEN

Colorado
October
Post-Harvest

The bright morning sun welcomed a beautiful Colorado fall day. The crisp clean mountain air, mixed with the changing colors of the leaves added to the celebration about to take place at the farm. She walked outside waving at the line of cars entering the front gate and motioned for the lead car to follow her.

Dani rented a large, enclosed tent for the early morning breakfast, knowing the mountains would be chilly and there would be children present. The tables, chairs, and standing heaters would make everyone comfortable for the workers and their families. This year's hemp harvest is the largest one to date, bringing an increased profit for the farm including the hair and skin products. The work José and his team accomplished made it possible to meet the food company's request and renewal for the next growing season.

Dani looked down at Koda who stood next to her. "Sorry, you'll have to stay inside today."

The dog seemed to understand and walked slowly through the screen door she held open for him.

José and his wife were the first to greet her. "Good morning, Miss Dani."

"Good morning, José. Everything is ready for you in the tent, including warmers for the food," she said.

José turned, pointed, and instructed everyone toward the tent.

"I wish you would allow me to pay for the food," she told him.

"No, Miss Dani. We are honored to bring the food. You do so much for us during harvest," he said.

Dani couldn't have a better foreman. She watched as the women quickly organized the food and lines formed for breakfast. Though she attempted to stop and take something from every pan, it wasn't possible to eat all of it. There would be plenty of leftovers to freeze for weeks to come. The best part of her morning had been visiting with the families, holding babies, and laughing while the smaller children run around playing outside. She found José and motioned for him to come over to where she stood.

"José, I guess it's time to make my speech could you help translate for me?"

"Sí, no problem, Miss Dani."

She walked to the front of the tent. "Good morning and thank you for being here. This celebration is for all of you, even though you did all the cooking."

Laughter came from the crowd.

"With your hard work and long hours, the harvest doubled from last year. None of this is possible without all of you and I am extremely grateful. I have a little something extra for each family. Thank you and see you next year," Dani said, handing José a stack of envelopes. "José, please hand these out."

As the envelopes were given out and opened the crowd grew silent. She could see several of the women crying and many crossed themselves placing hands together in thanks. Dani watched as a group of men gather around José having a conversation and pointing toward her.

He walked up to her. "Miss Dani, the men are asking me to thank you. We will pray for you tomorrow at mass in gratitude."

Dani nodded, not wishing to be impolite, but what lay ahead of her would nullify any prayers they raised to heaven for her. "If you and your brother could stay for about an hour after everyone leaves, I have the meat ready."

"He will be happy and we are both sorry you had to do more work with butchering a full beef. He must go home to Mexico and check on our parents, so he will miss deer season."

"It wasn't an issue."

"I'll let him know," José said and walked away.

Around noon the celebration ended with everyone leaving the farm. She scheduled the rental company to pick everything up at one, making this party nice and simple.

"Miss Dani, we're ready," José said.

"My tamales?"

"Here," Ruben said, handing a box to her. He reached into his wallet.

Dani shook her head no, holding up a hand. "Keep your money, give it to your parents, my gift."

Ruben turned to José. "Miss Dani, it was so much work for you."

"Thanks to you and your cousin the building is still standing. I found someone who will give you a good price to butcher meat next year."

"Thank you. You are too kind," Ruben said.

They drove up to the processor and loaded the meat.

"It's so pretty up here," Ruben said.

"Yes, it is. I'd love to build a home here one day. When I win the lottery, of course."

José walked around the building. "We did a good job on this building, but if there is a bad storm, it will not be here in the spring."

"It may end up kindling for the New Year's bonfire," Dani said.

When they returned, everything was gone and a bill was stuck in her screen door.

"José, I'll be taking my regular trip in a few weeks. I'll need some help with my other products. The orders are going to be too much for one person to fill."

He nodded. "All you need to do is tell me how many workers you need and when. Enjoy your trip and thank you again, Miss Dani."

"I'll try to bring back some good fish for us." She entered the house placing several containers of food and tamales in the freezer. Koda sniffed the air wagging his tail.

"Don't even think about it. Your gut doesn't do well with tamales," she said and patted his head.

She pulled a beer from the fridge and walked out, sitting on the steps, Koda at her side. Once the disposal of Charlie's problem was complete, the equipment would be dismantled and sold across the border in Wyoming for recycling. A few pieces might need to rust away at the bottom of the lake. She'd watched enough forensics shows to know DNA was the key to identification and human blood could be detected on everything. Dani knew the new disposal plan would be the best option for this issue.

She took a long drink of beer thinking of the harassment and publicity Charlie would face. Once Jon disappeared the principal focus of the investigation will be on her sister. The first suspect is always immediate family and that included her.

The phone started vibrating, and she smiled at the caller. "Tim, I was just about to call you."

"How's the harvest this year?"

"My biggest one to date. Are you and Cletus still selling hogs to the rendering plant for dog food?" Dani asked.

"Yep, I have a shipment going out around December first," Tim said.

"I just processed a whole beef and have another one coming at the end of the month. I didn't want to dispose of the organs on my property," she said.

"You can bring it out here, blood too."

"I appreciate that more than you know."

"Don't forget to bring your boots when you come. The pens are pretty messed up right now."

"The smell isn't that great either. The hogs won't have an issue digesting what I bring, will they?" Dani asked.

He started laughing. "No, never had a problem in the past. Hell, hogs have been known to eat a whole man."

"Good to know. What'd you call about?" she asked.

"I heard this might be your last year to butcher. What are you going to do with your equipment?"

"Most of it isn't worth saving. I'll be happy to work something out with you on anything salvageable."

"You going on your trip?" he asked.

"In a few weeks, we'll talk when I get back."

"Sounds good, bring what you need out here when you're done."

"Oh, I do have a favor to ask. Any chance I can borrow those two big pressure pots?" she asked

"Sure, you know where they are. Be sure to bring them back clean when you're done."

"Thanks." She hung up. "Problem solved."

Tim and his brother Cletus owned a hog farm north of Estes Park. The farm is so close to the Wyoming border counties from both states fight every year over the location of the farm. This made jurisdiction questionable and the farm a perfect disposal site. The brothers were moonshiners using the pig farm as a front, serving one hell of a product to customers in both states, and the sheriff. Their brewing setup at the farm appeared less than safe to her, making Dani worry the whole damn place might blow up one day killing them and their pigs.

CHAPTER TWELVE

Trick or Treat

Charlie leaned over the cold marble sink in the bathroom, feeling bile rise into her throat. The freedom from Jon's abuse all hinged on the success of tonight's celebration and her performance. She sprayed a small amount of perfume on both wrists, turning to stare into the full-length mirror behind her. The trembling of her hands made it difficult to latch the diamond earrings, and she worried Jon would disapprove of the snug-fitting black lace dress bought without his approval.

The loving and demure wife of bank president Jonathan Edwards III would play the part tonight, pushing him to the forefront of the celebration and bright lights of the media. She took a deep breath, forced a smile, and walked into the bedroom where he waited.

"You are exceedingly handsome in your new tux," she said.

He frowned, motioning for her to turn around. "When did you buy that?"

"Yesterday, it's a Dior, and on your list of approved designers for me."

He walked over and ran both hands up and down the lace stopping at her hips. She fought the urge to shiver and closed her eyes pretending to enjoy this moment by moaning slightly.

His expression didn't change. "It's definitely not something I would have chosen for you. I suppose it's appropriate for Halloween. You will need to return or dispose of it after tonight. Did the shop return the Mercedes?"

She prepared herself, praying he would control his temper. "We need to take the Escalade."

"You cannot be serious."

"There is a maintenance delay because of a part they didn't have available," she explained, stepping back, preparing for his wrath.

His face contorted for a moment then relaxed. "Well, hopefully, there won't be anyone outside when we arrive. A bank president really should arrive in a grander manner, but we'll discuss this mistake later tonight. You will need to do better, I'm confident with continued instructions you will do just that, get better."

"I'm sorry," Charlie said.

He reached out taking her face. "If it couldn't be avoided, all is forgiven."

Charlie looked at him. "Ask for Robert, he is the service manager, who apologized for not having the part in stock."

"I'll do just that on Monday," he said and released her.

Charlie fumbled with her watch. "We should leave or you'll be late."

He stepped back. "Things will be different after we move to California."

"I know this move is going to be a positive change for both of us."

He turned away from her. "It will be a satisfying change for me."

Jon left her alone in the bedroom. She could hear his footsteps on the stairs allowing her to run into the closet in her bathroom. Charlie checked the small cooler making sure there would be enough ice in it until she returned and took a moment to cover the two prepacked bags with a blanket. After Ginger's comment about additional alcohol present in the cocktail, she found a recipe using Scotch. The one item left would be removing his personal care kit in his bathroom.

"Charlie, where are you?"

• • •

Celebration

Jonathan drove in silence towards Houston, fighting the anger and urge to strike out across the console at Charlie. The constant battle inside him to verbally correct her instead of a physical remedy was taking a toll on him mentally. The continuing disregard of his importance and needs would cease after the first of the year. His immediate desire to release this anger and frustration on some new lovely would not be possible for another week. The Happy Companion compensated him nicely after the incident with Red. They extended access to their associate company in San Francisco where he discovered new clients were well treated. The women in California were eager to please and accepting of his demands.

He drove into the drive of the club concerned the only individuals to meet him were the valets instead of his father or at least one of the board members. He held up a hand stopping the valets from approaching and leaned across the console.

"You need to listen closely to what I have to say as I will not repeat myself. You will be seen and not heard this evening. No talk of your past life in my presence, even if asked. You need to remember who is the honored guest tonight."

"I will do my best," she said.

"See to the valet," he said and motioned for the young men to approach.

He proceeded to the front door of the club, waiting impatiently for her, extending his arm as she walked up.

"I know you would rather be in a morgue attending to the dead, but tonight, you are Mrs. Jonathan Styles Edwards III. If you forget that for one moment tonight it will be unpleasant for you when we return home."

"It's all for you, Jon."

The expectation of a Halloween carnival with orange and black balloons filled him with dread during the elevator ride to the top floor. He felt positive she intended to embarrass him with gore, including servers dressed as ghouls and goblins and smoking caldrons serving a garish punch. As they walked up to the main doors, he closed both eyes taking a final preparatory breath. The rage began building and almost exploded as the doors opened and a rush of air passed over him.

"How could she do this to me?"

It took a few moments for the scene before him to become reality. The main ballroom transformed into an elegant arrangement of sparkling crystals with oversized cut glass centerpieces filled with exotic flowers, sitting on every table. White twinkle lights and black satin tablecloths and chair covers completed the room. The thunderous applause, flash of camera lights, and cheers began as they entered. His greatness was being acknowledged and sharing this moment with anyone was unacceptable. He removed Charlie's arm, stepping forward toward his father leaving her alone at the door.

Styles shook his son's hand, motioning a server to come forward with a single drink on the gold-colored tray. "Congratulations son."

"Thank you, father."

Styles motioned for Charlie to move to his side. He placed an arm around her shoulders. "Gorgeous dress, my dear. You have accomplished the impossible. What do you think, son?"

"I'm sure your involvement is the reason this celebration is a success," Jonathan said.

"Nonsense, this is all Charlene. I had little to do with this tonight," Styles told him.

"I have my doubts," he said.

"Charlene, if you will excuse us. We have some distinguished associates in our circle who need immediate attention," Styles said, then squeezed her shoulders.

Charlie nodded.

"Mr. Edwards a moment, please," a male reporter said.

"Go ahead, after all, it is your night," Styles said and walked away.

Jonathan held a finger up to the reporter and motioned for Charlie to join him. He handed the empty glass to her. "Bring me another and keep my glass filled this evening. I don't want to see you drinking anything except tonic water tonight, understood?"

"I'll instruct the bartender to have these ready for you," she said.

He turned back, smiling at the cameras glowing in the attention everyone in the media was giving to him. The liquor poured freely from several bars set up for the night. An exquisite dinner and dessert were served on the best china the club owned. The time for toasts arrived with the club's most expensive champagne. The mayor gave a sad farewell, and made a point to say the city of Houston would feel his absence. Styles praised his son's accomplishments which earned the promotion and transfer.

Jonathan's speech acknowledged the politicians present, thanking everyone involved in the night's activities except the one person truly responsible for the night. His bravado continued, taking a moment to dance with his inebriated mother until the flashes ceased. He discarded her to a corner table where a server stood with a tray of drinks. The music played until midnight, then slowly the gala began to end. His glass was never empty thanks to a dutiful wife who remained out of his spotlight. When his eyesight began to blur, he weaved towards the bar discovering Charlie in the arms of a man.

"Charlie," Jonathan said, then recognized who held her. "Brian Deeds, how are you?"

Brian released Charlie and shook hands. "Congratulations. I appreciate the invitation."

"Donna informed me Brian recently returned to Houston. I simply sent an invitation to the local office," she said.

"How thoughtful of you. What local office?" he asked.

"I'm an agent for the FBI, transferred back to Texas from Florida."

"You always enjoyed being a public servant," Jonathan told him.

"Jon," she said, embarrassed by his comment.

Brian glanced toward Charlie, who bowed her head. "Well, it's late. Thank you for a lovely evening. Best of luck in San Francisco."

When Brian didn't turn back Jonathan grabbed Charlie dragging her from the bar.

"How dare you hug another man at my party?"

She jerked away. "For God's sake, he was our friend at one time, your best man. Stop acting as though we're having an affair. This is the first time I've seen him since our wedding."

"Don't think I've forgotten who you were engaged to before me."

"I'll get you another drink and call for the Escalade. It's time to go home," she told him.

He stumbled into a chair, his head spinning from the alcohol. A moment later his father stood in front of him, smiling.

"Charlene handed this drink to me and said it was your last request for the evening. I believe we are to meet her at the valet," Styles said.

"She left my Mercedes in the shop," Jonathan said.

Styles laughed handing out the glass. "One more for the road."

He reached out taking the glass. "Good a double. No ice?"

"Charlene said you asked for no ice."

"I don't remember," he said and downed the entire glass.

"I doubt you will remember anything in the morning. Let's get you to the car."

He stood up, leaning on his father. As they headed towards the elevator, he knew any chance for sex would be out of the question. He would be asleep before they left the driveway of the club. The Mercedes is a bitch to sleep in, at least the Escalade has extra padding in the back seats.

CHAPTER THIRTEEN

Escape

Charlie walked out the doors of the club, leaning against the valet podium, and breathing rapidly. The show was over and she survived his insults and denial all evening. It had been difficult to say goodbye to her friends and watch Brian walk away. He looked the same, six-foot-one, coal black hair and eyes the color of a blue sky. Brian always had a nice body and it appeared the FBI kept him in good physical shape. She closed her eyes, and thought of the life she could have had married to him.

"Charlene!" Styles called to her.

Charlie looked up and smiled at Styles pretending to be the dutiful and loving wife. The Escalade arrived as he and another man carrying Jonathan joined her. It appeared the extra dose of Ambien took a faster effect on him than planned.

She opened the back door on the passenger side. "Place him in here."

"Do you need us to follow you home?" Styles asked.

She smiled at them. "No. It's kind of you to offer; however, this will not be the first time he's slept in the Escalade."

"The party was an immense success. Charlene, be proud of all you accomplished here tonight for Jonathan."

"He deserved a memorable farewell," she said.

"He may need a few days to recoup," Styles stated.

"I agree."

Styles hugged her. "Drive safe, Charlene. Your future is in the back seat."

A slight grin appeared on her face. "You couldn't be more correct."

The young valet waited patiently on the driver's side assisting her into the vehicle. The fifty-dollar tip left him smiling and waving as she drove away.

Charlie kept checking the rearview mirror to make sure he didn't wake up. When she drove into the garage, the only sound after the Escalade motor ceased was his snoring. Instead of exhaustion, she felt exhilarated, pushing her forward to hurry. The uncomfortable high heels were left in the car as she entered the kitchen stopping at the sink to pull a plastic bag from behind the cleaning products. It held a pair of crime scene coveralls and personal protective equipment.

She hurried upstairs and then froze with a feeling of guilt, similar to a child entering their parents' bedroom for the first time. Charlie pulled the tight dress up over her hips, making it easier to put on the overalls. When completely dressed, she entered Jonathan's bathroom. His travel bag lay on the counter with just a few items removed since arriving home from California two days ago. She gathered only items he could not buy in a small-town shop including his work Rolex. It took her weeks to get enough of his clothes from the cleaners to pack. With all the traveling he just assumed those clothes weren't ready to pick up.

She backed out of the bathroom, stopping to look at his closet door. Maybe Dani was right, he could be hiding something, but it didn't matter, ignorance would be bliss and necessary for future purposes. She discarded the overalls, head, and shoe covers in a trash sack, taking everything including the suitcases, and cooler downstairs. The downstairs office had never been off limits to her and where his computer bag and laptop stayed when he came home. She checked inside making sure cords and chargers were not left, placing everything in the back of the SUV.

A final check to ensure the house remained perfect to greet the members of the crime scene unit when they arrive to process her home. Charlie retrieved a bottle of Scotch pouring the remainder into the sink, followed by bleach and hot soapy water. The small bag of medical supplies was removed from the shelf behind her cleaning supplies. With a quick spray of Febreze and a fast wipe of the sink using paper towels, she set the alarm and locked the door. She made one call.

"Charlie."

"I'm leaving now," Charlie said.

"Did you set the alarm?"

"Yes."

"What time is it there?" Dani asked.

"Three, I think," Charlie said.

"You have a long drive, between eighteen and twenty hours with stops," Dani said.

"I have planned stops where I will be out of sight and can rest," Charlie said.

"What about Jon? How do you intend to keep him out?" Dani asked.

"I crushed Ambien and Xanax tablets adding them in his drinks at the party. I made a liquid mixture that can be pushed through a syringe," Charlie said.

"What about the trash?"

"With me."

"Be careful," Dani told her and disconnected.

Charlie entered the car to the continued sound of snoring from the back seat. In two weeks, she would return alone, a murderer with a heart dark like the Texas night.

The Escalade hummed up I-45 on cruise control. Charlie removed the decorative clip from her hair, ran a hand through it, then checked the rearview mirror. The tight party dress was uncomfortable, but it could be changed later down the road. She needed to put miles behind them and checked Sirius for music that would keep her awake. Charlie heard him move and mumbled some words.

"My party, my life, bitch," Jonathan said.

"It was your party. It's my life now."

Thankfully, the Saturday traffic in Dallas seemed light. A sudden flash of the sun in the rearview mirror while she sped down highway 380 blinded her, causing the highway patrol sitting on the side of the road to be missed. He pulled in behind the Escalade, turning on his lights.

"Damn it."

Charlie immediately pulled to the side of the road, gathering all the paperwork he would ask for, including her license. She knew to be calm and respectful hopefully he would just give her a ticket and not ask to wake Jonathan. She lowered the window as he approached making note of his name.

"Good morning. License and registration please," he said.

"Good morning, Officer Brown." Charlie gave him the items requested.

He looked in the back seat of the SUV. "You seem to be in a hurry this morning."

"I'm sorry, Officer Brown. We're on our way to Colorado, a continuation of his promotion celebration," she said.

"There is quite a strong odor of alcohol. Have you been drinking?" he asked.

"No sir, but he has obviously."

"Can you step out of the vehicle," he asked.

"Absolutely," Charlie said, slipping on the Jimmy Choo shoes.

"I need his identification, please," Brown stated.

"It's in his jacket, may I?" Charlie asked.

They walked to the opposite side of the Escalade. The empty bottle of Scotch fell out of the Escalade when she opened the door. He waited patiently while she found Jon's wallet handing the license to him. She bent down picked up the bottle and gave her best-embarrassed expression.

"This wasn't quite what I had planned," she said.

"Would you wait here? I'll be back in a moment," he said.

Charlie checked Jon, pinching him to see if he responded. The snoring continued without a break. She moved to the back of the SUV waiting for the officer to check on them. All investigators for the medical examiners were required to ride along for two weeks with patrol officers. He was checking their licenses for any wants or warrants. Officer Brown would either give her the speeding ticket, which she deserved, or a warning. He returned shortly to Charlie's location with their identifications.

"Mrs. Edwards, I'm going to give you a written warning this time," he said, returning their licenses, and registration.

"Thank you," Charlie said.

"Please slow down," he said.

"I will, promise." She thanked him and walked back to the driver's side.

"Mrs. Edwards," Brown said.

She turned back to face him. "Yes, sir."

"Nice dress."

She smiled at his comment entered the SUV, placed Jon's license back in the wallet, and left. At one in the afternoon, Charlie pulled the Escalade into the Flying J truck stop in Amarillo. A much-needed break was in order and she wanted to put Jon's wallet in the computer bag. It took a few minutes to dig through her suitcase for a toothbrush and a change of clothes. The glares and stares of the patrons were extremely uncomfortable as she hurried toward the restrooms. After removing the tight dress and shoes, it took great restraint to not leave them in the trash. The thought of burning them later at Dani's brought a slight grin.

A few minutes later with fresh breath, a long-sleeved t-shirt, sweats, and beloved slip-on Sketchers no one noticed her. With the purchase of a large bottle of water and two sandwiches, she headed back. Her initial plan was to throw one sandwich away, but the hitchhiker standing in the parking lot outside might appreciate something to eat.

"Is there any place I could park and rest for a few hours?" Charlie asked the clerk.

"You might find a spot around back where the trucks park," she said.

"I won't be there long, just need to close my eyes," Charlie said.

"Just lock your doors," she said.

"Thank you," Charlie said.

She refueled the Escalade before pulling to the back of the truck stop and lowering two windows slightly, allowing the cool breeze to fill the vehicle. It was time to give Jon a closer check. He opened his eyes slightly, reaching for her.

"Oh, hell no, time for more drugs," she said and removed a small mixture from the center console. Charlie prepared several syringes of Ambien and Xanax, making it easier to feed them to him in a semi-conscious state. He coughed slightly swallowing the fluid, then shifted.

She removed his cell phone from the inside pocket of the tux, covering him with a blanket. The phone was turned off making a mental note to get a fingerprint later. Charlie set an alarm to wake in four hours, on her cell. The fleece-lined jacket became a blanket, once the driver's seat lowered.

"You have to rest," she said.

CHAPTER FOURTEEN

Waiting
November
Saturday

Dani pulled the four-wheeler into the metal building next to the garage after checking the processor. She walked out to see where Koda had run off to and could see him heading back to toward the house. He seemed to enjoy the cooler days and spent more time in the trees. She might worry if it weren't for his size. He proved many times to her the coyotes, even wolves were not a problem for him, but the cats still made him run. She checked the water pans in the storage building and garage, deciding it was time to buy some dry food to help sustain them during the winter. She shivered walking into the house and moved quickly to the small metal fireplace in the corner of the living room. When the chill eased, she removed the coat and gloves thinking a small glass of Jameson might warm the inside.

She moved to the kitchen table to look over the monthly bills. The increase in her consumption of electricity might be of concern except everyone knew she processed meat. The decision to move production of the hair and skin products into the garage, meant heating and cooling it to keep her and the women she employed comfortable, plus product stability. The generator she borrowed from the Boots brothers would be returned once the work had been completed. It would be nice to work in a warm building and smiled. She remembered all the hours working in the cold and though being a butcher was an honorable profession, just not one she wanted to continue. Old habits die hard and she'd spent extra time maintaining the equipment, seeing it cleaned, oiled, and new blades installed as she did with each new animal. The last thing she did was to move the burn barrels further away from the building for safety purposes.

She thought about the change in plans for Jon's disposal and should have kicked herself for not thinking of it sooner being a chemical engineer. Simple calculations for water, lye, and heat would make this an easier task. Tim and Cletus would never miss the small amount of lye she removed from their supply. She felt as prepared as possible, just concerned for Charlie. Dani checked the clock on the stove. The last contact from her sister was around noon Colorado time when she stopped in Amarillo to rest and sedate Jon again.

Her cell buzzed. "Hello, Tim."

"Dani, I wanted to call and let you know we need to send the hogs next week. I hope it won't be a problem?" he asked.

"No, not at all. The beef will be here tomorrow," she said.

"Knowing you, it won't take long to butcher it. Cletus and I are headed to Denver for the week. Any chance you could come by around Wednesday and feed the hogs?"

"Just one day? They'll need to be fed more than once."

"We have another neighbor who can handle all but Wednesday."

"I can do that for you. Have a safe trip," Dani said.

"Oh, we had a little issue with the plumbing inside the house."

"Is it serious?"

"It's the septic system, so we went old school and dug an outhouse behind the barn."

"Is it going to be permanent?"

"We hope not, but you know how Cletus is and well he had a little disagreement with the plumber. I told him to get busy and figure this out. I wasn't about to traipse out in the dead of winter bearing my butt in the cold wind."

Dani quietly laughed. "I agree with you there. Don't worry I'll tend to the hogs."

She poured another Jameson, then took a plate from the freezer placing it into the microwave. The smell of the carnitas warming made her mouth water as she moved the plate to the table. The situation at the hog farm might be a blessing and another problem solved thanks to the brother's plumbing issues.

Dani looked at the clock again as she washed the plate, Charlie had been lucky with only one incident since leaving Houston. It would probably be around midnight before she arrived, this gave Dani some extra time. She headed towards the bedroom closet and on the top shelf pulled a brown pouch down taking it back to the kitchen table. The leather worn from years of use was unwrapped with all the reverence of a holy object. The glimmer from the knives made her smile as these were training and work instruments not used since leaving Texas. Yes, she owned other knives, but these would always be special. Jon believed he held a position of importance and authority, so she would honor this belief with her very best work on him. Sadly, there would be no further use for them and they would need proper disposal. Dani took the worn wet stone and one by one sharpened each instrument, giving special attention to the knife that would remove the skin. It would be a long night for her.

• • •

Go Back

The short nap in Amarillo revived Charlie for the drive ahead. She drove west on I-40 taking 287 North and changed to Highway 50 into Pueblo. It seemed she'd been driving in the dark forever because of the time change making the bright lights of a roadside rest station a welcome sight. She took the last parking space at the end to avoid onlookers while checking Jon. The cold Colorado breeze didn't seem to affect him when the door opened. She decided another dose of Ambien and Xanax should suffice until reaching Dani's farm. This decision to wait until returning to the car to medicate him would be a grave mistake on her part.

After returning from the facilities the sight of someone leaning against the back doors of the Escalade stopped her from moving. Every beat of Charlie's heart could be heard pounding in her chest. Jon was awake and bent over holding his head in both hands against the vehicle. Approaching him slowly she reached out with trembling hands placing one on the shoulder of his wrinkled tux.

"Jon, are you alright?"

He raised his head, eyes filled with rage. "Do I look alright to you? What happened to me?"

"What do you mean?" She asked, taking one step back.

"Why am I here, why are we here?"

"Because you insisted, I drive us here," Charlie answered.

He straightened and before she could move further away, he grabbed and pinned her against the Escalade. Jon leaned into the side of her face. "Where are we?"

"Where do you think we are?" she asked.

He could feel his body shaking with anger and pulled her around to the driver's side of the vehicle to avoid any cameras. He placed one hand around her neck, backhanding her with the other.

Keeping his voice low as there were people coming and going at what he guessed was a roadside facility. "Bitch, I'm cold and my head is killing me. I will not ask you again. Where the hell are we?"

She felt the blood as it slowly oozed over her split lip and his hold continued tightening. Charlie grabbed at her neck choking out the answer. "We're on the other side of Pueblo on our way to Denver."

He released her, stepping back as if someone shoved him. It took a few minutes for him to speak. "Why are we going to Denver?"

Charlie coughed, touching her neck. "You wanted to go to a five-star hotel for a few days. The perfect ending to the celebration. Don't you remember?"

"I don't remember anything after the last drink at the party. How long have I been out?" He started back towards her.

She held up both hands preparing for another blow. "Sixteen hours."

He walked away from her and began kicking the back passenger door until he left a dent.

"Charlie, get in the fucking car. When I come back, we're going home. You can explain in detail how I managed to sleep sixteen hours."

"We're almost to Denver, wouldn't it be better—" Charlie said.

He was on top of her again, pressing her shoulders hard against the Escalade. "I don't care how close we are to Denver. You will turn the Escalade around at the next exit and go back to Houston." When she moved, he pushed her into the Escalade again, then walked towards the building.

"Where are you going?"

"After sixteen hours, I need the restroom," Jonathan said.

"Do you want to change clothes?" Charlie asked.

He turned around. "No, I don't."

When he entered the building, she opened the back door removing the thermos from the cooler. She shook the contents then opened it to make sure it had remained cold. Charlie wiped the blood away with the back of her hand and moved to the front driver's seat to wait for him.

Jonathan entered the passenger side slamming the door. "Leave."

Charlie drove out of the rest area, taking the next exit, and circled back towards Texas. The only noise in the car was his moaning.

"I don't suppose you thought to bring something for a headache?" he asked.

"I did, but the only thing to drink is a Scotch screwdriver in the thermos," she answered.

"Where?" Jonathan asked.

Charlie opened the console took the small bottle of Advil out handing it to him. He shook four capsules, then opened the thermos, taking a moment to smell the contents.

He tipped the thermos towards her. "Hair of the Dog." Jonathan took all four tablets at once followed by the Scotch. "I don't believe I've ever had one of these."

"Do you like it?" Charlie asked.

"It will do considering you made it." He continued to drink from the thermos until it was empty.

Charlie thought his reaction would be quicker, but the amount of Ambien and Xanax in his system could have slowed the effects of the vodka. As she drove through Pueblo, he began to clear his throat frequently.

"Are you feeling, okay?" Charlie asked.

He loosened his collar, rubbing his forehead. "I'll be fine when this damn headache is gone and I'm sleeping in my bed. Why do you care? It's your fault we're here. Stop talking and drive."

It wasn't long before his breathing became labored and he began to wheeze. Charlie pulled off Highway fifty, stopping on the shoulder, turning the motor and lights off.

He gasped for air, each word being forced from his lips. "Why did you stop?"

"I stopped to watch you die," Charlie said.

His eyes widened as she picked up the thermos. "What was in that?"

Charlie waved it back and forth in her right hand. "Just a little Scotch and a lot of vodka."

"I will kill—"

"No. I don't think you will," Charlie said.

She watched him attempt to unlatch the seat belt, but his hands were too swollen to accomplish the small task. He continued to claw at his throat as it swelled shut. With the doors locked and lights off, she waited until the only breathing heard was her own. Charlie reached behind the seat grabbed the blanket and wrapped it around him. She pushed his head against the window as the smell of urine and alcohol filled the vehicle.

She turned the emergency lights on and stepped out to make a call. "I had a slight problem."

"Resolved?" Dani asked.

"It is now, unfortunately, I lost about an hour, maybe more," Charlie said.

"I'm not going anywhere," Dani said.

"It may be two or three," Charlie said.

"Sis, listen to me, drive the speed limit the highway patrol here loves speeders. The last thing you need is to be caught with a dead body. He is dead?" Dani asked.

"See you soon," Charlie said.

She started the vehicle and circled back towards Pueblo, driving the same road once more. What did her mother always say?

"It's bad luck to travel the same route twice."

CHAPTER FIFTEEN

Plastic and Sharp Knives
Sunday

Dani looked at the cell phone and shook her head walking out into the cold mountain air to gaze at the stars. She wondered when Jon might die, and even thought it might be at her hands, but in the end, it was Charlie. A north wind ceased the viewing of the big dipper and sent her back inside. She placed another log in the small fireplace, then found a familiar spot on the couch. Grabbing a throw to cover up in, Dani thought about how stressful the next two weeks were going to be for both of them. A moment later a strange peace fell over the house, one she didn't expect but welcomed.

It seemed Dani had just closed her eyes when the sound of an engine woke her. She met Charlie in the dark. No words were spoken, just arms around one another, silent in their guilt as Koda stood guard protecting them.

"You made good time, any problems after you called me?" Dani asked.

"No. I didn't even see the highway patrol or a sheriff's vehicle. What time is it?"

Dani checked her watch. "Two."

"That's right, I forgot the change in time," Charlie said.

"I'll make some coffee," Dani said.

They entered the house where Charlie immediately moved to the corner, warming her backside. She pointed to the quilt and pillow. "I see you still prefer sleeping in here."

Dani smiled, pouring water into the reserve on the small pot. "I feel a kind of security in here, especially in the winter."

"I find that statement ridiculous with your hundred-pound guard dog and I'm sure a handgun within reach."

She pulled a bottle of Baileys from the cabinet and two cups. When the coffee finished brewing, Dani carried everything to the table turning on the overhead light. The sight of Charlie's face and neck made her face fill with heat.

"It's a damn good thing he's already dead."

Charlie took a cup waiting for Dani to fill it, then added a healthy shot of Bailey's. "I stopped at a rest station outside of Pueblo. I thought about killing him there, but my bladder said me first. Big mistake on my part. When I got back to the car, he was leaning against the Escalade waiting for me. To say he was a little upset, well you can see."

They drank in silence, listening to the wood popping in the fireplace. Time seemed to stop for a few moments for them.

"Sis, I know you're tired, but we need to get him to the processor. The longer I wait, the more difficult the job will be."

"I turned the heater up with all the vents towards him to help with the rigor. I'm ready," Charlie said.

Dani picked up her knives, joining Charlie outside. "I'll drive." When the driver's door opened, the stench of urine burned her eyes. Koda barked and backed away. "Good grief, it smells like the back alley of a bar."

"Pleasant, isn't it? I'm going to need a car detailer." Charlie took a place in the back seat.

"I'd turn on the heater, but it's a short trip. Charlie, I think it would be better if we clean the floor mat and seat ourselves. There's some cleaner and a spray in the house."

Dani pulled the blanket up over his head. "Death didn't improve him much."

"I have to disagree with you."

As they drove away from the house, Dani noticed her sister seemed quiet. "What are you thinking about?"

"We need to remember there must be forensic proof he was inside the car with me here at the farm. The highway patrol officer who stopped me outside of Denton can verify his presence in the back seat, drunk but alive. I'm positive there will be a video of him going into the rest station."

"I guess there were enough witnesses at the party to testify to him being completely wasted."

"When it takes two full-grown men to get him into the car, I'm good. Honestly, without a body to process forensically there isn't a lot to worry about," Charlie said.

"You mentioned his allergy in Houston. How did you discover a secret, not even his family is aware of?"

"I won't gross you with the details, but it involved a passionate night when we were first married. I made drinks with vodka, thankfully I had an EpiPen in my bathroom. He recovered, refusing to be checked out at the hospital, then swore me to secrecy."

"EpiPen? Why would you have that?" Dani asked.

"Early in our marriage, we actually had friends who would visit. One afternoon a wasp stung my friend sending her into anaphylaxis."

"Did she make it?"

Charlie nodded. "She always carried an EpiPen, her husband saved the day. After that incident, I keep one at the house."

Dani pulled up to the processor turning off the SUV. The hum of the generator and the light inside welcomed them. "How did you manage to talk him into killing himself?"

Charlie tried not to laugh. "On the way back to Houston the alcohol, drugs, and dehydration caused a severe headache. He moaned and groaned like a child, then finally asked if I brought anything that could stop the pain. The Advil and Scotch Screwdrivers stopped his headache."

"That's not all it stopped. Stay put until I return with the rope and table." She opened the building, pulling a metal table covered with plastic outside and to the passenger side. Pointing to the dent as Charlie exited. "I guess hitting you wasn't enough?"

"Can you fix it or trust someone who won't ask questions?"

Dani ran a hand over the damage. "Leave it. Physical proof of his temper will be useful when you go back to Houston."

Charlie moved to the front seat, unlatching the seat belt. They ran a rope around his upper torso. When his body hit the metal table, an echo could be heard across the valley. They could hear Koda barking from the house at the noise.

"Why didn't he follow us up here?" Charlie asked.

"Can't answer that, usually he goes everywhere I do."

"I forget how heavy dead weight is. I'm glad he wasn't lying down," Charlie said.

The wheels screeched and the table moaned slightly as they moved quickly inside the building.

"Did you hear that sound?" Charlie asked, continuing to look out the door.

"What sound?"

"I think Big Foot responded to your love call from the metal wheels. It's nice and warm in here." Charlie chuckled.

"You always get silly when you haven't slept, besides it's the wrong time of the year for mating season. I decided it wouldn't be necessary to work in the cold, he's not going to spoil." She handed a paper overall, gloves, shoe covers, and a plastic bag to Charlie. "Take off all of your jewelry, rings, watch, anything which might catch evidence and put it in the car."

She did as Dani instructed, knowing it should have been instinct, but she was tired. When she returned inside, his clothes were being removed. "There is no need to keep the underwear or socks. I washed the new ones in his bag, giving them a used appearance. The tux and shirt will need to be dried then dropped at the cleaners. I collected enough of his clothes and shoes to make it appear we packed quickly and left."

Dani leaned over his face. "Thanks, asshole, nice of you to help us out. There's a decent dry cleaner in town. He's fast, thorough, and a good friend."

"Do you know everyone in Estes Park?" Charlie asked.

"I butchered meat for people in town and the area those first two years when things were lean. The local meat and game butcher in town broke a leg. He knew I had a processor up here and sent folks my way."

"Are you worried about the local officials?" Charlie asked.

"The sheriff was my best customer. He'll be out for coffee tomorrow."

"I'm not sure about that," Charlie said.

"My friends need to know I have a twin, and you need to be seen for this to work. Don't worry about Luke."

"I see you two are on a first-name basis."

She nodded. "He is the first person who stopped out here to welcome me to Estes Park. Luke allows me to use his cabin when I hunt and fish. His deputies use my products, stopping by for a cup of coffee when the weather gets severe. One year the road back toward town became impassable and dangerous, the deputy bunked at the house. Any activities out here are my business. If an investigation takes place involving the farm, trust me. I will know before they knock on my front door."

"He sounds like a nice guy," Charlie said.

Dani watched her sister shuffle back and forth several times. "What are you looking for?"

"A place to hang this damn jacket."

"I put up a clothesline by the heaters, figured we might need it."

"I saw a dryer in the garage," Charlie said.

"It's mainly used in the winter. Do you remember mom hanging everything outside when we were kids?"

"I remember running through the sheets," Charlie answered.

"Thought I'd do my part when it's warm. You can't replicate the smell of laundry dried in the fresh air."

"No. No, you can't."

"Okay, time for you to go back to the house and rest. I'll handle things from here. There is nothing you can do to help me from this point forward," Dani told her.

Charlie nodded, then her eyes widened. "Wait, I forgot something." She ran out of the building, returning with a computer bag. The computer and cell phone were pulled out turning both of them on. Once both powered up, she took his right hand and pressed the thumb on both. "I almost screwed up."

"Print recognition."

"He hated changing passwords, give me a minute to reset both of them. I need access to send emails and texts. They'll need to be destroyed at some point."

They discarded the protective equipment, Jon's socks, and underwear in the burn barrel outside. Dani drove back to the house under a gray morning sky. It would be good sleeping weather for her sister. The house was warm, and she placed two logs on the dwindling fire. Charlie placed the computer bag on the kitchen table, and took off her coat lying down on the couch.

"Koda will watch over you, give him a nod and he'll snuggle."

"I'm going to just lay here and warm up. Are you sure I can't help you? I feel bad." She closed her eyes and was out.

Dani covered her. "Some things have to be done alone, sis."

The ride back to the processor on the four-wheeler was brisk. She checked the generator, stopping long enough to refill the tank. This time she suited completely up with cap, mask, and gloves with the overalls.

She wrapped chains around Jon's ankles, reaching for the switch. The motor moaned as his body raised off the metal table, swaying until she positioned him over a large plastic bucket. Dani stepped back thinking this scene reminded her of the Predator movies. Shortly, he would look exactly as they did. She moved a wall made of PVC piping and clear sheeting around the area including the floor.

Dani removed his Rolex and wedding ring placing them in a plastic bag. She raised his naked body higher where his nose met hers. Pulling down the mask, she looked at the pale face of her sister's abuser. She moved closer as if he might miss hearing the next words.

"When I'm finished, not even God will recognize you."

She stepped back, inserting two large trocars in major arteries on both sides of his neck. As the blood flowed down the plastic tubes into the bucket, she unrolled the leather pouch. The knives were removed one by one, placing them on the table like a skilled surgeon preparing for surgery.

CHAPTER SIXTEEN

Moving Forward

Charlie turned over on her left side towards the smell of coffee and bacon. Slowly opening both eyes, and pushing up on one arm, she was not sure of her surroundings at first. The reality of being somewhere safe and warm was confirmed by the crackle of wood, her grandmother's patchwork quilt, and Koda's wet tongue. She hugged the big dog's neck kissing him on the head then laid back down facing the ceiling, waiting for the wave of guilt or shame to claim her. It passed by like a white cloud on a hot summer day in Texas.

"You can't keep kissing my dog, you'll make him soft."

Charlie laughed. "I've missed having a pet."

"Well, you can change that now. Maybe not in Houston at least not right now, but later down the road."

"That will be a nice and welcome addition to my life. What time is it?"

"Almost four," Dani answered.

She sprung up, almost falling off the couch. "Why didn't you wake me up?"

Dani stepped over, handing a cup of coffee to her. "I didn't wake you because you would have been in my way."

"How long have you been here?"

"Almost two hours. I cleaned the floor mats, front seat, and disconnected the OnStar. There'll be enough evidence to prove he relieved himself in the front seat and you made it to the farm. It definitely smells better."

"I remember you said something about the GPS, I didn't know it could be disconnected."

"YouTube is pretty handy. You can stop and have someone check it on the way home. Or I can show you how to fix it either way just say it came loose driving up here on these narrow mountain roads."

"Good idea." Charlie drank the coffee and stared at the floor. "I should have been up there helping you."

Dani shook her head no. "You would have been in my way. I took a long shower, and now it's time for some hot food."

"I thought it might have taken you longer to finish?"

Dani turned around, waving a kitchen knife. "When have you ever known me to take longer than four hours to butcher meat? Once I started, the process moved quickly. He put on some weight apparently, there was more fat than I expected."

"It's nice to know for once in his life he wasn't a problem."

"Not anymore, I'd say the worst part of him is gone," Dani said, bluntly.

Charlie got up, grimacing with her first steps, wondering if his rough handling caused her soreness or sleeping on the couch. She turned on the light in the bathroom to a shocking sight. The finger imprints on her neck were defined, along with the increased swelling of her lip. She regretted not putting ice on the lip last night. She removed the party makeup, brushed her hair and teeth making things feel right for the moment.

"I feel like a new person," she said, returning to the living room.

Dani stopped cooking long enough to look at the damage on her. "You'll need a scarf or turtleneck sweater for a while. Luke can't see your busted lip."

"What time does he usually come in the morning?"

"Six, seven-thirty at the latest."

"Perfect. You can just tell him we're sleeping in. We can wait on introductions until the swelling subsides and I'll wear one of your sweaters."

"I have something in the garage which might help. I'll get it after we eat."

"How much time before it's ready?"

"I'm making a quiche and fresh biscuits, thirty minutes maybe forty."

"Breakfast for dinner, I loved it when Mom used to do that for us," Charlie told her then picked up the leather case. She pulled the computer and cell phone out.

Dani glanced around. "I'm not sure you should do that?"

"I have to check his emails, respond if needed, and get a word out to Styles. Jon is a creature of habit when it involves business."

"Don't you mean was?"

Charlie took a moment before speaking. "Sis, we can never, ever refer to him in the past tense. A mistake even once will set law enforcement on a search for a victim, not a suspect."

"Got it, the asshole lives," Dani said.

"I need to start the deception now. Give me a minute to look through this." Styles told her Jon would need a couple of days to recoup. This gave her a few options when writing the emails. They needed to be sent as a group, and she wanted to check the calendar for anything he might consider urgent. Charlie pushed the chair away from the table when his calendar appeared.

Dani turned around with the movement of the chair. "What's wrong?"

"He has nothing scheduled for next week on the calendar," she answered.

"I assume this is unusual."

"Yes. It is out of his norm," she said, then realized all his supposed meetings were excuses for something else. "The first appointment he has is a week from Wednesday, something isn't right."

"Maybe you should look through all his files," Dani suggested.

"I can't."

"Why not?"

"If I check his files, it will leave an imprint. I'm better off not knowing."

Dani turned back to the stove. "You have about ten minutes to send out emails before I put food on the table."

She nodded and quickly sent emails to his secretaries in Houston and California. The emails were a simple decision on his part for a two-week vacation before devoting all his time to the new promotion. Any business in his absence will defer to Styles. Charlie marked them as urgent so they would be read as a priority in the morning. The buzzer on the stove stopped her from checking the phone.

"I'll text his father after we eat." Charlie drooled as Dani placed the feast in front of her.

"You act as though you haven't eaten in months. Here, wipe your mouth," Dani said, handing her a napkin.

"I will have to be careful or none of my clothes will fit when I go back to Houston." She became silent, taking a moment to look at the peaceful setting of the house.

"What's wrong? Do you want something else?" Dani asked.

"I wish your house was bigger."

Dani smiled. "Thinking about staying, are you?"

"It wouldn't be all that bad, would it?"

"I'll start looking for twin beds, but your fancy clothes will have to go."

"You will get no argument from me," Charlie told her.

The food was more than delicious, with biscuits made from their mother's recipe. "I guess this jam is local?"

Dani nodded. "We'll stop by and pick up more this week in town. The woman who makes them usually sells them at the Farmer's Market. In the winter the shops help her out by stocking them on their shelves."

"I'll do the dishes."

Dani held up a hand. "Leave them, you need to take care of business first, then we need to make a trip to the processor."

Charlie nodded, checking text messages on his phone. "Well, this is interesting. It's pretty clear why he has no appointments next week."

"Lake Charles?"

"The Happy Companion sent a confirmation on his request."

"You have to cancel it," Dani told her.

"I'm doing it now." She waited for a response. "Bastard!"

"Sis?"

"Just a minute I need to send something." Charlie sent another text, waiting for the second confirmation. "It appears Jon was such a good client they referred him to their office in San Francisco. He has a standing appointment when in town."

"He must be paying for all this in cash. Call girls, casinos, where is the money coming from?" Dani asked.

"I can't answer you. He offered me a huge allowance to stop working and stay home."

"Wait, he tried to give you an allowance like a child doing chores?"

She waved Dani off. "I can't tell you the amount of his salary. We receive a set amount of money in our joint account every two weeks."

"The full amount is not being placed in the account."

"It can be the only answer to his cash expenditures. The problem is the escort service said there would be a cancellation charge on his card."

"Well, that isn't very smart," Dani said.

"Depends whose name is on it?"

"Did you ever check his closet?"

"No. I'll find out when they serve a search warrant. I need to text Styles, then we can go."

"Jonathan: I've taken Charlie on a trip to complete my celebration. Can you spare me for a couple of weeks?"

Styles: *"Of course and you should complete any home issues for the future, while you're gone."*

Jonathan: *"Without a doubt. Cell and internet will be spotty in some areas. Will check in when possible."*

Styles: *"Enjoy yourself and keep control of the home situation. Text me when you can. You will be a busy bank president once you return."*

Jonathan: *"Work is my life."*

She could not believe Styles was encouraging his son's abuse, though it didn't surprise her, and thought of Jon's mother. The woman appeared to be a shell, empty, lifeless full of pills and booze. Dani left the house as she started to text Styles.

Dani tapped the screen door with her foot. "Help me out here."

Charlie raised her eyebrows at the boxes in Dani's arms. "What's all this?"

She placed everything on the table. "The tube is a cream for your lip. The others are hair color. We need to decide before Friday."

"Nice, I love the items you sent me."

"Are you ready to go?"

Charlie nodded, leaving the house and moving towards the SUV.

"Not this time." Dani pointed to her old truck.

"I hate that thing."

Dani smiled as they hopped into the old black 1970 F100 Ranger, Koda jumped in the bed. "You can't keep going up and down the road in the SUV. The GPS shows location but with it not working they could expect you to give an account of mileage. We'll keep it simple."

Charlie loved her sister's property. It was so beautiful and serene here, without all the highways or heavy traffic to distract from nature. She leaned forward, glaring at something sitting away from the building.

"Is that a wood chipper?"

"It is, and before you get upset, I didn't use it. I thought it might work at one point," Dani said.

"What changed your mind?"

"When I put everything in perspective and did several experiments, I had the same issue with the end product. When pig bones were run through it too many large pieces were left making it a risky choice. The type of bone grinder needed is expensive and questions might arise if I purchased it for a one-time use."

They exited the truck heading to the building. Dani stopped and gave Charlie a set of hooded white paper overalls and a pair of shoe covers which extended to up to the knees.

"What did you decide to do?"

She handed Charlie a respirator and a pair of gloves. "I used lye. Koda back to the truck." The dog followed the command barking in disapproval.

They took extra time preparing before they entered the building this time. Charlie knew lye was a caustic and dangerous chemical, but trusted Dani had taken the proper precautions for their protection. When the door opened no sign of Jon's body appeared anywhere inside, only two of the largest cooking pots she'd ever seen.

She looked at Dani pointing at the cookers. "You want to explain all this to me, chemist."

"It's simple. A human body can be dissolved with lye when boiled at the right temperature for approximately three hours. The cooking process requires constant monitoring to maintain safety and completely liquefy the body. It takes a minimum of two hours to cool."

"In all my time as a forensic investigator, we never had a case involving lye though I have heard and studied cases where it was used. It's been a while since college, so if you wouldn't mind why this choice over meat processing."

"Lye destroys everything, DNA, RNA, breaking down the body with the smallest possibility of bone fragments or teeth left. I can easily crush anything left into a powdery substance."

"I assume we will strain the liquid for these pieces. What about the disposal of the liquid?"

"We can pour him down the drain or into a toilet," Dani said, waiting for a response.

"But we aren't going to do that right?" Charlie asked.

"No. I have something else in mind."

"Where did you find those cookers?" Charlie asked, still amazed at their size.

"I'll show you in a couple of days. They have to be returned."

"Wait, will someone be cooking food in them?"

"In a manner of speaking. I borrowed them from my friends who have a pig farm."

Charlie held up a hand. "As long as they don't cook in them for humans."

Dani laughed at her. "No."

She looked around the processor. Except for these two pots, and the tux hanging, there was no sign anything had taken place within the walls. The next two hours were spent straining all the heavy liquid from the cookers into plastic buckets. A few bone fragments, two teeth, and four small metal clips failed to dissolve.

"What are these?" Dani asked, handing them to Charlie.

"I don't have a clue."

"It appears he wasn't as perfect as everyone thought including him."

Charlie held them in her gloved hand. "They are all numbered. I want you to take a picture of these with your cell phone. Dani, do me a favor and check the library after I leave to see what purpose these serve."

"Well, he doesn't need them anymore. I'll do it later, and destroy them along with all the other things he no longer needs."

The freezer in the corner caught her attention. Dani stopped her as she moved towards it.

"Charlie, there is nothing in there, everything except the blood has been dissolved."

She nodded and turned away. "I'll get the tux."

They left the building disposing of the protective equipment in the burn barrels, leaving the respirators outside the processor.

"I need to start a fire. We'll need to stay a few minutes to make sure there are no embers."

Charlie took the keys and started the truck. They didn't speak to each other for a while, simply watched the yellow and orange glow of the fire.

"I'll never be able to repay you for all of this."

"Charlie, there's nothing to repay. I should have been stronger and said something when Jonathan proposed so quickly after you started dating."

"In my hurry to make Brian jealous over our breakup, I accepted Jonathan's advances. He was charming at the beginning, trips, gifts, anything I wanted he bought. It has been one huge mistake on my part," Charlie told her.

"We'll make it right," Dani said.

"What's next on the to-do list?" Charlie asked changing the subject.

"We need to get you settled in the rental. The code to the key lock will not be available until four tomorrow."

"Which house did you rent?"

"The big one, continuing the Jonathan Edwards lifestyle. Wednesday will be a full day for us. The hog farm is a couple of hours driving both ways. You'll need to follow me and we'll drop the Escalade off at a local lake, picking it up on the way back."

"Additional mileage and places we visited," Charlie said.

"Yes. I have hair appointments for Friday."

Charlie smiled. "I guess we should make a decision from the hair colors you left on the kitchen table."

"Over the weekend we'll take the SUV into town. We'll make several stops from the salon to downtown, then have dinner at the Stanley Hotel."

"What will be our story?" Charlie asked.

"Your loving husband wanted you to spend as much time with me as possible. We'll buy to-go orders for him when we leave the restaurants."

"I'll need to use the computer at least once at the rental house for proof of life at least electronically."

"You should be able to handle everything with his phone." Dani pointed to the barrels. "I'm going to check them."

Charlie watched her stir the barrel, then turn giving a thumbs up. She knew as an investigator there were no perfect crimes. The best criminal always made mistakes according to her professors and law enforcement instructors. They would continue to be cautious and stick to the protocols they set for this situation. Their lives now and in the future depended on it.

CHAPTER SEVENTEEN

FBI Investigation
November

Brian Deeds weaved through the boxes making his way into the kitchen of his apartment. He found his Keurig and box of pods last night setting it up for today. He placed the FBI coffee cup on the platform and closed the lid making his choice of strength and amount. He leaned against the counter and picked up the invitation to Jonathan's party laying on the bar. Had it truly been almost six years since he'd seen them? He took the coffee and picked up the card walking back into the bedroom to finish dressing.

He looked in the mirror thinking of how Charlie's beauty and the sparkle in her eyes were the same as when he'd first met her at a fraternity party. Brian never admitted this to anyone, but he fell in love with her that very moment. Charlie told him she had a twin sister and they would attend Sam Houston State next year. This would be the perfect solution for driving over an hour to see her. When they began to date, both agreed education would be their priority. His goal was to be an Agent for the FBI, if he had been more considerate of her aspirations, they might still be together.

The pressure of completing their education, working in different cities, and having little time to see each other caused the relationship to struggle. With the accidental death of her parents, the situation escalated. When he suggested they take some time apart, she agreed and returned his ring. Six months later he realized his mistake, but it appeared Jonathan quickly took his place and proposed to Charlie. He lost her and instead of being angry agreed to be best man. Brian remembered how close the three of them were in college. He ended that friendship with Jonathan after discovering his infidelity after marrying Charlie.

He walked towards the front door turning back wondering when he would have the time to unpack. It felt good to be back home and as he drove through the traffic smiled thinking it wasn't much different from Orlando. He thought again about Charlie and how Jonathan's drunken demeanor hadn't changed. He couldn't count the times he stopped Jonathan from saying the wrong thing or picking a fight with a bigger individual. This is probably why Charlie's spirit seemed diminished, at least to him. He wondered if the twins still looked the same and why Dani wasn't at the party.

Since he had no parking space assigned Brian parked in the visitor lot, made his way to the front door, and buzzed for entry. He took the elevator to the floor he'd been instructed by security and located the office.

The woman at the front desk smiled at him. "Good morning, Agent Deeds. I'm Leesa Garrison and will be your assistant. It's a pleasure to have you in the Houston office. If you'll follow me, I'll get you settled." She picked up a packet and stepped out in front of him.

"Thank you." He walked past her desk and took a quick glance at the photographs on the desk.

When she stopped in front of a large office, he hesitated for a moment. The transfer back to Houston was a promotion, but his own office an unexpected perk.

"Is there a problem, Agent Deeds?" Leesa asked.

They entered with Leesa closing the door. "No. I didn't know I would have such a nice office."

She smiled. "Agent Woods briefed me before your arrival and felt this might be preferable to a cubical. I'm happy you approve, Agent Deeds."

He turned to face her. "Leesa, I would prefer Agent Deeds when in proper and outward situations, it's Brian when we're working together, please."

Leesa nodded. "I have your schedule for today. You have a meeting in the conference room in twenty minutes."

"Any chance there is coffee anywhere?"

"Do you take cream or sugar?"

"Plain, with a lot of caffeine."

I'll be back in a moment," she said leaving a packet.

He moved behind the desk and looked over the standard office information. He would receive a computer, iPad, company cell phone, and badge once a trip to security was completed. His assistant is a well-dressed woman somewhere in her early forties, with shortcut blonde hair and hazel eyes. The photographs on her desk displayed older children and a husband.

Leesa entered the office with another file and coffee. "There will be more coffee in the conference room and food. You need to go, it's down the hall turn right, the first room to your left."

"I hoped there might be a tour first, but duty calls," he said smiling.

The conference room possibly meant an important case or investigation. When he entered the room twenty-five to thirty agents stood drinking coffee and eating pastries. He recognized several, moving towards them to shake hands and reconnect. The majority of the agents present were from fraud units across the state. Mark Woods, his supervisor, entered the room with an assistant.

"Agents take your seat. We're ready to link with the other cities," Mark said.

His assistant lowered a screen, checking her iPad. "San Francisco and Albuquerque are ready."

Mark moved to the podium. "Good morning. Approximately six months ago, our office received anonymous information in regards to bank irregularities involving Edwards Bank and Trust. Through an investigation of the initial complaint, several of the allegations have been verified. This unit will execute multiple search warrants on all facilities associated with the bank. This will be a three-state operation, executing warrants all on the same day."

"What is the time frame for execution of the warrants?" Brian asked.

"One week from today," Mark said.

The sound of surprise echoed through the room from several of the agents. The out-of-state representatives immediately motioned for their assistants and issued critical orders to be sent out. Brian leaned back into the chair, concerned with the enormity and improbability of this deadline.

"How will this be possible?" an agent asked.

"Agents, you are here to make it happen. Bren is handing out packets specific to your assignment. Partner assignments with city and bank information are in them. I will give agents in charge of the larger banks additional help from local and county officials," Mark advised.

"Will these local officers be brought in before the execution of the warrants?" Another agent asked.

"I don't believe any advanced knowledge outside of this building would be wise," Brian responded.

Mark nodded in agreement. "Everyone associated with the bank is a suspect at this time. We will share no information outside of this building. Our next meeting will be here, Thursday morning at 07:30, dismissed."

Brian ignored the immediate rise of decibels in the room. Men and women were moving about, locating their partners, discussing the task before them. He looked through the packet discovering his assignment and partner was a blank space.

"Agent Deeds."

He turned towards the voice. Mark's secretary stood next to the chair. He immediately stood up. "May I help you with something?"

"Mr. Woods is requesting to meet with you in his office," she said.

"When?" Brian asked.

"Immediately."

He picked up the packet, following her out of the conference room. When they arrived at the office, he respectfully knocked on the door frame waiting for his boss to complete a phone call. Mark motioned for him to enter.

"Come in and shut the door. First, I wish to apologize for the improper welcome this morning. This is not the usual greeting for a new agent to my office," Mark said.

"No apology necessary, I'm assuming an immediate call to your office doesn't concern unit orientation."

"You are correct. What I am about to ask will define your involvement in this case. I need every agent I can trust," Mark said.

"You're concerned about my association with Jonathan Edwards."

"You were seen Friday night at a party."

"Along with about a thousand other individuals. Friday night was the first time we have seen each other in almost six years. I will be happy to step back if you feel it will jeopardize any faction of the case."

Mark nodded. "I spoke with the attorneys about your involvement in the case. They would like to speak with you this afternoon."

"I'll be happy to answer questions to secure there is no conflict of interest."

"I'm pleased to hear this as it appears Jonathan is the focal point of this investigation, but his father cannot be excluded. What do you know about his wife?" Mark asked.

"Charlie? A lovely lady, an investigator for the medical examiner's office. Do you believe she is aware of his involvement?" Brian asked.

"The entire family is suspect. Everyone will be brought in for questioning," Mark said.

Brian held up the packet. "I didn't see a partner for me."

"There isn't one, you are in charge of the Houston execution at the main bank downtown. I need someone familiar with the area who can handle the local officers. I've read your record from Florida and believe you to be the best choice for this. Welcome home."

Somewhat shocked Brian simply nodded. "I'd like to meet with the agents assigned to me, so we can begin putting a plan together."

"They'll be waiting in your office. I want your plan on my desk before you leave tonight," Mark said.

Brian raised his eyebrows. "No pressure."

"One last item. I want you to interview and press his wife hard. She may break and give us the information we need," Mark said.

He left the office standing for a moment, unsure of which direction to go.

"Two rights, then a left," Mark told him.

"I'll get orientated in a couple of days."

He knew Charlie had testified during her time as an investigator on cases and was sure she'd been cross-examined by Houston's toughest defense attorneys. Brian would need to visit the district attorney's office and speak with the attorneys who knew her best. They would be able to give him an insight to Charlie's skills into court and interview settings. If his suspicions were correct, he would have a better chance of changing water to wine than breaking Charlie.

CHAPTER EIGHTEEN

Colorado

The coffee was brewing when Dani heard the sheriff's Jeep pull up to the front door. She peeked out the window to see him walking around the Escalade with Koda at his heels. Luke Hills was a nice-looking man at fifty-five, with a slender build for his six-foot frame. A thick head of salt and pepper hair complemented his baby blue eyes, their friendship started the day she moved into the house. Over the first year, he stopped in to check on her, giving information on the area. The impressive wealth of knowledge he had for the area helped her that first year.

During their conversations the subject changed from work to fishing and the offer to use his cabin. A career officer, Luke began his time in Denver, where he met the only woman who could put up with him. Luke and Wynita moved to Estes Park five years after they married for a slower pace of life. He confided one evening on their wish for children, though it never came to be for them. The one-time Dani noted sincere emotion from him was during Wynita's last days at the cabin. The man's devotion to his wife allowed her to die surrounded by peace and beauty at the home they built together.

"Cancer may have taken her body, but it will never take her spirit," Luke told her.

Dani could see he appeared hesitant to approach the door. She stepped out to keep him from leaving. "The Escalade belongs to my family and they never get up this early. Come in, I have sweet rolls in the oven."

Luke walked inside removing his hat followed by Koda. "I thought you might have company and didn't want to bother you."

She laughed, pouring him a cup of coffee. "When have you ever known me to have a male visitor out here besides you and José?" she asked, checking the oven.

"Heard a rumor you had a visitor, a few months back."

"Old friend from college found me and stopped by for a few days."

Luke held his hand up. "None of my business as long as they weren't a wanted criminal." He took a sip of coffee, taking his spot at the kitchen table. "What happened to the door out there?"

"Not sure. Jon, my brother-in-law, is a little perturbed over it. I decided it might be better not to ask."

"It doesn't look too bad, have him stop by Benny's towing. He can pop it back into place before it leaves a crease. How long are they going to be here?"

Dani took the sweet rolls out of the oven, turning around. "Let me see they arrived Sunday morning early. My sister said they were taking a two-week vacation and wanted to stop here for a few days. I'm guessing a week, plus they want to go into Denver before heading back. Jon received a huge promotion at the bank in Houston. They will move to San Francisco after the first of the year."

"I guess congratulations are in order then. I'd like to meet them, especially your sister," he said.

She took a small bowl stirred the contents and poured an orange sauce over them "There you go fresh from the oven and just a hint of Grand Marnier."

Dani filled their cups again, joining Luke at the table. He bit into the roll, leaving a small amount of icing on the corner of his lip.

"This really hits the spot this morning, thank you. I wanted to make sure my deputies can stop here again this winter to warm up?"

She stopped eating. "You don't even need to ask. There'll be a fire and coffee for them when I'm here."

"Appreciate it, Dani. You should take your family up to the cabin. Even if it's for a day."

"I planned to call and make sure it'd be empty, didn't want to intrude on your time up there," she said.

"Seeing as you always take some time up there after harvest, it's all yours. Replace the coffee as usual. I spoke to José yesterday, he said the harvest was good this year."

Dani nodded. "I believe it doubled from last year. If it continues, I'll need more help or have to buy a mechanical harvesting machine."

"Sounds like a good problem to have," he said.

"True, but what I really need is more land. I signed a contract this year with a food company making this the second business requesting my crops. I'm being contacted weekly by companies wanting hemp and willing to pay a nice price for it. Unfortunately, the price per acre here is higher now than five years ago and less of it."

"Dani, I have a better chance of hearing first about land sales. How much are you looking to buy?"

"The bank is willing to loan me enough money for another five acres I might push them for ten."

"I'll keep an eye out and let you know if something comes available. Oh, I stopped by Luna and Bobbie's shops over the weekend. They said your personal care products are flying off their shelves. They said their online orders from Denver and Pueblo have doubled."

Dani leaned back, smiling. "It's a good problem to have, I'm going to hire José's wife and some of her family to help me out. I wasn't expecting such a huge response, it's been difficult to keep up."

"A blessing for folks who need work and the community. Guess I had better get busy and leave you to your family. I'll check back with you on visiting."

"Not a problem, Luke, you're always welcome. I'll tell Jon about Benny's."

She followed him to the door, waving as he drove off. Charlie was pouring coffee when she turned around.

"He's a nice man."

"Yes. He kind of reminds me a little of dad," Dani responded.

"Nice story on my earlier visit and the Escalade." Charlie took the coffee and moved to the table. She picked up a roll, looking at it pensively. "Did you make these?"

Dani pulled the can out of the trash. "Not this time, don't tell Luke."

Charlie laughed. "What's our plan for today?"

"I thought we could drive into town, and make sure people see the damage on the SUV. We need to pick up a few groceries for the rental, including Scotch."

"We should color our hair here before heading to the rental," Charlie said.

"Agreed. Sis, the rental house is enormous inside."

"You understand this is simply for appearances."

"So, are saying the three of us couldn't be cozy in my home?" Dani teased.

"Anyone who knows Jon would be suspicious. I'll cook at least a couple of meals, leaving leftovers for the cleaning crew to throw out and use in the master suite. Jon's personal items will happen to spill out on the counter, hairs in the sink, and shower. You should plan on staying at least two nights. You have a multitude of bedroom choices."

Dani nodded in agreement. "It's rented for a week, and remember you need to be out Monday by noon. Once you leave, I suggest a couple of days up at Luke's cabin. We'll go our separate ways afterward. Did you ever finalize your story on his disappearance?"

"I did. It's simple, and leaves him to never be seen again," Charlie responded.

"Good. We'll discuss the specifics tonight over beer and pizza."

CHAPTER NINETEEN

Wednesday

It had been years since an alarm awakened her before eight. When the second annoying buzzer refused to cease, she left the warmth of the bed. It was five in the morning and still dark outside. She stumbled into the bathroom, turning on the light revealing their choice of hair color seemed to be a nice one. The Colorado Autumn and Stanley Sienna were the original two top choices. Dani worried there were too many red tones in the Sienna and pushed for the other. She quickly brushed her teeth and hair, dressing warmly, then out the door.

Dani spent the first night with her at the mansion which comprised of five bedrooms, three downstairs, and two upstairs, each with a private bath. They slept in the family room on the large sectional with a fire keeping them warm all night. She spent most of Tuesday morning alone while Dani headed back to the farm, returning around noon with a pickup full of her product to be delivered. They spent the afternoon meeting friends and associates of her sister's, laughing each time, her twin received a scolding for keeping Charlie a secret.

The Escalade thankfully no longer smelled of urine and alcohol. The chemical to remove the odors lived up to its advertisement on the outside of the bottle. Arriving at the farm, the lights of the SUV lit up the back of the old pickup. The huge pots and plastic buckets filled the truck bed. She entered the warm house where Dani stood dressed and ready to go.

She frowned at her sister. "When did you load the truck?"

Dani turned around from the microwave, handing her a burrito. "Good morning to you, too. Coffees ready and to answer you, I did it yesterday after you went back to the mansion."

"You should have let me help you. Those pots weigh too much for one person to lift." She said taking a bite of the burrito. "This is good."

"I didn't need you, the wench and screeching Bigfoot table did the heavy lifting. Cleaning these monsters was another story."

Charlie handed her a small black bag containing the Ambien and Xanax mixture along with the syringes. "These need to be disposed of with everything else."

Dani nodded. "You have a first aid kit, correct?"

"Yes. I always have an extra blanket and the appropriate medical items needed for emergencies, why?"

"Just making sure, because any medical person would have some type of kit on a long trip."

What did you do with the teeth and bone?" Charlie asked.

Dani took out a small bottle from her pocket, shaking it. "I have something planned for this after you leave. The clips are in the bedroom, safely tucked away for now."

"Where are we headed?"

"First, we'll drop the SUV off in the Red Feathered Lakes area for the day, then head to Tim and Cletus Boots hog farm south of Laramie, Wyoming. It's so close to the border they have issues every year with both states claiming their property for tax revenue." She laughed.

"What's so funny?"

"They're moonshiners using the hog farm to cover their second business. We need to leave it's going to be a full day's work for us." Dani handed Charlie a to-go cup.

The drive to the recreation area took almost an hour. She followed Dani to a secluded area and left the Escalade.

"Are you sure this will be, okay?" Charlie asked.

Dani took a tag, placing it where any park employee could read it. "It will be fine, this will handle any issues until we return this evening. I come several times a year."

Charlie grudgingly moved to Dani's old truck crawling up next to Koda. She hated this vehicle more than the Mercedes. "It's a little tight."

"No room in the back for him, at least not until we're through and I've hosed out the back bed."

"I wish you'd let me buy you a new truck," Charlie said, as they hit a dip exiting the lake area.

"I might consider it."

As they continued north, the sun turned the darkness into light. As they drove through the gate Charlie turned towards the door gagging.

"Oh, you better get used to the smell. We're going to be here for a while," Dani told her.

"What are we going to do besides empty buckets?"

"Tim and Cletus are out of town and asked me to feed the hogs today," she said, pulling up to the barn.

Charlie's eyes widened as she stared at all the pig pens. "Holy Jesus, I thought this was a small place, maybe five or six pigs. How many are out here?"

"I think Tim said they had close to eighty.

"And we're going to feed all of them?" Charlie asked.

"Yes, all of them. When we first discussed this, three options for disposal made my list. We could make hamburgers out of him, feed him to the hogs, or turn Jon into liquid. The chance for DNA being discovered was too great with the first two. I made the right decision." Dani moved to the back of the truck pulling down the tailgate.

Koda bolted from the front seat and headed to the back of the pens.

"Will he be, okay?" Charlie asked.

Dani watched for a moment. "Chasing rabbits, he knows better than to get close to the pens."

"I'm sure there is a story that goes with your comment, but I don't care right now. What's first?"

"Grab a pair of boots. We'll feed the pigs, then empty the truck. One more thing."

"What's that?" Charlie asked.

"Don't go into the pens. The bigger sows will attack you."

"Well, that's good to know."

It took all morning to feed the pigs in each pen. If it hadn't been for the four-wheeler and trailer, they would have been there late into the evening. Charlie headed towards the last pen when Dani pulled behind the barn, backing up to the temporary outhouse.

"Do you need to go before I start this?" Dani yelled.

"No!"

Charlie completed feeding the last pen of hogs unsure the stench would ever wash away. She returned to the barn immediately turning on the water to hose the mud and hog crap off the boots. Dani joined her taking the hose.

"I will never eat bacon again."

Dani laughed. "Well, if it's any consolation, the outhouse wasn't that great either. There were two holes inside which is a little concerning for me."

"I assume there was plenty of depth for everything?"

"Yes. It appears they have had some issues for a while, it's deep. I cracked the door to help with the additional odor. I doubt they will notice with the hogs being so close."

"Give me a decomposing corpse any day compared to this. Ugh, I would prefer not to drive the Escalade until I bathe. Can we leave it until tomorrow?"

"It will be fine, even if there is a question, I'll claim to have taken you camping overnight. The last thing is to get the pots inside the barn," Dani told her and backed the truck inside the barn.

Charlie stood back as her sister drove a small forklift toward the truck. "Who are these guys?"

"You didn't expect them to pick up a five-hundred-pound hog with their hands, did you? Everything out here including the lye has a purpose. Would you rinse all those plastic buckets out and stack them? I'll leave them for slop buckets."

"What about the one with the blood?" Charlie asked.

"I'll take it out to the pen where Blossum is standing, they have a blood barrel out there. It goes in when they have a delivery of hogs, it's disposed of all neat and clean."

"Wait, they name their hogs."

"Blossum is their breeding sow. She's special."

Dani placed the pots back where Tim and Cletus could find them all shiny and clean. Charlie rinsed the white buckets, stacking them next to the pots. After returning from the blood barrel, she held up the bucket.

"Burn barrel." They said together

"I'm ready for a hot shower and some food," Charlie said.

"I guess you'll be spending the night?"

"Unless you'd rather stay in the mansion."

"I have better food," Dani said.

The drive back was unpleasant as a result of the day's activities. Charlie felt it seemed a small price to pay for the use of the outhouse for Jon's disposal. The small house appeared dark as night when they returned but quickly became the safe place she needed with a warm fire and the thought of food.

Charlie turned on the kitchen light, opening the fridge. "What can we warm up to eat?"

"I have leftover pork roast," Dani said.

"What else?" Charlie asked.

"Ham and pork ribs," Dani said.

Charlie stood up, turning back towards her sister who was laughing. "You never change."

"Worth it just to see you gag again. Go shower, I'll fix something besides pork."

Charlie finished, hoping there would be enough hot water for Dani. She took cotton swabs, dipped them in alcohol, and rubbed them in her nose. She learned this trick with her first burned victim. It took repeating the process three times before the smell of pig crap disappeared.

She entered the kitchen. "Your turn. What's in the pot?"

"Beef stew."

"Where is Koda?"

"I bathed him in the garage, there is a shower with a ten-gallon hot water tank out there. Put it in for emergencies."

"Like him rolling in hog crap," Charlie said.

"That and he's been skunked a couple of times. He should be ready to come inside."

"I'll get him, go, you stink."

When Dani returned, the table was set. Charlie opened a bottle of red wine pouring it into two glasses. They ate their meal in silence.

Charlie picked up the empty bowls. "Can we wait until at least nine or ten before heading back to the lake?"

"I guess, Luke will be by in the morning so stay in the bedroom until he's gone."

"I'll never know when he comes or goes. I'm tired."

"We'll run up to the burn barrels, do a little housecleaning, then head out. I'll stay the night at the mansion. We can go in and get some food-to-go for the three of us."

"I heard Jon say sushi, with a side of Crab Rangoon," Charlie said.

"Extra sauce in case of an accidental spill."

CHAPTER TWENTY

Time to Lead
Thursday

Brian waited patiently as Mark read over his additional requests and needs for the Houston team. His plan was solid, and the agents assigned to him were working together, well. One concern would be his request for an additional agent from the Louisiana office. Jonathan's activities in Lake Charles needed to be investigated and a local agent would have a better handle on the area leaving his team free for the job ahead of them.

Mark leaned back in the chair, removing his glasses. "It seems you are saying this office purposely ignored the activities in Lake Charles."

He shifted in the chair. "Not ignored, just overlooked. This may or may not have a direct connection, regardless, the current situation concerns me. I would prefer an agent check this activity before we read about it in the newspaper."

"You're positive it will not interfere with the execution of the warrants on Monday?"

"No, sir."

"Then I approve your request, have Bren send the official request."

"Thank you. I have a second meeting tonight at seven, with my team to troubleshoot any issues before your Friday deadline." Brian stood to leave.

"I understand you spent yesterday morning at the district attorney's office, followed by a trip to the medical examiner's," Mark said.

"A little professional courtesy is necessary and expected before I request to speak with attorneys or associates who have cases with Charlie. Once a proper introduction had been made, I spoke with the individuals who know her best. Your suggestion to break this woman will not be an easy task and should not be taken lightly."

"I expect you to try, and one other thing. Be careful you do not make enemies with her friends. We will continue to work with all of them after this is over. The last thing we need is animosity between these offices," Mark stated.

"Understood."

He stopped by Bren's desk, leaving the formal request to be sent immediately. In the past few days, he'd become comfortable moving around the building and spent less time asking for directions.

The information requested on the local officers to be assigned was on his desk. Brian insisted these individuals have no association with Edwards Bank and Trust. They would all sign warnings of prosecution if they revealed information outside the agency office.

The light knock on the door frame made him raise his head seeing Leesa. "I thought you had left for the day."

"I took off at three and went home to see my family," Leesa answered.

"Thank you for coming back," he said.

"One thing you will learn is I prefer orderly chaos. If I stay this evening, it will make the next few days' transition smoother for both of us," she told him.

"I have an agent who needs to be contacted. Please ask her to come tonight, if possible," Brian said.

"Monique Aubuchon," Leesa said before he could say the name.

Brian nodded his head smiling. "Monique will be in charge of the Lake Charles investigation."

"Is the entire team expected this evening?" she asked.

"Yes. Monique will need a full file," Brian said.

"I'll set up the east conference room. You haven't changed the time for the meeting?" Leesa asked.

"No. It's scheduled for seven."

"Nice to have a little more time tonight," she said, leaving his office.

He could not believe how fortunate he was to have an assistant like Leesa. She seemed to be one step ahead of him, making his new job easier. A definite raise would be in order once this case was settled. The thought of Charlie being involved with any type of fraud seemed out of character and difficult for him to believe. He made a trip to The Woodlands last night around eleven checking to see if they were home. When he didn't see the trash receptacles out like the rest of the neighborhood that answered his question. Their absence concerned him, though they could be in California looking for a new home. He wandered into the break room, pulling a sandwich and power drink from the fridge. Leesa entered the room as he finished the last bite.

"Brian, the team is arriving. I've sent them to the conference room and contacted Agent Aubuchon. She's in Clear Lake visiting family and will arrive in thirty minutes."

"You are a miracle worker." He left the break room, making two stops before heading to the conference room.

Brian entered, walking directly to the podium. "Good evening, you have updated information on the plan we discussed Tuesday in front of you. I need to remind everyone present again we will follow all Bureau protocols, no exceptions."

Twenty minutes into the session, the door opened and Monique entered the room with a packet. She moved to a seat at the back table. Brian went through the team's immediate needs, multiple scenarios, and was pleased with the questions and suggestions from everyone.

He glanced at his watch, realizing it'd been an hour. "Let's take a break. When you come back, we'll try to wrap up everything so you can go home before midnight."

Monique approached him shaking hands. "It's good to see you, Brian."

"I'd like to catch you up on the case. Can you stay for a while after the meeting is over?"

"My sister said the couch is waiting if I come back," she told him.

"I'm almost wrapped up here. It's nice to find you back home in Louisiana," Brian said.

"I read over the file Leesa gave me. I assume you need me to secure subpoenas for the escort service in Lake Charles," Monique said.

"Yes. Let me finish here and we'll talk in the office. Please tell Leesa I'm going to need her for a couple of hours longer."

"I'll do that and see you in your office," Monique said, leaving.

Brian would be happy to have her working on this case. She would be invaluable in Lake Charles as a native with local contacts. As his team returned to their seats, he spent the next hour troubleshooting for the Houston execution. The men and women assigned to him were all experienced agents along with HPD's top fraud officer, Dorian Torrence. He was a seasoned officer with fifteen years on the force and went through the FBI academy program.

Dorian walked up to Brian. "Good briefing."

"I feel the team is ready for Monday morning. Could you do a check for me?" Brian asked.

"Sure," he said.

"I need to know where Charlene Edwards' sister is located?" Brian said.

"What about parents or other siblings?"

"Her parents died years ago. I think the only family she has is a sister," he said.

"Charlene's maiden name?" Dorian asked.

"Parks. Her sister's name is Danielle."

"Do you need it now or can I do this tomorrow?" Dorian asked.

"Tomorrow will be fine. Go home," he told him.

It took a few minutes to gather all his paperwork and head back to the office where Monique was highlighting pages from the packet. She graduated number one in their class at the academy, a brilliant woman and like Leesa, always one step ahead.

"Did I miss something in your packet?"

She smiled. "You know me always looking for another angle on things."

"Where's Leesa?"

"Her husband is running a pizza by for us. She ran downstairs to get it. You have a super star for an assistant."

"I'm thankful she was assigned to me. Leesa kept me from appearing completely inept the first two days I was here."

"How long have you been back?"

Smiling at Monique. "Four days."

She dropped all the papers on the floor. "You're kidding."

"Monday morning, I walked through the front doors straight into lead agent on a major fraud case."

"Damn." She knelt down and picked up the papers.

"Pizza anyone?" Leesa asked.

Brian motioned for her to come in. "Bring it in here."

Leesa entered with two large pizzas and a six-pack of coke. "My husband thought we could use a snack. He usually checks on me when I work late."

"Sounds like a good man," Brian said.

"I think so," she said, smiling.

Monique took a piece biting into it. "Brian, I've dealt with the owner of The Happy Companion in the past. An agent is standing by in the office waiting for me to send the paperwork. He'll process the search warrants and have them signed first thing in the morning."

"The reason you're here is to take the lead in Lake Charles for now. The paperwork for your assignment on this case should arrive in the morning," Brian stated.

"I'll oversee the interviews and check through their records. It will take me a few days to put everything together once we're finished. If they refuse to cooperate, the threat of a detailed check into their financial records should help," she told him.

"The quicker you can do this the better. It's going to be busy for a while after Monday. If you find anything out of the ordinary, I need to know immediately."

"I have you on speed dial. Leesa, grab another piece, and let's do this. You have a husband waiting for you," Monique said.

"He's used to my crazy hours."

"You may want to warn him about Monday," Brian said.

"Already have, Agent Aubuchon, I'm ready," Leesa said, picking up another piece of pizza and a can of coke.

"Good, and it's Monique."

"Monique, thanks for coming," Brian said.

"Glad to help," Monique said.

He took a few minutes to finish eating, then picked up the trash and headed toward the break room. Brian found Monique sending paperwork through the fax machine and Leesa walking out the office door.

"Done?" he asked.

They both nodded. Monique turned back for a moment before leaving with Leesa. "I don't guess I can speak to the informant?"

Brian smiled at her. "I haven't even talked with her, maybe him."

"Didn't think so, but I had to ask."

CHAPTER TWENTY-ONE

Dani's Farm
5:00 a.m.

Charlie stared at the ceiling in her sister's bedroom thinking of the last week together. She couldn't remember smiling and laughing so much as they primped, drank, ate, and shopped. While they were in town Dani suggested she wear designer clothing on their excursions. This helped to present the image of a bank president's wife, replacing any memories of her relaxed manner earlier in the week.

In almost every shop they entered Jon's name would be mentioned. She purchased a crystal decanter, filling it with his favorite Scotch. They both commented on it being the perfect gift for his new office in San Francisco. Charlie asked the shop clerk to wrap the decanter in a decorative sack with black and gold ribbon.

The day she left the rental the sack was pushed off the counter to the tiled floor crushing the crystal and spilling the Scotch. A shoddy attempt had been made to clean it up making sure a fair amount of liquor remained on the floor. This left an image of either an argument or an unfortunate accident.

First-class reservations were made for him on a flight Monday afternoon from Denver to San Francisco. She made several comments through a chat option about the importance of him being in first class. The biggest issue had been car service from the rental into Denver. After several emails and text messages, one finally agreed with a large charge for coming to Estes Park. The driver would arrive at the rental home at eleven and leave without a passenger. These two reservations will be the last time anyone will have electronic contact with Jonathan. She left the key to the rental on the kitchen counter.

After arriving at Dani's, they made a couple of trips to the burn barrels disposing of clothing, shoes, and his luggage. The addition of lighter fluid to the fires assured the heat would consume everything, or leave pieces so small they couldn't be identified. The small black bag containing Ambien liquid and syringes met a similar death. The smell of coffee brewing meant it was time to join Dani in the kitchen. She grabbed the blue flannel robe from the end of the bed and opened the bedroom door.

"Good morning. I thought you were going to sleep late," Charlie said.

"I planned to, set an alarm for seven just couldn't sleep," she said, placing a small casserole in the oven.

She looked at Dani's hair, flipping it off her shoulder. "I love our new hairstyles and color. It adds an air of mystery to our appearance."

Dani began laughing. "Maybe I should change the name of the color to Mystery Brown. It is one of my top sellers in town."

She took the cup of coffee from Dani. "What time will the cleaning crew arrive at the rental?"

"The information packet the company sent me said to check out promptly at noon. No exceptions unless prior arrangements are made. I'm guessing someone will be there around twelve-thirty, or one at the latest. This assures the house will be ready for the next rental at four."

"I would hate for them to come early," Charlie said.

Dani held up a finger. "I thought about that too. I called and made sure no one would not arrive before noon."

"Good to know. Now, I have a question for you. What are your plans for the farm?"

Dani leaned against the kitchen counter. "I'd like to purchase more land."

"With the collateral you have, it shouldn't be an issue."

"True, but all of my inheritance is invested."

"Again, the bank will know you are a good investment," Charlie told her.

"We'll see. What I do know is I've definitely outgrown the garage with the increase in my sales. I need something similar to the metal building outback, it just needs to be insulated."

"Are you thinking of a large building for bigger production or keep it small?"

Dani laughed. "I'll say medium size. I love working the land, so anything big means a business suit over my jeans and flannel shirts. I'm not ready for that type of change."

"I understand."

"Property in this area is expensive, and none for sale at the moment. It will come when it comes. Sis, grab some plates and forks."

Dani carried the casserole to the table where they sat down to eat.

Charlie looked up between bites. "What time do you want to leave here?"

"I thought once the sun is up. We'll take one last trip to the processor and make sure the burn barrels are cold."

"I'll pack the cooler with enough food for two days," Charlie stated.

"There's a bag of ground coffee marked Luke's Choice, make sure you pack it. It's our payment for using the cabin."

Charlie ran a hand over the soft bathrobe. "I'm going to miss your clothes."

"Well, you have a couple of days to still enjoy them. I packed a couple of sweaters since it will be cold where we are going."

Smiling. "Maybe a little snow?"

"It wouldn't surprise me at all. Oh, the ladies in the shops complimented your style of clothing and jewelry over the weekend. Luke called and apologized for not meeting Jonathan. He said it had been a busy week at the office."

"One less excuse to make on his behalf. Is there anything to do at the cabin besides hike and fish?"

"Do you still remember how to handle a canoe?" Dani asked.

"Of course. It took a while for all those calluses to go away from rowing Dad out to fish every weekend. Do you remember how much fun we had in the beginning?"

"Until we realized he was using us to do all the work," Dani said, laughing. "I miss them."

"They would have loved coming up here to visit," Charlie said. "Why the question about the canoe?"

"The Sheriff has a small one. I thought you might like to take it out," Dani told her.

Charlie thought the peace of a mountain lake would be therapeutic with the trials ahead. "I think some time alone on a lake will be enjoyable. Any chance someone will check on us up there?"

"There is a county deputy who makes rounds, it's nothing to worry about."

"I assume you will know whoever shows up," Charlie said sarcastically.

"Probably."

CHAPTER TWENTY-TWO

Final Check
Monday
6:00 a.m.

The barren walls and stacks of files on the floor reflected Brian's first week in the Houston office. He picked up a file folder and ballistic vest heading out the door to the large conference room. Every conference room available on two floors would be used today. A sea of black vests, jackets, and hats with the FBI logo in clear view greeted him as the door opened. This morning local officers and deputies assigned to him were receiving radio equipment from an agent.

Two large screens connected the conference rooms of New Mexico and California, to the offices in Houston. He smiled at the early morning faces in the other states, every team a busy hive of men, and women preparing to serve their warrants. The multiple pots of coffee and boxes of donuts could be seen on tables as the camera panned the rooms. The appearance of Leesa, Bren, and three other office assistants suggested it was time for the last check. Brian motioned for his team to move together. Mark Woods entered the room followed by the Houston Police Chief, Sheriff, and District Attorney, Abe Gutierrez.

Mark walked to the podium. "Good morning and please take your seats." He gave a moment for the noise to settle. "Today we will execute multiple search warrants on Edwards Bank and Trust facilities, simultaneously across three states. I will expect professionalism from every agent involved. All team members, including local officers and deputies, will defer to their leaders for questions that arise at the locations. Agents, it's time for everyone to go to work."

Brian motioned for Leesa to join the team. "I suggest you take a few minutes to recheck your equipment. We'll reassemble in twenty minutes at the vehicles. Dorian, were you able to get the information I requested?"

"I did, Charlene's sister, Danielle Parks, owns a hemp farm in Estes Park, Colorado. I contacted the local sheriff," Dorian said.

"Any issues?" Brian asked.

"Dani, as he called her, is an active member of the community since arriving almost six years ago. She's described as a level-headed, hardworking businesswoman. He visits the farm occasionally."

"Is he aware of any visitors in the past few days?"

"He didn't say, and I never asked. Do you want me to recontact him?" Dorian asked.

"If we have time, you can contact him later. See you downstairs." Brian waited until he left before turning to Leesa. "I need a search warrant for the house in the Woodlands."

"It's on my computer, ready to print. Agent Aubuchon called, and said the Lake Charles warrants were executed about an hour ago."

Brian smiled. "Good to know."

"Agent Deeds?"

He turned around to see six officers, men, and women in Houston Police Department uniforms. "Yes."

"We're assigned to your team," the man said.

"Leave your cell phones with my secretary and proceed to the garage." He turned away then stopped when several comments were made from the officers regarding giving up their phones. "Is there a problem? If you have an issue with this request, you are relieved of duty and will take a seat minus your phone until the warrants have been served. Any further comments or questions?"

"Sir, how long will we be with you?" Another officer asked.

"Until we're finished," Brian said.

At eight sharp, all teams in three states began their executions based on central standard time. Brian knocked on the front entrance of The Edwards Bank and Trust. All phone systems in the bank ceased to function and cell phone service was disrupted. The security guard at the front door of the bank hesitated to allow them inside. He quickly explained the consequences of his actions for impeding a federal search warrant. The older man nodded, unlocking the door, and stepping aside.

Agents entered immediately ceasing all transactions including employees attempting to make phone calls. Men and women were moved towards him, their expressions varied from fear and anger to worry. When several of the women began crying, he de-escalated the situation quickly.

"Ladies and gentlemen, I need everyone's attention." The room became silent. "I am Agent Brian Deeds of the FBI, our purpose this morning is to execute a search warrant. Is there a senior bank officer here?"

A short, balding man in his fifties stepped forward. "I believe that would be me."

Brian could see beads of sweat across his forehead. "Your name, sir."

"Jay Hamilton."

"Mr. Hamilton, you are served," Brian said, handing the warrant to him. "Is there a large conference room on this floor?"

He turned around, looking at the employees. "Not for this many people. There is one on the third floor."

Brian motioned to Dorian and one of the female officers, then turned back to the group waiting. "Please follow this agent and officer to the third-floor conference room. All cell phones are to remain off and given to the investigators."

"When can we have them back?" A frantic young woman asked.

"Once your interview is complete. Any individuals with medical issues, appointments, or children to pick up from school will be interviewed first," Brian announced to calm any hysteria.

Dorian slid over to Brian. "We're going to need extra help upstairs with all these people."

He nodded. "I'll send someone once things settle here. Be sure they have water, and bathroom accessibility. Any issues contact me channel one."

"What are you going to do with Mr. Hamilton?"

"Keep him here." He started towards the small man when an all-clear came across his radio. This notification meant the drive-through areas and ATMs are no longer accessible.

"Excuse me, Agent."

"Deeds."

Jay held the papers out toward Brian. "You have no authority to do this"

Brian wanted to smile at this man who believed he could intimidate him. "Mister Hamilton, the papers in your hand with a federal judge's signature, gives me the authority. Where is the bank President?"

Jay glanced at his watch, then at the agents who were stacking laptops and iPads in large boxes. "Styles Edwards has not arrived this morning."

"Follow me," he said, leading him to a desk where one landline was active and picked up the receiver. "Please call and advise him to come immediately."

Jay nodded, turning away to make the call. A moment later he motioned for Brian. "Mr. Edwards will be here in thirty minutes. May I join the others on the third floor?"

Brian pointed to the chair behind the desk. "I prefer you remain here, this officer will see to anything you might need."

The small man, sweating profusely took a seat. "May I have a bottle of water?"

He nodded towards the officer who left returning with a bottle. Brian turned around as the front door opened, allowing three FBI agents to enter. He walked over to greet them.

"Are you Agent Deeds?" the young woman asked.

"Yes."

"Agent Sylvian Garza." The two shook hands. "They assigned us to one of the other teams this morning. The facility was smaller and required fewer agents. We were released and sent here to assist you."

Brian smiled at her. "I'm extremely happy to see all of you."

"What can we do to help?" she asked.

Brian called for Dorian to come to the lobby. "Agent Garza, there is a conference room full of employees who are nervous and want to leave. The officers need help with their interviews."

Dorian smiled seeing the three agents, then looked at Brian. "I hope they're not here delivering coffee."

"Dorian Torrance, you haven't changed since the academy," Sylvian said.

"Nice of you to say since that was in my younger days. I hope you haven't forgotten how to do interviews Agent Garza?" he teased.

Brian stood for a moment watching them banter. "I see it isn't necessary to introduce you. Dorian with the extra help you should be able to get everyone in the conference room cleared quicker. Once you have Agent Garza and the others settled upstairs with interviews, I'd like for you to locate Jonathan's secretary. Go to his office, contact me and I will meet you there."

"Yes, sir. We have four employees ready to release, all women with school-age children. One man being interviewed now has a medical appointment at noon," Dorian reported.

"Agent Garza, thank you for coming," Brian said.

"We're here until you release us." She motioned for the others and they left the lobby with Dorian.

He moved to the area where agents were stacking laptops to speak with one of his team. The front door opened allowing Styles Edwards to enter followed by another man he felt would be his attorney. They stopped long enough for Jay to point toward Brian. The two men turned, moving in tandem across the lobby, followed by Jay waving the warrant.

"What gives you authority to close the doors of my bank?" Styles asked.

Jay handed the paperwork to Styles. "They have a search warrant, sir."

Styles took the warrant, passing it to the man standing next to him. The elevator opened to the lobby where ten employees stepped off with Agent Garza. Brian pointed to the side door.

"Excuse me for a moment," Brian said, heading towards the employees about to exit. "Ladies and gentlemen, until further notice the bank is closed. Thank you for your cooperation. Agent Garza, please see me before returning upstairs."

"Yes, sir."

Brian returned to where Styles stood.

"Agent Deeds, I understand the bank attorneys are remaining in their offices upstairs," Styles said.

"Yes, that is correct."

"My attorney and I would like to go upstairs and counsel with them. I believe they need to see the warrant and inform them of the situation in our lobby."

"I see no problem with your request. One question before you go," Brian said.

"What can I help you with Agent?"

"Where is your son?"

"On holiday with his wife."

"Where are they?"

"He didn't inform me of a location. Jonathan's text said they would be away for two weeks."

"Please contact him now. They're to return immediately."

Styles attempted to use his cell phone and then looked at Brian. "Is there a reason my phone will not work inside the building?"

"No one's cell phone will work. We've blocked the signals, and the only line available is at the desk you passed at the front door."

"This is unacceptable!" the man said next to Styles.

"It's protocol. Please call your son," Brian said.

"I will do my best, Agent Deeds."

"I'll have an officer escort you upstairs. When everyone is ready to leave, he'll bring you downstairs."

Agent Garza returned, waiting for Brian to finish speaking. "The news media is set up outside."

"Styles probably called them. Did they bother the employees?"

"They all park in the employee garage, so not yet."

"Anything noteworthy in the interviews or on their phones?" Brian asked.

"No sir, nothing questionable at this point."

"Thank you, how long before you release everyone?"

"If we find nothing through our questioning or on the cell phones, by three at the latest."

"Nice job, thank you."

Dorian called on the walkie for Brian to come to the sixth floor.

He exited the elevator which opened to a waiting area with a reception desk. The double doors opened into a huge office with windows displaying I-45 and the downtown area of Houston. Jonathan seems to have made the change from flamboyant playboy to bank Chief Financial Officer over the last five years.

"I see it pays to be related to the owner of the bank."

"I checked the other offices of the senior bank officers, none are this large and most have little or no view," Dorian said.

"Did you find anything?" Brian asked.

"It's what I didn't find."

"Explain." Brian rubbed his forehead, preparing for the next words.

"The bank transferred all desktop computers to laptops, iPads, and top-of-the-line cell phones."

"Jonathan's laptop is missing," Brian said.

Dorian nodded. "Before you ask, he didn't have an iPad according to the assistant. His secretary showed me an email Jonathan sent to the Houston and California offices advising of a two-week holiday. All bank business is to be referred to his father. We'll check the IP address at the office."

"What's the date on them?"

"Last week," Dorian answered.

Brian frowned. "I need information on their phones and vehicle descriptions."

"We're going to be here for a while. The floor-to-floor checks on all the other businesses in this building are taking time, we need more agents," Dorian told him.

"Once Agent Garza is finished, they can help. Clear anyone who has no association with the bank and secure the offices. If there is any question, I'll contact Styles who is still upstairs with the bank attorneys. We have one opportunity here, if we miss something we may not have a second chance."

"What shall we do about his son and wife?" Dorian asked.

"Styles is attempting to locate them. I'll allow him a limited amount of time to contact them. If there is nothing to hide, they'll return."

CHAPTER TWENTY-THREE

Luke's Cabin

Dani loaded the old truck with camping and fishing gear, adding a duffel bag of clothes and Koda's favorite blanket. She made a quick call, thanking the sheriff again for the use of his cabin, and motioned for Koda to go get in the truck. The trip wasn't a long one from the farm, but with the winding roads it seemed longer. They left later than planned because one of the burn barrels continued to smolder. She poured water over it making a note to check for any identifiable pieces later. The Escalade appeared to be packed with enough food to last a week instead of two days.

Luke's cabin didn't have an address or location on a map which made her happy. The man appreciated his privacy, especially after Wynita's death. The secure location of his property was perfect to keep out the prying eyes of strangers. Dani knew with the colder morning there might be a light dusting of snow which would be nice for her sister. When they arrived, the sun was bright with a definite chill. She parked the truck jumping out to point to a location for Charlie to park. This spot would completely hide the Escalade.

Dani walked up waiting for the window to roll down. "Grab a jacket."

"Sis, the drive up the mountain with the pine trees and snow makes me want to live here forever."

"If you liked the drive, wait until we walk around the corner. Get your bag, and we'll open the cabin."

"Where is the cabin?"

"Around the corner, come on," Dani told her, maneuvering down a small path through several trees into an open area. She turned back to see Charlie standing with her mouth open. "If it wasn't cold, I'd tell you to shut your mouth or eat a bug."

Charlie took a moment to stare at the snowcapped mountains circling the lake. The pine-scented air was clean and brisk, and the lake appeared like glass. "Now I know for positive, I'm never leaving here, this is beyond beautiful."

"You need to see it in the summer and when the leaves change. You're about three weeks too late on fall foliage." Dani told her as the door opened and Koda rushed inside.

Charlie strolled up, taking a moment to look at the cabin and read the sign. "Luke's Lakeview. I like the matching chairs and firepit, nice."

"We'll sit outside if it doesn't snow." She entered the house, dropping everything on the table, and heading straight to the fireplace. "It appears Luke's been by, there's a fire starter set up for us."

Charlie looked over Dani's shoulder. "You are so lucky to have a supportive community and good friends."

She used the butane lighter and lit the kindling. "Let's get everything unloaded and remind me to light the water heater or no hot showers."

It took two trips before all the supplies were brought inside.

"We're never going to eat all of this food," Charlie said.

"Don't worry about it, I'm still going camping for a few days what isn't eaten can be taken back home. Why don't you head down to the lake and see if the canoe is still out?"

"Sounds like a deal. I'll be back in a little while."

"I have a .380 under the front seat. Take it with you," Dani suggested.

"Bears?"

"I haven't seen any around here, mainly bobcats."

Charlie nodded and grabbed Dani's duffel, rummaging through until she found the items needed. "Hat, gloves, scarf, good to go."

Dani checked at the front room window making sure Charlie stopped at the truck. The fire warmed the small two-bedroom cabin quickly. She put away the groceries placed water and food down for Koda, then began a pot of chili. The water heater lit up without a problem, all that she needed to do now was put sheets and lots of blankets on the beds. It'd been about an hour since Charlie left when Dani heard the front door open.

"I'll be out in a minute, want to finish this up. Did you have a nice walk?" she asked then heard the dog barking.

"I ran into a little issue with the canoe," Charlie answered.

Not liking the sound of her statement Dani hurried into the front room, stopping to stare at Charlie's face. "What the hell did you do, run into a tree?"

"All I am going to say is I seemed to have had a slight disagreement with one of the oars."

"I see the oar won," Dani said, opening the fridge door, and pulling out the bag of ice they brought.

The left side of her sister's face was red, and slightly swollen, which would increase later. Blood oozed from a small laceration on her cheek and busted lip. The worst area seemed to be over her left eye, where a bruise was forming.

"I can't believe this, all the bruises were healed. Now, look at me."

Dani handed the ice pack to her. "This might be a blessing in disguise."

Charlie took the ice pack. "You're not serious."

"Hear me out. This will go nicely with my intervention Sunday at the rental. I stepped in when he hit you, then brought you back to my house for safety. With the dent in the car, and these injuries it all speaks to his volatile demeanor."

Charlie didn't speak for a moment, then turned her head towards Dani. "It could work if there are no imprints from the oar."

"We'll know more tomorrow. If anyone shows up here, you will need to stay hidden. We don't want to explain why you didn't make a report on Jon's abuse."

"Agreed. From now on you can fight the oars in the canoe, I'm done. What smells good?"

"Chili."

"Can you add a beer and Advil to my order?" Charlie asked.

"Gotcha covered."

She closed both eyes placing the icepack on the injuries, wincing each time the pack changed locations.

"Look up," Dani said, taking a picture.

"What are you doing?"

She continued to take a few more. "These will look good blown up the size of this cabin if you ever end up in court."

"Are you finished?"

"One more and I'll get the Advil. You should have been doing this every time he hit you."

Charlie lowered her head. "I did."

"Don't say another word. Keep that little secret for another time." She started towards the bathroom then stopped turning back to Charlie. "The key you put in the package I brought home, that's mothers key to her lock box at the bank, isn't it?"

"Yes."

"I'll get the Advil and the chili is ready."

"And beer."

Dani dropped the bottle in Charlie's hand. "Can you give me twenty minutes and I'll make cornbread?"

"Go ahead, me and Modella Dark are going to get acquainted with the fireplace." She curled up in the soft, worn chair.

Koda moved next to her raising his head and whimpered.

"I know it looks bad, hurts too," she told the dog.

Dani took a prepackaged mix, added milk, eggs then poured it into a greased cast-iron skillet. She placed it in the oven, setting a timer. "I brought Jon's wallet. Thought we'd look through it and make a fire outside later."

"Do you think that's safe?"

"I'll bag up the ashes and take them with me."

Charlie smiled. "Did you bring the lighter fluid?"

"Luke has some under the kitchen sink." The oven bell interrupted their conversation.

"Eat first, then we'll investigate," Charlie said.

They ate in silence except for Charlie's occasional moan or ouch. Dani placed the bowls in the sink, grabbing two more beers. She placed Jonathan's wallet on the table, neither of them moved to open it at first. Koda walked up smelled it and growled.

"I feel the same way, boy. Do you want me to open it?" Dani asked, but didn't wait for an answer removing all the contents.

She placed several plastic cards, cash, phone numbers on paper with no names, and two driver's licenses on the table. They each took items to check.

"Who is Styles Parks?" Dani asked.

"What?"

She turned the card around, pointing to the name at the bottom. "This Discover card has the name Styles Parks on it."

"What a low-life bastard using our name," Charlies said. "Ouch, ouch, ouch."

"Calm down," Dani said, counting the money.

"How much?"

"Five hundred."

"He always has a thousand on him."

"Did you use any on your way here?" Dani asked.

"No. I used my credit card. Are those two driver's licenses?"

"You need to look at these," she said, pushing them toward her sister.

"What the hell. License to carry."

"Check the date," Dani told her.

"He's had this about a year looking at the expiration date."

"Have you seen a gun in the house?" Dani asked.

Charlie shook her head no. "It's probably in the damn closet with everything else he's hiding from me."

"Your license to carry is active, right?" Dani asked.

"Yes." She picked up a piece of paper with numbers on it. "Dani, do these look like phone numbers to you?"

"No. Don't have a clue."

"We have to burn the money," Charlie told her.

Dani sighed. "I figured, always wanted to know what it felt like to burn cash."

"Money isn't always traceable, but I don't want to take any chances. We're destroying everything else might as well burn it."

"I know you're right, give me a few minutes to get a fire started outside."

Thirty minutes later they sat outside burning everything from cash to cards on sticks like marshmallows for S'mores. Koda didn't seem interested in the fire and wandered off toward the lake.

Charlie stood up holding the wallet. "We're burning a four-hundred dollars wallet."

"Jesus, sis."

"It was an anniversary gift. There are no photographs of me or his mother, just the things he loved the most, money and lies." She threw the wallet in the fire turned and hugged Dani. "I should have listened to you."

"Don't cry, at least this time you did. Head in, I'll stay out for a little longer to make sure there is nothing left."

"I might take a shower and go to bed," Charlie said.

"Don't use all the hot water." Dani teased. She smiled holding back the anger for every abuse and degradation Charlie suffered at the hands of Jonathan. She took the small can of lighter fluid, pouring a steady stream on the wallet causing the fire to blaze up hot. Koda walked up and stood next to her.

"Burn in hell you son-of-a-bitch!"

Koda growled and barked as if agreeing with Dani's statement.

CHAPTER TWENTY-FOUR

FBI Houston

The agents finished the floor-to-floor search of the bank gathering all items within the parameters of the warrant. The bank attorneys left with Styles leaving behind all technology including cell phones. He closed the doors to Edwards Bank and Trust with the news media outlets filming him for the ten o'clock news. The multitude of reporters bombarded him with questions all at the same time.

He held up a hand. "I have a statement. At this time all questions will need to be directed to the Houston office of the FBI, please contact Agent Mark Woods. I have nothing further at this time." The continued questions bombarded the area as he walked away. It was nice to leave the media to someone whose pay grade exceeded his.

When Brian arrived back at the office, he went straight to the conference room where agents were busy unboxing and logging evidence. As he looked around the room the job ahead of them seemed to be massive. It would take weeks and months to process the information in this room.

He walked over to Dorian. "How much longer before you're finished?"

"I honestly can't say for sure. The boxes can be left until morning. Mark stopped by to say all the computers, iPads, and cell phones would be logged in tonight."

"I'm going to split the team, decide on a team leader for the night shift, and let them finish up," Brian told him.

"You're going to split us up?" Dorian asked.

"This is going to take weeks to go through, and I have found tired agents make mistakes. This case will be under constant scrutiny from the media, bank attorneys, to the court system. I want you on the day shift so make a decision and be back here at seven a.m."

"I know several who will be happy to work nights to stay away from all the daytime hassle. Did Mark advise you a group of forensic auditors will arrive tomorrow?"

"He didn't, I assumed there would be others to go through the accounts," Brian answered.

"I am more than thrilled we don't have to mess with that headache."

"We're to assist them in any way possible and remind everyone it will be their job to find the irregularities. Have the night team secure the doors when they leave."

"I'll see you at seven," he said, then watched Dorian move towards the rest of the team with two signs as he left.

Dorian waved the day and night signs at the group. "Come on guys, we have to make this an even split."

Brian arrived at his apartment thankful to be on the first floor. When he opened the door moving boxes of all sizes greeted him. It would be weeks before he could even think of unpacking and after the day's activity, all he wanted was a shower. He searched through a box marked clothes pulling out a pair of sweat bottoms to sleep in, then opened the fridge door.

"Beer and cold pizza it is."

"He stretched out on the sofa thinking about Charlie and the possibility of her involvement in this case. Over the next few hours, he drifted in and out of sleep, never truly resting. At four-thirty he dressed and headed back to work.

He discovered Monique at his desk going through files when he arrived after five a.m. It would be nice to have her in the Houston office permanently. The chances of any transfer weren't in the cards with her family living in Louisiana. He found Monique beautiful with her five-foot-five build, dark brown hair, and eyes. They met in the academy where she excelled in all classes, proving to be an effective leader when called upon. After several weeks, he approached her for a date. She smiled, explaining the long-term relationship with her partner, Lyssa. As time passed at the academy, they became the best of friends and spent time in Monique and Lyssa's Lake Charles home.

"How long have you been here?"

"Not too long, maybe an hour. I wanted to get a head start on the employee interviews from the bank. You might want to look at these," she said, holding up a file folder.

"Interviews from The Happy Companion?"

She shivered. "They are disgusting. The amount of money he spent on…well, you can read it. Oh, it sounds like Jonathan has a little drug issue, too. Do you know a man named Lonnie Walker?"

"Good morning, everyone," Leesa said.

Brian turned around shaking his head. "Doesn't anyone sleep?"

The women both laughed. "We could ask the same about you," Leesa said.

"Yes, I know Lonnie Walker, why?"

"We discovered some interesting text messages on records we subpoenaed on Jonathan's phone in our jurisdiction."

"I could have gotten those for you, Monique," Leesa told her.

"True, but I have a friend who is always happy to help and is fast. Brian, we need to bring him in for questioning."

"I'll look at the texts. Any word on their location?" Brian asked.

"I checked before leaving last night, and nothing. I'll start the usual list of searches on phone records, credit card activities, and the GPS locator on both vehicles shortly," Leesa said.

"I need information as soon as you have it. If things get too bad, Monique will help you," Brian said.

Monique smiled. "Anything you need, Leesa."

"I'm expecting a visit from Styles and his attorney sometime today."

"I'll contact you when they arrive. A busy day for all of us." The phone at the front desk rang. "Duty calls," Leesa said, leaving.

They watched as she left the office a moment later her voice came through the intercom. "Brian."

"Yes."

"Video call in five minutes from Lance Bellows out of San Francisco."

"Thank you, Leesa."

"I guess you want your desk?"

"If you don't mind," he said.

Monique logged off Brian's computer. "Lance graduated in the class ahead of us, didn't he?"

"Yes. I hope they have news on Jonathan," Brian said, sitting down.

"Good morning, Houston," Agent Bellows said.

"Good morning, or should I say night?" Brian asked.

"Is that Monique? I thought you were in Louisiana?" he asked.

"I am, Brian needed my expert help, so he kidnapped me to help here in Houston."

Brian looked up as Dorian entered the office. "I hope you have some information for us and the location of Jonathan."

"He isn't in California, at least not as of yesterday. My agents discovered several offshore accounts set up with nonexistent companies," he said.

"Jonathan Edwards III as CEO?" Monique asked.

"No. There is a Jonathan Edwards, Sr., Jonathan Edwards II, and someone named Jay Hamilton," Lance said.

"Lance, just a minute." He put the computer on mute, pointing to Dorian. "Contact HPD and have officers check the airports. Find Hamilton and bring him here."

"I'm on it," he said and ran out of the office.

Brian unmuted the computer. "Sorry for the interruption."

"Sending someone to round up the suspects?" Lance asked, smiling.

"I'm worried about Hamilton disappearing, Jonathan Edwards II will be in today, the other has been deceased for some time."

Lance shook his head. "Man, that's cold to use a dead relative."

"What else did you find?" Brian asked.

"We're still searching records here, what we found is two million missing," Lance said.

"That doesn't seem like much," Monique said.

"I didn't say that is a total amount, it's the amount we found on a quick audit. All of this since he took over the bank here," Lance added.

"I expect you will find more," Brian told him.

"Any transfers from the main Houston branch?" Monique asked.

"No, mainly the smaller branches in Texas and New Mexico," Lance answered.

"Did you find anything in his wife's name?" Brian asked.

"One item. A new life insurance policy for five million," Lance said.

"What was the amount of the previous policy?" Brian asked.

"One million."

"How new?" Monique asked.

"It's dated October 1ST," Lance said.

Monique stepped back, speaking in a low voice. "He's going to kill her."

"Could you fax a copy of the policy to me and keep us updated here on what you discover."

"Will do, and Brian send any information you find on transfers of money Jonathan sent out here from Texas. Be sure to note if it is his personal account," Lance requested.

The conference ended with Brian turning to Monique. "I need you to contact Styles attorney and request their appearance by ten this morning. Do not allow any arguments. If he's not here, we'll send an agent with officers to bring him to the office."

"I hope he refuses, neighborhoods always enjoy our early morning shows," she said.

"He won't take a chance on something which would appear on the news. Would you see if Leesa needs help and explain we will have company shortly?"

"No problem."

"What do you think he is doing with the money?"

Monique walked over and circled the text messages from Lonnie Walker. "I think it has something to do with their conversation on a project in Las Vegas." She headed out the door turning back. "I'll bring that new insurance policy once it arrives."

He left the office heading towards the break room for a much-needed cup of strong coffee. Voices were filling the hallways as agents arrived to begin work in the conference room. Several of the team members appeared with sacks and boxes of morning delights for the work ahead dropping them in front of him. Smiling, Brian grabbed a donut and left discovering Monique standing at his desk licking her fingers.

"How did you get food before me?"

"I caught them coming in the door. Here's the policy, it's pretty interesting."

He placed the donut on the desk. "Let me guess double indemnity for accidental death."

Monique nodded. "It appears Jonathan is sloppy and didn't take the right lessons on hiding evidence. Dorian called from his car. He received information Hamilton is on the way to Hobby airport."

Brian looked surprised. "Well, that was quick."

Monique began to laugh. "Jay's wife said he left this morning on bank business. She is being extremely helpful. Dorian contacted airport security who will hold him for us."

"Where's he headed?" Brian asked.

"The Dominican Republic, and I would bet money he'd be leaving there for another country that doesn't have extradition laws," Monique added.

Brian leaned back in the chair. "I'd love to sit in on this interview, but I have a ten o'clock appointment and we have a lot of work to do. Check with Dorian when they arrive and see if you can assist him."

"I always enjoy watching other agents' interviews, seeing the different techniques. Leesa advised the forensic accountants will be here between eleven and noon," she said, leaving the room.

Brian checked the time, it was almost eight-thirty. How could time go so fast? He picked up the two files on the desk. The Happy

Companion or employee interviews weighing them as if his hands were scales.

Leesa entered the office. "Dorian has Mr. Hamilton in custody. He should be back in an hour, maybe longer due to traffic. I have a warrant ready for his luggage."

"Monique has gone to help in the conference room, I'll go tell her to come and get the warrant from you."

"One more item, Linden Smyth called and said they would be here at ten."

"I'm sure he meant more than the two of them, it should be interesting. I guess these files will have to wait." He left the office, watching Leesa head back to her desk.

The morning team set up multiple tables for the accountants. The computers on one, iPad and phones on the others. He walked up to Monique.

"Brian this is going to take a lot of time," she said.

"Agreed, and be happy we aren't having to search through all of this. I have a job for you. Leesa is printing out a warrant for Hamilton's luggage, can you run it to the judge?"

"Not a problem, be back shortly," she said and left.

He took a moment to walk around looking at the evidence collected yesterday, now that it was out of the boxes. His cell phone rang. "Agent Deeds."

"I'm on the way with Hamilton and he won't stop talking."

Brian could hear the noise of Hobby in the background. "Monique just left to have a judge sign a search warrant for his luggage."

"He'll probably give us permission without it, though it's better to be safe," Dorian said.

"You did Mirandize him?"

"I did, but he made several statements before I could finish."

"Has he asked for an attorney?"

"No."

A smile grew across Brian's face. "All admissible. A recorded and signed statement will be a plus for the case."

"I don't believe it will be an issue. This guy sweats a lot. Do you want to interview him?" Dorian asked.

"Any other time, I'd love the opportunity. This one is all yours," Brian answered.

"The traffic is heavy out here," Dorian told him.

"Drive safe, when you're finished with Hamilton, I have someone else you need to bring in for an interview," he said and disconnected.

Brian left the conference room and headed back for a coffee warmup and another donut. He forced himself to sit down and stop wandering around. A bad habit that started in the academy of wasting time instead of using it in a productive manner.

Leesa leaned around the doorframe. "Styles Edwards and his attorneys are here."

"They're early. How many did he bring?"

"There are four gentlemen and Mr. Edwards. Do you want me to bring in more chairs?" Leesa asked.

"No."

She grinned, leaving to go direct the crowd into Brian's office. He refilled the coffee cup and fought the urge to take the rest of the jelly-filled donuts with him. Moving closer to his office, he heard the conversations between lawyers echoing in the hallway. Brian entered his office, ignoring the initial comment.

"Agent Deeds, this is bordering on harassment of my client," Linden said.

He placed the coffee on the desk and took a seat. "Good morning, gentlemen."

"We need more chairs for everyone," Linden demanded.

"You may decide on who sits or stands. Any additional furniture in this room is a fire hazard," Brian said.

Styles and Linden sat down, while the others stood. "Agent, explain this urgent summons, instead of the scheduled afternoon meeting."

Brian took a moment to look at his watch. "I've been here since five-thirty, so my day began early after a late night. The reason for this meeting is we received information from San Francisco this morning on a number of fraudulent accounts."

Styles turned to Linden shaking his head. "We're listening."

"The names on these accounts include your client, his father, and Jay Hamilton. We found Mr. Hamilton at Hobby airport attempting to leave the country an hour ago," Brian said.

"My client denies any involvement," Linden said.

"I expected his denials."

"Why are we here?" Linden said.

"Mr. Edwards is the only person I requested to see. The rest of you are here voluntarily and free to leave at any time. Sir, have you heard from your son?" Brian asked.

"No, my client has attempted several times to contact him with no response. The situation has become alarming. We believe he has been kidnapped," Linden said.

"By who, his wife?"

Linden stuttered for a moment. "They've both been kidnapped."

Leesa entered the room with a report on the location of the Escalade and Mercedes. He took a moment to read over the location of the SUV and recent credit card charges.

"Why is the Mercedes at the dealership?"

"I believe it's being serviced," Styles said.

"Mr. Edwards, do you know anyone in Estes Park, Colorado?"

Styles held up a hand as Linden started to speak. "I do not know anyone personally, though I understand Charlene has a sister there. Why do you ask?"

"The last GPS location of the Escalade shows it was there two days ago."

"Where is it now?" Linden asked.

"Unknown, as it appears the GPS is no longer active," Brian said.

"They've been kidnapped! Agent Deeds, we need to return to the Edwards residence and wait for a ransom demand," Linden said.

"Mr. Edwards, I do not believe this story your attorney is spinning for me. I am concerned your son is planning to murder his wife," Brian said.

"Absurd," Styles said. "He loves Charlene."

"Why would he kill his wife?" Linden asked.

"Five million in life insurance, double if accidental."

"Jonathan doesn't need money. We are Edwards," Styles stated.

"Then can you explain this new policy purchased shortly before they left town?" Brian said, handing his copy to Linden.

"You'll have to ask him," Styles said.

"Agent Deeds this means nothing. Insurance policies are updated every day," Linden told him.

"True. Can you explain why his policy wasn't increased, just hers?"

"You can ask Jonathan when the kidnappers return them," Linden said.

Brian sighed. "I'm going to ask you to try again and contact him, here in my office. If he doesn't answer leave a message, this is his last chance to respond," he said, placing a phone in front of Styles.

"Or what, Agent?" Styles asked.

"I'll send out the troops."

CHAPTER TWENTY-FIVE

Contact

Wednesday afternoon

Brian spent Wednesday morning with the forensic accountants making notes on accounts they believed to have unusual activity on them. Jonathan appeared to be transferring large sums of money in and out of them with no explanation or detailed reasons. They seem to fit within the time frame in question. They would continue to search for the initial date of irregularities and connect it with the report from the informant. He returned to his office where Leesa left reports on cell calls and credit card purchases. It appeared Charlie and Jonathan were spending time with Dani. The sheriff needed to be contacted again and ask more detailed questions. If they were truly there, someone in town must have seen them.

Linden Smyth reported there were no calls to Styles and believed both were victims of foul play. Brian found this interesting as no demands from said kidnappers were received. He updated Mark on the progression of the case and asked to set a deadline at the end of the day on locating them.

"Brian, contact the sheriff before putting out any information to the media on them. Call her sister and check all avenues, then call me with what you discovered," Mark told him

"What's your concern?"

"Styles Edwards is accusing us of interfering with a kidnapping case, endangering his son and daughter-in-law's life. I'm willing to wait another day, to avoid any incident," Mark stated.

Leesa knocked on Mark's door and then entered. "The Escalade is back in service."

"Where is it?" Mark asked.

"A Cadillac dealership in Pueblo, Colorado," she answered.

Mark motioned for them to go. "See if you can contact them."

As they walked down the hallway Brian could hear the phone ringing in his office. Leesa ran in answered it and placed it on hold.

"It's Charlene Edwards, asking to speak with you."

Brian nodded, then waited until Leesa left. "Charlie, are you okay?"

"I am. What can you tell me about these emergency texts and emails Styles is sending me?" she asked.

"Is Jonathan with you?"

"No. He's in California."

"Where are you now?" he asked and sat down at his desk.

"You know my location."

"What happened to your GPS?" he asked.

"The mechanic said it probably came loose while we were up in the mountains. I want to know what is happening. Styles texts are frightening. He keeps saying he'll pay any amount to get Jonathan back. Apparently, I'm not so important."

Brian raised his eyes towards the ceiling. He didn't believe Styles cared about anyone except his son. "We've served a warrant on Edwards Bank for embezzlement. Jonathan's computer is missing, and he hasn't checked in with the bank in California. When did you last see him?"

"Sunday. We argued over his decision to cut our vacation short and go back to work. He proceeded to get drunk and hit me in front of Dani. She stepped between us stopping the attack. I've been staying with her until this morning. You may want to check the hotels in San Francisco for him."

"Can you make a suggestion on where he might be staying?" Brian asked.

"I suggest you call the most expensive one in town."

"Can Dani confirm what you've told me?"

"Send your cell phone number. I'll give you something better."

He gave the number to her. A moment later several photographs appeared on Brian's cell phone. He grimaced at the injuries on her face, swelling around one eye including purple and blue bruises. A scab over her upper lip and cheek.

"Did you make a report?"

"I haven't made any reports on his physical abuse over the last two years. Brian, am I a suspect?"

"We need to talk to you," he said.

"I'm planning to stop in Amarillo tonight, then drive into The Woodlands on Thursday morning. Have you searched the house?" she asked.

"Not yet, we have a warrant."

"Have your secretary and another agent come to your office. I'll give you verbal consent to enter."

"Hold on a minute, Charlie." Brian walked out to Leesa's desk. "Where is Monique?"

"Conference room."

"Go get her and both of you come back to my office." He returned placing the phone on speaker. "Charlie, I have people coming."

Leesa and Monique entered the office.

"What's up?" Monique asked.

Brian held up a hand. "Charlie, I have Agent Monique Aubuchon and my secretary Leesa Garrison present in the office."

"Agent Aubuchon, please record this," Charlie said.

Monique looked at Brian, who nodded. She took out her cell phone. "Go ahead, Mrs. Edwards."

"I, Charlene Leanne Edwards, give the FBI permission to enter my home in The Woodlands, and are free to search any and all rooms, closets, and garage. Styles Edwards has an extra set of keys and security codes that will allow you to access entry without damaging the property."

"You give this permission of your own accord without promise or persuasion of any type?" Monique asked, then repeated Charlie's full address in The Woodlands.

"Yes. May I speak privately with Brian?" Charlie asked.

Brian motioned for the two women to leave. "How long before you leave Pueblo?"

"I'm going to fill the Escalade with gas, eat something, then head to Amarillo. Unless you are going to send someone to take custody of the vehicle and fly me back to Houston?"

He thought for a moment knowing any other agent would make her stop where she was in Pueblo. "I'm going to allow you to drive in, but you will need to contact me when you stop tonight. I need you to promise me there will be no changes in the car's condition, and keep all the trash. You know the routine."

"I'll take photographs now and send them to you. I'd appreciate it if someone would contact Styles, and let him know I'm alive not that he cares," Charlie said sarcastically.

"I can do that, I'll speak with you tonight, drive safe." Brian hung up, handing his cell phone to Monique as she walked back in.

She frowned. "These are ugly. Who's going out to pick her up?"

"No one. I'm allowing her to drive back."

"Alone? I probably would have sent someone to ride back with her to make sure evidence isn't destroyed," she told him.

"You're probably right. Think about public opinion once she's photographed arriving at the airport beaten and bruised with one of our agents. I think this time it's better if she comes back alone."

She made a face. "Double-edged sword. Do you think Mark will agree with you?"

He shrugged. "Guess I should update him. She's sending timed and dated photographs of the Escalade and promised to bring all the trash back with her."

"She gave us consent to enter the house, what criminal does that? Are we going to wait until she arrives to search the house?" Monique asked.

"Yes. We can take custody of the Escalade and all her belongings. She's a witness at this point."

"Monique sat down across from Brian at his desk and ran through Charlie's pictures again. "Weren't you three friends at one time?"

Brian nodded. "I allowed my selfishness and pride to make the wrong decision. I ended up a best man instead of the groom."

"Ouch, that would have ended it for me. I can tell something else happened, what was it?"

"I discovered him out one night with another woman after marrying Charlie."

Monique took a moment to look at him. "You should have said something, especially if you truly loved her."

"I wanted to, had her number pulled up ready to call," he said.

"Why didn't you?" she asked.

"I can't answer that except I believed she might see it as sour grapes," Brian answered.

"He's quite the player. After reading all those interviews from Lake Charles, I would've dug a deep hole and left him in it. Never to be found," Monique said, returning Brian's phone.

"The Charlie I know, isn't capable of killing anyone."

Monique leaned forward, placing both arms crossed on his desk. "Brian, everyone is capable of murder under the right circumstances. Are you going to contact Styles?"

"I'll give a courtesy call to his attorney shortly after she arrives back home."

Monique raised her eyebrows. "On that note, I hear the conference room and accountants calling me. When you talk to Mark tell him these people need to be making more money," she said, leaving the office.

Brian leaned back, turning towards the window. Was Charlie a victim or an accomplice? The answer didn't seem to be clear at this point in the investigation.

"Daydreaming?" Mark asked from the doorway.

"I need to update you. Charlie contacted us and is voluntarily coming back, alone."

Mark sat down in a chair. "You're not concerned she'll—"

"Destroy evidence, bolt? No." Brian passed his cell phone to Mark.

He frowned at the pictures. "I intended to tell you to push hard when you interview her, not sure about that now, after seeing these. We'll have to document all the injuries before any interview. Where is Jonathan?"

"According to Charlie, in California. I'll press her for more details tomorrow. Oh, we have verbal permission to enter the house, recorded."

Mark shook his head. "This doesn't make any sense, something is out of kilter here." He stood up to leave and hesitated.

Brian looked up at him. "What are you thinking?"

"I think we should change tactics on your interview. Be thorough, don't push too hard and contact Styles or Linden. We need to remember she called us."

"I will."

"Brian call one of them before she arrives home," Mark said.

Brian smiled. "Any particular time?"

"Reasonable," he said and left.

"Monique said the accountants need a raise," Brian told him.

Mark laughed. "Their pay grade is above mine. Get some answers tomorrow."

"I'll do my best."

CHAPTER TWENTY-SIX

Home
Thursday
6:00 p.m.

Charlie stayed in a Marriott on the east end of Amarillo, texting Brian the location although it didn't seem necessary with the GPS working. This morning she took time to eat at the breakfast bar in the hotel, then left refueling on the way out of town. The drive from Amarillo to Dallas was desolate with small towns decreasing the seventy-five miles per hour to a sudden thirty-five. At least the music from Sirius kept her mind from constantly thinking of what waited at home.

She wanted to call Dani just to hear a friendly, reassuring voice, but couldn't take the chance someone might accuse her of being involved. Charlie contacted Brian as she left the city limits of Huntsville. Arriving at the house, she parked out front where a van and several cars were waiting. Thankfully, the news media wasn't there, though it would be a plus for them to document her beaten face. As she exited the Escalade, Brian and a smaller woman left a dark-colored car joining her on the sidewalk.

Charlie smiled and grimaced at the same time. "Hello, Brian."

"Charlene, this is agent Monique Aubuchon," he said.

"Mrs. Edwards," Monique said.

Charlie nodded, holding out the keys. "The keys to the house for the search warrant. My suitcase is in the back, the only item of Jonathan's I have is his tux hanging in the back seat."

"Thank you, now, if you will—" Monique never finished.

"Charlene!"

The calm scene at the house turned into chaos. Styles Edwards bulldozed his way by Monique, knocking the small woman to the ground. He grabbed both shoulders, shaking her hard. She always thought he could be violent, and this certainly proves him capable.

"Where is he? Where is my son? You know!" Styles said, then suddenly backed away at the sight of her face. "What happened to your face?"

Charlie stepped forward, pointing at it. "Your son did this to me!"

Styles face turned red pulling back his hand. "You lying bitch! What have you done with my son? He's missing and you know what happened to him. You're hiding something, what is it?"

Brian helped Monique up, then stepped between Styles and Charlie. He glanced around to see the sidewalks were now filling with onlookers and cell phones.

Charlie leaned around Brian. "The only thing I've been hiding is the years of abuse your son inflicted on me! Look at the car, he kicked in the door."

"Liar, you're lying!"

Monique took Styles's arm, moving him to their car.

Charlie took a moment to compose herself, then looked at Brian. "What is he talking about? Jon went to California."

Shaking his head no, Brian told her. "He isn't in California."

"Where is he?" she asked.

"We were hoping you could tell us."

Charlie stepped away from him. "You knew when I called, didn't you?"

"Yes."

"Then you believe I'm involved. You're wrong, Brian. You're wrong," she said, following him to the second car.

He opened the front passenger door, joining her. "Stay here and calm down. I need twenty minutes to get things settled here. We'll talk about all of this at the office, away from this circus."

She turned around, looking at the car behind her where Styles sat. "I knew he could be violent. Can you please lower the windows it's stuffy in here?"

Brian turned on the car long enough to lower the windows. "Anything else you need?"

"If it's possible, I could use something to eat," she said.

"We'll stop on the way back. Stay away from Styles." He left the car, heading to the front door of her home, stopping midway to speak with Monique.

"Are you okay?"

"Just bruised my ego, I sure didn't see that one coming. What is wrong with that old man?" Monique asked.

"He's concerned for his son, regardless of our suspicions. I'm going to head back with Charlie. Stay here, make the initial walk-thru with the team, then come back and report," he said, turning when a black BMW screeched to a stop. "You can handle Linden."

Charlie heard their conversation. Linden's arrival meant another headache for Brian. She placed a hand over her face, laughing as he escaped the attorney, leaving Monique to fight the battle.

She covered her face as they drove through the onlookers. "Thank you for not handcuffing me."

"I think the neighbors thought we should cuff Styles. Where do you want to stop?"

"Sonic."

He laughed. "Chicken sandwich on a brioche bun, cheddar peppers, and a large cherry lime."

"I'd pay, except Monique has my purse."

"I'll have Linden cover it later."

Charlie looked back as the forensics team started towards the front door. They wouldn't find anything, just a spotless house. Her bag would reveal little if nothing of interest, and the tux remained in the cleaner's bag. Now the games begin.

• • •

Entry

Monique waited for the team to remove their equipment and for Linden to finish speaking with his client. She regretted talking Brian into contacting him when Charlie called with an arrival time. The first thing he did was notify his client, which caused an incident. The neighborhood came alive with all the shouting and soon videos would be streaming across social media. At least the news media hadn't been there to film her being knocked on her ass.

"Agent," Linden said.

"Monique Aubuchon."

"Agent Aubuchon, a moment, please."

"What can I do for you?"

"Under the circumstances and my client's concern for his son. I'd appreciate an opportunity to enter with you."

"You wish to enter the house with us," she said.

"We are all worried about Jonathan," Linden said.

"You didn't seem to be worried about his wife."

Linden straightened his stance. "Of course, we're concerned about Charlene, and I see she is well."

"Beaten, and bruised, you mean," she said.

"I don't understand."

"A moment." She opened her phone sending a text requesting Charlie's photographs. When she received them, the phone was given to Linden. "I suggest you look at these, then speak with your client about his son's actions."

Linden took a brief view, handing the phone back. "I'm unaware of any such activity in their home. I repeat my request to enter the house."

"Do you think she killed him and left the body parts where we could find them?" Monique asked.

"Agent, please."

"This goes against my better judgment and protocol."

"I assure you if there is no disturbance I will leave," Linden assured her.

"Stay with us, don't touch anything."

"Did Charlene give you the security code?" he asked.

"No. I'll text them for it."

"I have one and will be happy to use it."

She nodded unlocking the door and allowing Linden to enter his code. As they entered each room turning on the lights, Monique couldn't believe two people lived there. The house appeared spotless, nothing out of place, and even the kitchen towels appeared new.

She turned to Linden. "Who cleans all of this?"

"Charlene."

"Excuse me. This is between three and four thousand square feet. It would take at least two housekeepers working two days a week to keep it this spotless."

"I assure you Jonathan doesn't allow anyone to come in and touch anything of his," Linden told her.

"You're done here. Please take your client home and keep him there," she said.

"If you discover anything."

"Agent Deeds will contact you with any updates." Monique walked him to the front door.

"Shouldn't I be with Charlene?"

"It's a simple interview, I'm sure she will call if you're needed." Monique closed the door, watching through the side window until Linden and Styles left.

Dorian moved up next to Monique. "Finally gone?"

"For now, I still can't believe the media isn't here."

"They bombarded the main office, Agent Woods is handling it."

They walked back into the family room. "You have to love upper management," she said.

"I have a wrecker coming for the Escalade," Dorian said.

"Search the house thoroughly, take your time, and document everything. You're in charge. Call if you find anything out of the ordinary."

Dorian turned around, looking at the kitchen. "Like what, a speck of dust?"

She held up both hands. "I've never seen a house like this except in magazines. It's not our usual crime scene."

"I want to hire their cleaning service."

"Then call the office, Charlene Edwards, cleaning extraordinaire."

Dorian tilted his head. "No."

"According to Linden, she is the only one allowed to clean it. I need to head back."

"We'll let you know if we find a cobweb anywhere," he said.

"Good luck. Oh, you did a nice job handling Hamilton."

"Thanks, tell Brian I have people looking for Lonnie Walker. The information I'm receiving is he learned of the subpoena and has disappeared. His phone is no longer working so we're unable to trace his movements."

"Disappeared as in…dead or left town?" she asked.

"If he's involved with any of this mess, we might only find parts of him."

"Explain."

"Lonnie Walker and Jonathan have been working a deal in Las Vegas. A lot of money is involved in this with people I want no part of," Dorian told her.

"If it's who I think you're talking about, this case just became even more interesting. Call if you find anything besides cleaning products."

CHAPTER TWENTY-SEVEN

A Dark Place

The white Sonic paper bag still held half the chicken sandwich and a couple of cheddar peppers when they arrived at the field office. Charlie's first stop was the ladies' room before being ushered into a typical interrogation room. The chair reserved for the suspect is always metal, stiff, one leg shorter than the others, and uncomfortable. Charlie took the interviewer's chair, exchanging metal for padding, and positioned her back to the mirror. She couldn't change all the rules but could arrange the setting. Brian entered with two bottles of water, and a local female HPD officer who took photographs of the injuries.

He didn't react to the change of seating or arrangement she made to the room. "Charlie, I need to read you your rights," he told her sitting down in the metal chair.

"Not the simple interview you implied earlier, then?"

"This isn't something new for you. This situation requires a Miranda warning."

"I wave my rights and am aware this conversation is being recorded," she said, leaning back into the chair.

"You are refusing to have Linden Smyth here?"

She raised both eyebrows, leaning forward. "I have no use for an attorney at this time. If one becomes necessary, it will not be him."

"State your full name for the record," Brian said.

"Charlene, (Charlie) Leanne, Edwards," she stated giving a full address in The Woodlands, including her date of birth.

"Tell me what happened after the celebration party on Halloween night."

The next four hours she described the impromptu trip after the party, including the traffic stop by the DPS trooper.

"We'll check on that," he said.

"The warning ticket is on the visor in the Escalade. He was professional, cordial, kind, and liked my dress, too."

"I'd like to get back to the trip," he said.

She described the stop in Pueblo at the rest station, the temporary stay at Dani's farm, and their time at the rental. Charlie discussed the issue between her and Jon that led up to the argument on Sunday causing the injuries. She kept the information generalized, with no specifics unless asked for by Brian.

"Who rented the house?" he asked.

"Dani."

"Do you know the name of the company or individual she contacted?"

"No."

"Dani has all the information?"

"Yes."

"Let's talk about Sunday. Tell me again what happened."

"Dani and I spent the day together on Saturday. I bought Jon a crystal decanter in a specialty shop in town and filled it with his favorite Scotch. I wanted to give him a special gift for his promotion. Sunday morning, he decided to cut the trip short and go to California."

"Did he say why?" Brian asked.

"No. I believe spending extra time with Dani upset him. He began drinking, and pushed the crystal decanter off the counter, shattering it. I called Dani to come to the house. She entered the house as he attacked me. Her intervention stopped any further injury though you can see the damage. I took the car and left."

"Did he have transportation to the airport?"

Charlie held up a hand. "I cannot answer anything further on what he thought, did, or how he left the rental." This last comment stopped any further questioning of her knowledge of his location.

"What was he doing when you left?" he asked.

The door opened, and Monique entered giving Brian a file. Charlie refused to play this game and waited to answer until the agent left.

"Jonathan did what he always does when we argue, drink more, and curse me."

"There are parts of your story I'll need to confirm with Dani. Will you take a polygraph?" he asked.

A smile appeared on her face. "You already know the answer to that question."

He leaned across the table. "Charlie, you cannot go home. There is no access to money, credit cards, or a vehicle. Until I am convinced you are not an active participant in this case, you'll be our guest."

"A guest of the county you mean? Am I under arrest?" Charlie asked.

"At this point material witness," Brian told her.

"Aren't you being a little heavy-handed with this?"

He sat back. "In what way?"

"You know exactly what way. I have several friends who will be more than happy to allow a comfortable stay while being investigated."

"I assume you're talking about the assistant district attorney, director of the medical examiner's office, or Dr. Harrison. Unfortunately, your close relationship with them makes such accommodations unethical."

She started laughing, "You think these women would take a chance of losing their careers helping me to escape? And go where with no clothes, money, or transportation?"

"They have the ability to give you all three." He motioned at the mirror.

Charlie took a couple of deep breaths, calming the anger building. She prepared for his next words. The door opened and Monique entered.

"Agent Aubuchon will escort you to county."

Charlie stood up. "I hear the breakfast over there is pretty decent."

"Mrs. Edwards, if you'll follow me."

As they reached the front door, Charlie turned around. "Thanks for dinner."

She didn't speak on the way to the basement, following Monique to the black sedan. The agent opened the front passenger door, allowing her to enter. They drove from the office to an entrance, known as a Sally Port. Charlie remained composed on the outside, shaking inside.

They stepped up to the counter where a female guard stood. "I'm Agent Aubuchon and this is Mrs. Edwards, our material witness."

Though not a criminal, the removal of jewelry, shoes, and clothing including her underwear is standard procedure at the jail. She placed everything in paper bags knowing they would be processed for evidence. Charlie held out the oversized jumpsuit, putting it on without complaint including the oversized shower shoes.

"Very chic, at least I won't get too hot in this," Charlies told the guard.

Monique took a thin blanket from the guard, handing it to Charlie. The three of them walked down the hallway to a single isolation cell. She faced away from the cell door for a moment, turning back to face Monique.

"When you want to tell us what really happened, have the guard call us," Monique said.

Charlie smiled, stepping away from the door to a hard, cold concrete bench. She sat down, covering up with the thin blanket. Never did the thought of being here enter her mind. Brian would keep the door shut and locked to break her. His total lack of empathy, or common sense that she wanted to be abused further, was unreasonable. The funny thing about this present situation had to be the embezzlement. Go figure. They believe Jon is off somewhere sipping Margaritas or Pina Coladas. If they only knew the truth that his ooze was soaking into the ground of a Wyoming outhouse on a pig farm.

She wondered what Styles would do now. Maybe Agent Aubuchon would file a formal report, and have him arrested. With the mess at the bank, he didn't need another Houston front-page story. Charlie hadn't noticed the time when they arrived at the county jail, it didn't matter as there were no windows in isolation. She knew this situation is what Dani tried to prepare her for, the legal games to be played out. What she didn't expect was for Brian to leave her in a dark place.

• • •

Follow-up

Brian waited in his office for Monique to return contemplating his decision. His actions to hold her as a witness would not go unnoticed by anyone who knew Charlie. Hopefully, her friends would not learn of the incarceration, since he promised Mark a gentle interview. Charlie's evasive answers were frustrating, though he expected it. Maybe he did treat her as a suspect instead of an abuse victim. It would take some time to verify the location of the rental and send agents to process it. Three or four days in the noisy county jail might encourage a truthful and informative story. He heard Monique's voice as she entered the office.

He looked up waving her into the office. "Charlie didn't say a word when they shut the cell door, did she?"

"She just smiled," Monique said.

"This may have been a mistake," Brian said.

"Give it the weekend. I'd confess to get out of that cell," Monique said.

"Did you get her rings and shoes?"

"And clothing." Monique held the paper bags up. "I'm on my way to log them into evidence."

"We need to verify what we can of her statement," he said.

"Hold that thought until I get back." Monique left to make sure evidence remained in the proper chain of custody returning empty-handed. "Okay, all taken care of. I listened to the interview, it won't be difficult to check what she said."

"Seems a little too easy."

"A DPS trooper, her sister, and a broken GPS is not a lot to go on here. Any movements outside Estes Park will be tough to prove without something to compare it with. Cutting you off once she left the rental house was a brilliant move," Monique said.

Brian laughed. "She caught me off guard for a moment. I'm surprised more criminals haven't figured out how to do this."

"Criminals don't have the advantage she does with interrogation tactics. You were right about her being tough, the file ploy didn't make any type of impression," she said.

"I knew it wouldn't," Brian said.

"What about the sister?"

"Dani is family and will give us minimal information. I'm interested in getting into the rental and interviewing the cleaning crew. We need to know what the condition of the house was on the Monday he left. There will be evidence inside if they stayed in it."

"Brian," Leesa interrupted through the speaker.

"Yes."

"Agents at the house are requesting you and Monique."

"Any details," Monique asked.

"None," Leesa said.

Monique looked at Brian. "Body parts?"

"It would make our job easier to close the case. I doubt it though."

They stood to leave. "I have a question?"

"Why didn't I ask more about the abuse?"

"The approach Mark suggested might have given you a different outcome," she said.

"Abuse is a personal issue, best discussed with counselors. I could have pushed harder on it, then she might have asked for an attorney. We're investigating fraud, not abuse. I will contact The Woodland's police and give them the information on his abuse. "

"I checked to see if there were any reports," Monique said.

"There aren't any, I contacted Houston Police Department and The Woodlands after the party Friday night. Charlie isn't the vibrant woman I knew five years ago," Brian said.

"Abuse will change a person," she said.

"I believe it did."

"Dorian has people searching for Lonnie Walker. He discovered information Lonnie and Jonathan were dealing with an unsavory group of people in Las Vegas," she told him.

"Organized crime," Brian said.

"If that is true, we may not find either of them."

"It's possible, but something doesn't feel right."

"What did Mr. Morgan tell us about feelings at the academy?" she asked

"They aren't science-based, and a gut doesn't hold up in court."

CHAPTER TWENTY-EIGHT

Discovery

Brian and Monique arrived at the house in The Woodlands, parking out front. He thought it a little out of character the neighbors weren't still outside wandering around asking each other questions. The next odd situation was the absence of the news media. This had to be Styles or Linden's doing to keep further front-page articles from focusing on him or the family.

He glanced at his watch. "I am praying the situation inside will not turn into an all-nighter for us."

"I'd like a few hours' sleep myself and a hot shower," Monique told him.

"Let's see if they found anything." Brian opened the door. "Anyone home?"

Dorian stuck his head over the railing. "Up here! I hope you brought some food we're all about to starve."

Brian shook his head. "Monique, call in an order to Dominos for them."

"Something with lots of meat on it," Dorian told her.

"Got it, four vegetarian pizzas coming up," she said and walked away smiling. "I'll meet you upstairs. Hello, I need an order to be delivered."

Brian left her downstairs and walked up the marble staircase entering the large master bedroom. He took a few moments to view the entire room. Everything he looked at or touched was perfect, not one thing disturbed in the room. He then moved to the windowsill running a finger over it.

Monique walked up next to him. "It's like this over the entire house, all three or four thousand square feet of it."

"Who?"

"Cleans it. She does," Monique answered.

Brian seemed stunned and then turned around moving toward the team.

"Here, you need to put gloves and shoe covers on. Don't touch anything until we get another warrant," Dorian told them.

"Charlie gave us permission to search every room," Brian said.

"Then she didn't know about this one or hoped we wouldn't find it," Dorian said.

The three entered a bathroom the size of a small apartment, with only one sink in the vanity.

"One sink? Isn't that a little unusual?" Monique asked.

Dorian turned to her. "This isn't their bathroom. I believe it's his. There is another one on the opposite side of the bed with women's clothing and accessories."

Brian shook his head. "This doesn't surprise me at all knowing Jonathan."

"What do you mean?" Monique asked.

"He hated sharing a bathroom in college."

"You're telling me he didn't have some plush apartment off campus?" she asked.

"No. His father told him living with the common people would make him appreciate his life later. We pledged the same fraternity, and lived in the frat house, do I need to go on?" Brian asked them.

"Man, that's cold on his father's part, especially with all the money they have," Dorian said.

"I don't think it helped his attitude," Monique said.

"Did Mrs. Edwards give you permission to open the safe?" Dorian asked.

"She didn't mention a safe at all. Show me," Brian told him.

"We missed it on the initial search. It wasn't until one of the agents pulled out all the bureau drawers at the same time that a door opened," Dorian said.

The walk-in closet like the rest of the upstairs seems to be oversized for one person. The drawers were still out, leaving the door unlatched. Dorian walked over opening it to a medium-sized wall safe with an old metal two-drawer filing cabinet below it.

"Did anyone open the filing cabinet?" Brian asked.

"It's locked once we discovered this everyone backed out. The decision on how to proceed is above our pay grade," Dorian smiled.

Brian closed both eyes, rubbing his forehead. "Monique, the original warrant and verbal consent should cover this."

"I think we should be cautious and process another search warrant for this just to be prudent," she said.

"What about the second bathroom?" Brian asked.

Dorian held both hands out. "We couldn't find anything similar."

"I'll include it in another search warrant." Brian looked at his watch. He sent Leesa home for the weekend. "What about the rest of the house?"

"If there is a speck of dust, we can't find it. His travel bag is missing, which isn't unusual since they are on a trip. We obtained fingerprints from the liquor bottles and hair samples from a brush in the second bathroom. I will take any clothing which is not in a cleaner's bag and all his shoes."

"Take her work shoes," Monique said.

"We haven't found them or her work scrubs, but the shoes in her closet are worth more than what I make in a year. I don't think taking any of her clothes will help us and leaving all this jewelry here isn't a good idea," Dorian said.

Monique walked away.

"Where is she going?" Dorian asked.

"Holy mother of God!"

Brian and Dorian ran to find her. "What did you find?"

"A Hermes clutch, Mark Jacobs bag, two Louis Vuitton, and a Hilde Palladino," she rattled off to him.

"Purses," Brian said.

She looked up at him, shaking her head. "No wonder you're not married. These aren't just purses, they are fashion worth a lot of money. This Hermes bag alone is worth over forty thousand dollars."

"Leave them and bring the jewelry to the office. Dorian, how much longer will you need?" Brian asked.

"Not a good idea to leave these here," she told him.

Brian waved her off.

Dorian laughed at them. "Maybe two or three hours. This was our last area to check. What about the safe and filing cabinet?"

"I'll go talk with Charlie and see if she will permit us to open them. Any refusal will mean Monday morning," Brian told him.

"We could all use a day off and drink a beer." Dorian made a mug motion with his right hand.

"Finish with what we've discussed get everything logged in and be in the office Monday at seven."

"It would be nice if we could get a key or combination," Dorian said.

"That might have been possible until I locked her up in the county for the weekend. Jonathan probably has the key. I'll do my best to get a combination," Brian said.

Dorian made an ugly face. "I'd give it up to get out of the county, though they have a good breakfast I'm told."

He and Monique walked downstairs to the foyer. "While you and Dorian were talking, I contacted Woodlands PD for security until Monday."

"Always one step ahead."

"Dispatch is sending a supervisor and officer out here. They should be outside when we leave," she said.

"This is not exactly what I hoped they'd discover."

"You realize she's not going to cooperate," she said.

"Yeah, hindsight which means we're going to have to do it another way. She might have given permission if I'd gone the gentle route."

She slapped him on the back. "Glad I'm not the one updating the boss on Monday. Woodlands PD is here."

"Will you take care of setting up security until Monday? If there's an issue with their personnel, contact Conroe PD or Willis to help them out."

"Got it covered. See you in the car." She left the house.

Brian took a tour of the downstairs, checking the bedrooms, the formal living area, ending up in the family room and kitchen. Dorian hadn't exaggerated, no dust or dirt inside the house, including the garage. Who cleans the garage? The image of Charlie being a type of indentured servant came to mind. He wondered how she managed to escape him to work at the medical examiners. He needed to speak with her friends, hopefully, they wouldn't burn him at the stake.

The doorbell rang and a multitude of footsteps began heading in his direction. Brian laughed and paid for the food. "Everyone outside. Where's Monique?"

"Here," she said carrying a roll of paper towels. "I didn't think they would mind if we borrowed these."

CHAPTER TWENTY-NINE

Clearing Up Loose Ends

Dani stopped by the Boots brother's farm Friday on the return from a short fishing trip. She walked to the back of the pickup, grabbed her green rubber boots, and locked Koda inside the cab. Opening the cooler lid, she removed a gallon bag of raw hamburger. Since it was early and not wanting to be shot, she called out for Tim and Cletus. It seems they were away with deliveries since neither of the men responded to her call.

She walked out to the first large pen, crawling up on the fence. "Blossum! Here pig!"

A moment later a huge sow weighing five hundred pounds ran up to the fence. She reached over, patting the animal on its head. "I brought something for you, girl."

The sow backed up snorting then rooted forward. Dani opened the plastic bag and took out a large piece of hamburger throwing it where the hog devoured the small treat.

Dani smiled. "Who said Jon wasn't good for anything?" With the small pieces now disposed of the watches were next on her to-do list. She thought about taking a picture with her phone of the metal clips, but sketched them including the numbers. They were still a mystery at this point and didn't have to be identified. He no longer needed them and there would be time to research them later.

One evening while camping, she dismantled his cell phone and burned the sim card. The rest met a watery death in the lake. The plastic parts of the computer lay in the bottom of the burn barrel, leaving the internal sections to destroy. She arrived home at noon, driving straight to the processor.

As she entered the building a north wind blew through rattling the sides. "This place will never make it through a harsh winter," Dani said out loud.

Over the next few days, Dani would dismantle the equipment, selling or giving it away. She walked out to the burn barrels digging through them since the recycler would be out today with replacements. After digging through both of them the only thing there was ash. It didn't surprise her to see Luke's jeep, knowing he would be interested in the trip.

Dani opened the door letting Koda in first, then removed her coat. "Afternoon, Luke. Anything interesting in the paper?" She washed the black soot off both hands before pouring a cup of coffee and joining him at the table.

Luke rubbed the dog's head. "Thought I'd better come out and check on you. I heard about your sister and the issues in Houston."

"What issues?" Dani asked.

Luke passed the paper to her. Dani's mouth dropped open. "I didn't know, been out of reach, fishing."

"How did the fishing go this year?"

She put the paper down. "I should have stayed home and fished out of the freezer."

He picked up his cup and took a drink. "Got a call from FBI Agent Brian Deeds."

"What did he want?"

"Information on you. This is the second time the FBI has called me. The first guy just wanted to know if you were here. This agent Deeds seems more inquisitive and I didn't appreciate his attitude or the accusations he made about you."

Dani put down the newspaper. "I guess he thinks I have information. I've known Brian for a while as he and Charlie were engaged at one time. According to the paper, this is a huge fraud case, guess he thought a heavy-handed approach would impress you."

"Well, it didn't, and I told him, so."

She pointed to his cup. "I have something that will warm your coffee up a bit if you're off duty."

Luke nodded. "A healthy pour will be fine. This Agent Deeds needs to be a little more courteous when asking questions on an upstanding citizen and friend."

She pulled a bottle of Jack Daniels out of the cabinet, pouring some into both cups. "I appreciate that. What kind of accusations?"

"It seems he believes you're involved in this fraud case by helping your brother-in-law disappear. He used words like accomplice and motives. He then asked me if you'd made any large purchases including airline tickets out of the country over the last six months. Mr. FBI kept asking if I knew for positive, they were both in town during those dates. He demanded if you can believe it. Demanded, I bring you into the office for interrogation and talk you into allowing a search of your home."

Dani shook her head and smiled at him before sitting back down. "Luke, I have nothing to hide out here. Don't even lock my doors most of the time and you are free to search my house anytime you'd like."

Luke shook his head no. "No need Dani. Agent Deeds blew smoke in the wrong man's face."

"My sister came here to see me and hope to save her marriage, unfortunately, I caught him beating her at the rental. We packed the Escalade and I brought her here for safety. Can't say what caused the argument, but he was drunk so any reason is possible. Don't know or care where he went after we left."

Luke frowned at her. "I wish she'd made a report, don't take kindly to anyone beating a woman."

Dani nodded. "I tried, but she refused, too embarrassed over the entire situation. The few days at your cabin helped both of us. I'm hoping she will file for a divorce."

"It sounds like a good idea to me," he said.

"I knew Jon could be a jerk." She picked up the paper. "This means jail time when they catch him and my sister is alone facing all this without any support from people who care about her."

"Anyone questioning your integrity better have more than just words. Our conversation ended with my suggestion to not bother my office again without proof," Luke said.

She smiled. "He will probably send an agent out to speak to me from the Denver area."

Luke sighed. "Dani, don't talk or allow anyone inside the house. If someone shows up out here, call me immediately. We'll drive into the office where I can oversee what they're doing."

"Thank you, it's nice to have a friend," Dani said.

"I protect my community and friends, plus you are the best damn butcher, I've ever seen," he said.

"It's nice to be a part of a community. I have sad news though, just processed my last animal," Dani said.

"Hate to hear this and I won't be the only one upset over the news," Luke said.

"The success of the farm is taking all my time," Dani said.

"Happy for you but it doesn't mean I can't complain."

"Do you need another cup?" Dani asked.

"No. I just wanted to let you know we're here for you. Let me know if I can help you or your sister." He stood up, putting on his jacket.

Dani looked at the paper again. "I may need to leave for a while."

"Family first."

"I'll let you know. Do you know where the Boots brothers might be? I stopped by on my way back, they weren't home," Dani asked.

"Can't say, hope someone is watching the livestock."

"I'll call tomorrow. The hogs can't go long without food or they'll turn on the little ones," she said, frowning.

"Let me know and I'll have a deputy drive over with you to help. My guess is they're making a shine run, probably be back late tonight or early in the morning." Luke smiled.

Dani walked with him outside. "I kind of thought the same, still need to make sure someone feeds the livestock."

"Let me know if you go to Houston. We'll watch the house for you and Koda, keep it safe from Mr. Deeds."

The honking of a horn made both of them look toward the gate. Luke looked back at Dani.

"New burn barrels, it's time to replace them," she told him.

"Don't last long when you're processing."

"These lasted longer than the others, usually change them out regularly because of the wildlife. This company takes care of the ash, recycles the barrels, a win, win."

"Talk to you in a day or so, remember what I said about any snappily dressed strangers."

Dani held up her phone. "Got you on speed dial."

The truck stopped as a burly man jumped out of the cab. "Looking for a Mr. Daniel Parks."

Luke laughed while getting into the jeep and drove away.

"It's Dani, and that would be me. The barrels are up the hill."

"Sign here and you're done."

She took the clipboard, signing the receipt. "This happens more times than I can count. All anyone hears in Daniel, not Danielle."

"Maybe you should use your middle name," he said, walking away from her.

As he drove up the hill to get the barrels, Dani unloaded the fishing and camping equipment from the truck. She stopped to look around the garage for a place to store them. At least for now she had a corner still available, but it wouldn't be long before hemp products would fill every inch of space. She will be forced shortly to decide on more land or a bigger building for employees and inventory. The driver honked as he passed by her walking back to the house. She smiled as he drove out the gate taking away more evidence of Jonathan's existence.

Dani walked by the oven, turned it on for dinner, and picked up a small bag of clothes ready to wash from the trip. Since there wouldn't be fish on her menu, tonight's meal would comprise of eggs, ham, and biscuits. While dinner was cooking, she sat down with a fresh cup of coffee and scratched off two tickets, both losers. She held them out to Koda. "Trash." The dog took them and dropped both, into the trash can.

Dani looked at the newspaper shaking her head. "Wish we'd known this shit two weeks ago," she said to Koda.

Charlie was now a person of interest with his absence and the embezzlement. The wife always knows the location of her husband, at least they think she knows. She finished dinner placing the dishes in the sink. She opened the freezer door on the fridge and reached back behind the multiple cartons of Rocky Road.

She found the one marked "HANDS OFF" taking it out. A small tool kit from beneath the sink was removed and placed on the table where the Rolex watches and his wedding band were removed from the carton. A couple of hours later both watches lay in pieces, the diamonds, and wedding band on a small plate. Dani could see the numbers on the watches associating them with Jon. Everything would be destroyed with a high heat source. His money burned easily, and her research says the diamonds would too.

She walked back out to the garage, reaching up next to the hair products, and removed a box. The watch pieces and diamonds joined the computer parts and metal clips in the container.

Dani made a call to see if the brothers were back. "Tim, good to know you're home. I stopped by earlier and checked on the hogs."

"Appreciate that, Dani. What can I do for you?"

"I'd like to come by tomorrow and use the welder," she said.

"Any time, do me a favor and take it out back away from the barn," he said, chuckling.

"Not a problem, see you early."

CHAPTER THIRTY

Trifecta Plus One
Sunday

Brian worked late Saturday preparing the information needed for the additional search warrant on the discovery of the safe and filing cabinet. His bed never felt so nice as it did when the cell rang at nine, Sunday morning. He reached for it and remembered it had been left on the kitchen bar. By the time he found it, the ringing ceased. Mark left a message and urgent text requesting his presence at the office post-haste.

He sighed and rubbed his head. "No rest today." Brian couldn't understand the urgency on Sunday, but it warranted a shower and run to Mark's office.

His arrival seemed uneventful, and Leesa's absence meant no active situation was in progress. The eerie silence in the office made him slightly uncomfortable as he eased towards Mark's office. Instead of knocking as he usually did, Brian entered the room stopping at the sight of three women. The answer to his question of urgency was seated in front Mark's desk.

"Brian, we've been waiting for you. Join us, please," Mark said, motioning for him to come closer.

The three women were professionally dressed and turned towards him at the same time with total annihilation in their eyes. He knew this could not possibly be a social meeting.

"Good morning, everyone." He took a position on a wall thinking this might be his only support. It appeared these women were about to be the judges at his inquisition.

"I've had the most enlightening conversation with the assistant district attorney and her colleagues over the last two hours. You're acquainted with them, I believe."

"I am. What brings you here so early this morning?" Brian asked.

Donna and Ginger started to rise. "Ladies, please," Namisha said in a calming voice, leaning forward in the chair for a moment. "Agent Deeds, you know damn well why we are here. The actions you've taken against Charlie are inexcusable, bordering on coercion."

Brian opened his mouth to speak when Namisha held up a finger. "I'm not finished."

He looked at Mark, who agreed with her.

"Do not think for one moment, your insinuations and deplorable actions have gone unnoticed. It's inconceivable and insulting that you would accuse three highly respected city employees of a conspiracy to interfere with a federal investigation."

"I assure you—"

Donna interrupted him. "I understand you have Charlie sitting in the cold, dark isolation cell with a thread-worn blanket, in an oversized jumpsuit."

"I'm not—"

Ginger leaned over, throwing Charlie's picture on Mark's desk. "This will not look good to a judge or the news media."

"I can explain—"

"We will be filing a formal complaint on this office's treatment of a material witness. Charlie is being treated like a criminal," Namisha said, turning to the others. They all rose to leave. "Mark, your agent has damaged the collaboration we've gladly shared over the years. I'll be speaking with the district attorney in the morning. It would be prudent for you to join us for this discussion."

"Send a time and I will be there," Mark said.

The three exited his office. No words were spoken until the office door slammed shut.

"Mark—"

"Have a seat, Brian. The scene you just observed was mild compared to the heated call I received at six this morning, demanding this meeting. The two hours of listening to the three of them roast you over the coals appear for the most part to be deserved. Without an update, I couldn't back your decisions," Mark said, pushing a file across the desk to him.

Brian scanned the information which included two additional life insurance policies besides the one they knew about on Charlie. "Who brought this to you?"

"Namisha, and before you ask. No. She didn't reveal how or who sent them. I believe she is holding back something else, but this is all she gave me. Can you explain how the assistant district attorney has this information?" Mark asked.

"No. I wish she'd said who sent them to her. I intended to update you on everything we've discovered tomorrow."

"Since we're here, you can update me now. I'm interested in the incident with Styles and additional find at the house," he said.

Brian raised his eyebrows. "Who?"

Mark raised a hand. "There isn't much in this office I'm not aware of, and no one is subverting your authority. Why don't you start with the interview? Explain what happened to my suggestion of being gentle?"

"My interview turned from gaining information to suspicion. She's been trained by the best in the city. Charlie knows how to answer and when to stop. We can't trick her into telling anything she doesn't want us to know. I am aware any of those ladies would be happy to see to her comfort and medical care, but that will not get me the answers on Jonathan's location or her involvement."

"You believe she's involved."

Brian shrugged. "I can't say for sure, something didn't feel right."

"Did you accuse them of interfering?"

"I may have alluded to that possibility," Brian admitted.

Shaking his head in disbelief. "I would have preferred you checking her into the most expensive hotel in Houston with a guard at the door.

Styles called an hour after Namisha, screaming about the incident at the house. He felt this office should have notified him the moment Charlie contacted you."

"He lost it at the house, knocking Monique down, then attacked Charlie. He'll be lucky if they don't file assault charges."

Mark stood up, walking over to the coffeepot he'd brought from the break room pouring two cups. "He failed to mention the assault on a federal officer. Brian, I have to say I have never had an agent hit a trifecta of complaints like you did today."

"It wasn't my intention. Have you ever been to the house in The Woodlands?" Brian asked.

Mark shook his head no. "I try to stay away from social gatherings for obvious reasons. I have never heard of any parties at that location. Why are you asking?"

"The house resembles those in The Paper City magazine of Houston."

"A showcase home?" Mark asked.

"Yes, spotless, nothing out of place, and according to Monique the only person allowed to clean it is Charlie."

Mark scratched his head. "That doesn't sound right. Did she say anything about the safe?"

Brian shook his head no. "Something isn't right in the house, you can tell."

"Explain," Mark said, leaning forward.

"She gave us verbal consent before arriving, but never mentioned the false wall or how to open it."

"Do you think she knows about it?"

"A good question to ask her." He leaned back in the chair. "There is a possibility the initial search warrant and her verbal consent might cover this."

"It depends on what you find, a judge might not agree later. I think you're correct to wait and secure another warrant. Do it first thing in the morning so we can release the officer out there."

"Locals calling?"

"It's hard to have an officer sitting all day and night when they're backed up on calls."

"I could call Leesa in," Brian suggested.

"What about your team?"

"Gave them the day off."

Mark thought for a moment. "Hit it hard tomorrow."

Brian stood to leave. "I'll be here early."

"One more thing. See if Charlie will talk to you, if not, I want her out of the county by Tuesday, not a day longer."

"And put her where?"

"Take your choice. I know three individuals who will be happy to have her as a guest. Run by county this evening, be charming, apologize if you must, and see if she'll talk."

"That old adage of using honey never worked for me," Brian said, smiling.

"I suggest you try."

• • •

County Jail

Charlie finished the second baloney sandwich for the day. By the meals served, it must be Sunday evening. One of the night jailers stopped to check on her and during their conversation said Namisha was a good friend. The guard promised to get word to her on Charlie's location and situation, with a photograph.

She understood this game and knew Brian could hold her here indefinitely. The FBI didn't have any evidence involving her with the bank or she would have been arrested at the house. If there had been a nice stack of books to read, a heavier blanket, and a pillow, she'd just stayed for the duration. The deal breaker on these accommodations was the concrete bed, blanket, and apparel. Dani needed to be called and informed of her situation, with any luck she'd arrive on a red-eye flight tomorrow.

Charlie yelled down the hallway. "Guard!"

A large female officer opened the cell door. "Mrs. Edwards, Agent Deeds called and is on his way to speak to you."

"I would like to make a phone call," Charlie said.

"You can do that after he arrives," she said.

"I'll make this easier for you. I want to contact my attorney, please," Charlie said.

She nodded, taking out a set of large keys to open the door. "Follow me."

The guard led her to a location where three phones hung on the wall. "Number three."

"Thank you." Charlie waited, then picked up the receiver, giving the operator the information. She took a breath praying her voice wouldn't crack when Dani answered.

"Charlie," Dani said.

"I'm in the county jail as a material witness. Bring an attorney, clothes, and a set of underwear, when you come," Charlie told her.

"Are you okay?"

"The breakfast is good."

"I'll take a morning flight, be there before noon with a good friend," Dani said.

"See you tomorrow."

She disconnected, waiting for the guard to return her to the cell. Charlie took the thin blanket crawling onto the concrete bed to wait. Twenty minutes later the door opened again, this time allowing Brian to enter.

"Charlie, I'd like to talk with you again."

She stood up, wrapping the thin blanket around her shoulders. "Agent Deeds, I invoke my right to an attorney for any further questioning. Dani and my legal representation will arrive tomorrow," Charlie said.

"I'll wait for your attorney's call and make arrangements to have you released once they arrive." He turned around, moving out of the cell.

She could see him walking away, never turning back to look. Charlie pressed her head on the door, closing both eyes, and hearing Dani's voice.

"Keep to the plan."

CHAPTER THIRTY-ONE

New Plan
Monday

Brian spent a restless night thinking of the scene at the jail. The one chance to correct his mistake was twenty minutes late, according to the guard. He thought she would accept his apology and agree to talk. The moment she stood up, he knew. What surprised him was the hard, stone-cold expression on her bruised and battered face. The last few days had not been stellar for him.

He stopped at Shipley's Donuts, arriving at the office around six smelling coffee. Leesa stood in the breakroom and smiled as he entered.

"I heard you didn't have the best day off," she said.

"No, I didn't and it's going to be a long day for everyone in the office." He placed the boxes on the counter. "The coffee smells good this morning."

"I ordered it in from Farmville, North Carolina. A good friend lives in Greenville and swears it the best," Leesa said, handing him a cup.

Brian took a sip and nodded. "Your friend is right, this is incredibly smooth."

"I have the warrant ready on the discovery at the Edwards home."

"Thank you. Where are the accountants and the night team? There is no way they have gone through everything."

She laughed. "They complained about all the noise and interruptions on this floor to Mark. He moved them, the lead agent stopped by my desk Friday and said they will be ready to shut down the night shift in a couple of days. They seem to have narrowed down their search."

"Good to know. When everyone comes in this morning, we need to meet in the conference room."

"I'll move the donuts and make more coffee," she said.

Monique entered the break room grabbed the coffeepot, then looked towards Brian. "You look like a truck ran over you this morning. Did something happen?"

"Follow me and I'll fill you in on my Sunday."

"You worked?"

"I wouldn't call it work more like damage control," he said, taking a donut.

Monique took two and followed him out. "Things backfired, didn't they?"

"More like a nuclear explosion. On Sunday Charlie invoked attorney privilege refusing to speak further with anyone. My actions during her interview may have damaged our working relationship with the district attorney and medical examiner's offices."

"Ouch." She took a bite of her donut, then sipped the coffee. "Do you have any butt left?"

"Wait, I'm not finished. Styles blames us for the incident at the house. As for my butt." He turned around, looking back. "I still have most of it."

"I want more details as this all sounds interesting," she said.

"I don't believe calling it interesting is the best description. First, Namisha Johnson made an early call around six yesterday morning to Mark, demanding a meeting. It was followed by Styles screaming in his ear over our late notification. His Sunday didn't start well. He's a little upset over the incident at the house and believes you should file assault charges."

She shrugged. "Styles has enough issues right now. I'll hold it in reserve."

Brian heard Dorian and several others coming down the hallway. "Monique head everyone to the conference room. Leesa set up coffee and took the donuts there. I'll be in shortly."

"What about the night crew?"

"See if you can catch them before they leave, this concerns everyone," Brian said.

"I hope they're still here," she said, leaving.

Brian walked to Leesa's desk, picking up the warrant. "Call the county jail and send over a release for Charlie once her attorney arrives. I'm sure we'll be hearing from someone soon."

"Do you know who she contacted?" she asked.

"She didn't say."

Monique returned with the night crew. "Found all of them."

The morning meeting included the announcement the night shift would end in a few days. This met with several cheers. He gave an update on the possibility of agents being sent to process the rental house and interview witnesses in Colorado.

He looked over at Dorian and Monique. "I need both of you to head to my office. The information left on his agenda concerns the rest of the team members." The two nodded and left. Brian informed the night shift he would give them two days off once relieved to adjust back to days, then released them. "The dayshift will check to see if the accountants need help, if you are released return here. The forensics team will also remain here until the search warrant is signed for the Edwards' house. Take a break, it's going to be another long day for all of us."

He gathered the files, and walked back to talk with Monique and Dorian.

"My wife said to thank you," Dorian told him.

"I'm glad because it's going to be another hectic week. I need you to take the warrant, get it signed, and pick up your team. Relieve the officer at the house and thank him. This search warrant is for the safe and filing cabinet only. If you discover anything else, it must be in plain sight."

"See you at the house," Dorian said, leaving.

"Dorian. Any word on Walker?"

"No, he's a ghost for now."

Brian nodded.

"If you send someone to Colorado, I want to be the first to volunteer," Monique said.

"Don't hold your breath, Mark will probably not sign off on it since the Denver office is only sixty-five miles away. I'm hoping they haven't rented the house more than once."

"We might get lucky," she said.

"I could use it after Sunday."

"Brian, line one, Linden Smyth," Leesa announced over the phone speaker.

He held up a hand to Monique. "Agent Deeds."

"Why is Charlene Edwards in jail?" Linden asked.

"Material witness," he answered.

"I want her released."

"You will need to consult with her attorney," Brian said.

"I'm the family attorney."

"Apparently, you're not hers," Brian said, hanging up the phone.

"My, my, discord in the family," she said.

"Their problem, not mine," he said.

"Do you know who she hired?" Monique asked.

"She didn't say. The involvement of another attorney complicates the investigation."

"We have no proof she's involved," Monique said.

"I can't believe she doesn't know where he is or went," Brian said.

"She probably doesn't care. I wouldn't after the abuse."

"I want to believe her," he said.

"Brian, Kiara Marshall on line one," Leesa announced through the phone speaker.

He dropped his head. "And I just thought the day or my situation couldn't get any worse."

"Who is Kiara Marshall?" Monique asked.

"You don't know her because there isn't enough money in your bank account. She is the number one defense lawyer in Houston." He picked up the line. "Agent Deeds."

CHAPTER THIRTY-TWO

Released

Charlie exited the county jail with Dani's arm around her. It felt nice to be wearing anything that didn't allow the cold air of the jail to blow through. She took a breath and followed Kiara Marshall away from the building. The tall African American attorney was the top defense lawyer in Houston, with a six-digit retainer. Her beauty had often been misjudged for weakness in the courtroom, causing attorneys to fall hard for their mistakes. Few of her cases ended up in court unless they were high profile or the district attorney's case was strong enough to win. Kiara's tough and ruthless demeanor often left unprepared witnesses running from the courtroom in tears after her cross-examination. Charlie's one encounter with her in court left her with admiration and high respect for the woman.

When they reached the sidewalk, Kiara turned to Charlie, "I wish you would have called me sooner."

"Honestly, I didn't know who to call," Charlie said.

Dani smiled at Kiara. "Kiara, and I have been friends for several years."

"Dani has always been there for me when I needed a friend." Kiara looked at Dani. "I hope that will never change."

Dani nodded to her. "It won't."

"You never said anything all the years I've known you," Charlie said.

"Professional reasons. Now to our present issue. My conversation with agent Deeds was brief. This type of treatment is unacceptable and my complaint will be on Mark Woods' desk in the morning," Kiara said.

"I don't have the information they want," Charlie said.

"You should have never been placed in jail. I understand we cannot enter the house, and another search warrant is being signed."

Charlie looked at Dani. "Why do they need another warrant?"

"He wouldn't say, we'll find out later today," Kiara stated.

"I need a shower, more clothes, and a decent toothbrush," Charlie said.

Dani removed a key card from her jean pocket. "We have a room at the Marriott."

"I have no money, no credit cards, they took everything. They placed a hold on every account, including my private one," Charlie said.

"It's covered, sis," Dani said.

Kiara walked up placing a hand on Charlie's shoulder. "I want you to go shower, eat something besides baloney and have a glass of wine. Try to rest, then be in my office at five. I need to know everything you've told them."

"Ask for a copy of the tape they made," Charlie said.

She stepped away from Charlie. "Agent Deeds didn't offer that information. I'll have it in an hour."

They headed to the parking lot where Kiara climbed into a Jaguar, waving as she drove away. Dani pointed to the black Town Car dangling the keys.

"I see you splurged," Charlie said.

"We need a special treat now and then."

Dani drove the town car to the Marriott at the Woodlands Mall area, taking Charlie to the suite.

She ran into the bathroom, found the new toothbrush waiting, and brushed for five minutes. "I've needed that for the last three days."

"There are pajamas on the bed in the large bedroom. Order anything you want from room service, then go to bed. I'm going shopping for you. What stores do you use?" Dani asked.

Charlie walked over to the window and motioned for Dani to join her. "Go over to the Woodlands Mall. I have accounts at Macy's and Nordstrom with the brand of clothing Jon set up with the fashion consultant. I'll need slacks, silk and cashmere tops. Find a leather jacket and lingerie."

"Jewelry?" Dani asked.

Charlie nodded. "Buy a simple gold necklace and earrings. Carmen should be working at the Mac counter in Macy's, ask for a travel set of makeup. Buy a pair of short black boots and a pair of black high heels. I will need two purses, anything from Michael Kors."

"What about a black dress?" Dani asked.

"Yes, try everything on and adjust the styles you feel will be best. I can't afford to dress casually at this point. I'm so sorry you have to pay for all this. My charge accounts will probably be suspended."

Dani shrugged. "It's fine, I could use a couple of nice outfits to match yours. It's been a while since I've worn cashmere."

"Dani, how are you affording Kiara Marshall, I know what she charges an hour?" Charlie asked.

"Don't worry about it. I'm calling in a favor, there will be no cost to you or me. No more questions because I will not answer them."

"Tell me there's a jacuzzi tub," Charlie said.

"Go soak. When you're out, order a couple of bottles of wine for us. It will take me a few hours to fill the list. Oh, I called your friends, we're meeting them for drinks at nine in the hotel bar," Dani said, hugging her sister before leaving.

"Koda?"

"Spending time with Luke at the cabin."

"I wish I was at the cabin."

"Go, bathe," Dani said.

Charlie moved to the bathroom in the master suite, filling the tub over the jets. The darkness faded with the bubbles as she slid down to wash away the stench of the county jail away. After refilling the tub twice, she slipped on new pajamas and slept peacefully until Dani returned. Christmas came early with the multiple sacks being brought into the suite by the bellman.

She laughed at all the sacks. "You got a little carried away, didn't you?"

"You will not believe the sales I found there. Thought we could both use the treat so I broke in my new Discover card. You seem to have friends at the stores. I lost count of all the samples they added for you. Did you order anything from room service?"

"No. Bathed and slept," Charlie answered.

"It's fine, I called on the way back. We need to eat something before the meeting." The knock on the door made Dani smile. "And there they are." She opened the door, allowing the server to set up the appetizers and open the bottle of wine. Dani signed the ticket, giving him a twenty.

They drank a toast to being free, devouring the appetizers.

"This sure beats the baloney sandwiches," Charlie said.

"Brian is such a dick for doing this to you."

"It's his job, Dani. I just didn't expect to be sent to jail. He looked a little sad yesterday when he came to visit. I couldn't decide if it was because of where he put me or the fact, he didn't break me."

Dani frowned, taking Charlie's hands. "You can't feel sorry for him. Brian isn't your friend, regardless of the past. He's an agent in charge of a high-profile case with a job to see someone ends up in jail. Keep to the plan."

She nodded. "You're right. What should I wear?"

Dani emptied the wine glass, pouring it full again. "I think we should wear cashmere."

CHAPTER THIRTY-THREE

Questions
4:30 p.m.

Brian checked his watch, trying to understand how the day slipped away so fast. He agreed to Kiara Marshall's demand to allow her client recovery time after the weekend. The harsh treatment Mrs. Edwards incurred required additional time before any further questioning. At ten this morning he updated Mark on the warrant, Kiara's phone call, and a request to send agents to Colorado. It took a second for Mark to deny the request, reminding Brian the Denver office is full of agents.

The rest of the day he and Monique went over Charlie's initial interview. The Trooper remembered Charlie describing her down to the shoes. He placed Jonathan in the back seat on the passenger's side, alive and drunk. Monique confirmed this is where Styles and another man placed him the night of the party. The video from the rest station where Charlie stopped had been requested from Colorado. They couldn't do much with the statements involving the rental or shops in Estes Park. The owners or managers remembered their interactions involving Charlie and Dani. It appeared the office in Denver would need to help with the investigation and he made a note to have them ask about the amenities at the rental.

He knew it was going to be non-stop today and was positive a late night remained ahead of him. Brian stood up to stretch then walked to the break room. Mark opened the fridge removing a cold drink. "When is your interview?"

"In about an hour. I have a team at the house, waiting for information from Charlie on the safe. I'm hoping there will not be a need to force it open."

Mark leaned against the counter. "I'd suggest you bring the filing cabinet here to go through the information inside."

"Agreed. How did your meeting go with the district attorney and medical examiner?"

Mark looked at the ceiling for a moment. "I suggest you not expect any favors for a while. Kiara made a formal complaint about the appalling treatment of a material witness today. This makes five complaints in twenty-four hours, a record for the Houston office."

Brian took a power drink from the fridge. "Suggestions for this afternoon?"

"Kid gloves, you do not want to face Kiara Marshall in court."

Monique followed Leesa into the breakroom. "Brian, Ms. Marshall is here with her client."

"They're early. Is Danielle with them?"

"Yes."

"Have her wait in the front with you, please. We'll do this in the small conference room with a video camera."

"Did you get any information from the team at the house?" Monique asked.

"Are you referring to prints in the bathroom?" Brian asked.

"Yes."

"Jonathan's only," Brian said.

"Do you think she knows the combination and where the key is located?" Mark asked.

"I suggest we ask her," Monique answered.

They stopped by to pick up a file from Brian's office and then headed toward the small conference room. Monique stopped and made a small gasp at the woman in the waiting area.

Brian touched her arm, moving them out of hearing range. "Danielle Parks, Charlie's mirror image twin."

"If it weren't for the injuries, I'd swear it was Charlie," she said.

"Charlene and Danielle Parks are in the Guinness Book of Records."

She smirked. "For being twins?"

"No. They are unique, one in millions," he answered.

"Unique in what way?"

"Carbon copy of each other, same DNA patterns, prints, hair, the list goes on and it could be a forensic nightmare."

"A clone. This is a huge problem," she said, leaning against the wall.

Brian reached for the door. "Kick me if I start to throw down the gauntlet again. I have strict, orders to be kind this time."

They entered, taking seats across from Kiara and Charlie. Brian noticed she looked rested, with new clothes and makeup delicately applied over the injuries.

"Agent Deeds, we are here out of courtesy," Kiara said.

"I appreciate your presence and acknowledge this and the complaint you filed," Brian said.

"I've watched the hours-long interrogation of my client who cooperated and continues by coming in today. She informed me of her bathroom breaks during the interview and your purchase of food."

"We're not barbarians," Monique said.

"You aren't? Let's discuss this for a moment. Arriving home Thursday, she is brought here and interrogated for hours. You have denied access to her home, money, credit cards, or personal transportation. Please explain the threat which sent her to the county jail where you stripped her naked and provided inappropriate clothing. Agents, there were other options available."

"I believe she purposely held back information that could lead us to her husband. Through associations with certain individuals, she might—"

"Yes. I've spoken with Namisha Johnson and the others about your absurd accusations. It's your job to find her husband."

Brian changed positions in the chair, reminding himself to keep calm and not lock them both up. "I expect Mrs. Edwards to tell the truth. The reason for this meeting is to serve another search warrant on the safe room, in the front bathroom," Brian said.

"We would appreciate the combination of the safe and key to the filing cabinet," Monique said.

Charlie raised her eyebrows, turning to Kiara, shaking her head no. "What safe, what filing cabinet?"

"Are you going to tell us, you have never seen the room inside the walk-in closet?" Brian asked.

Brian handed Kiara a folder with photographs of the room and its contents. They both looked through the photographs.

"In the four years we have lived in the home, he never allowed me to enter his bathroom. Not even to clean it. Your forensics team will not find one piece of evidence showing my presence in there," Charlie said.

"Who cleans it?" Brian asked.

"Jon."

Monique laughed. "I find your explanation difficult to believe."

"Agent Aubuchon, have you ever met my husband?" Charlie asked.

"No."

Charlie leaned, forward-pointing. "Then take a long close look at my face. This isn't the first time I've had these injuries. He expects things in the house to be kept a certain way, His! He dresses me from underwear to jewelry, checks my makeup before I leave the house, and my hair cannot have one piece out of place."

"How many years has this been?" Monique asked.

"Don't answer that," Kiara said.

"Agent Deeds, you may tear up, rip out, or blow up the house for all I care. The one item in the house which means anything to me is my mother's wedding ring. I cannot give you, what I do not possess," Charlie said.

"I have a question. Why are there no personal photographs in your home?" Monique asked.

"Ask Jon when you find him," Charlie said.

"It is our belief Jonathan became aware of your investigation and disappeared of his own accord. He left a wife to face the embarrassment of his actions and harassment of authorities," Kiara stated.

"We would appreciate the name of the rental company in Estes Park," Monique said.

Charlie leaned over, pulling a piece of hotel stationery from her purse. "Since Dani took care of the arrangements, she is happy to provide the information. The additional names and numbers are the shops and restaurants we visited."

Monique reached across the table, taking it. "Very kind of her."

"As both of you can see, my client is being extremely cooperative," Kiara stated.

"Can you explain why the sheriff never saw or met Jonathan while you were at the farm?" Brian asked.

"Make your point, Agent," Kiara said.

"We believe he never made it to the farm. Your client dropped him off somewhere under threat should she say anything," Monique said.

Kiara leaned back in the chair, crossing her arms. "Give it to them."

"Give us what?" Brian asked.

Charlie reached into the purse again, pulling out a plastic bag with a toothbrush and Jonathan's special brand of toothpaste. She placed it on the table.

"Where did this come from?" he asked.

"Dani's house. He left it there when we checked into the rental. I won't go into his accusations of me purposely leaving it. He complained every day of having to use a disposable toothbrush and generic toothpaste provided by the rental. Agent Aubuchon, are you finally getting the image of the type of man he is?"

"We would like for you to take a polygraph," Monique said.

"Hell will freeze over first. You have all the information you need, do your job. Do you have any evidence proving my client is involved in the bank fraud?" Kiara asked.

"No, not at this time," Brian said.

"I'm filing a motion in the morning to have Mrs. Edwards' private account released, so she can at least buy food. I'm assuming the file with the photographs is mine, or shall I file for discovery?" Kiara asked.

"They're yours," Brian said.

"Charlie, we're done here. If you need any further contact with her, you will call me," Kiara said, picking up the file and standing next to Charlie.

"Ms. Marshall, until we open the safe and look through the files, Charlie needs to remain in Houston," Brian said.

"You'll find her and Danielle at my home starting tomorrow night," Kiara said, turning away from them.

"That's profoundly thoughtful of you," Monique said, snidely.

Kiara whipped around, leaning across the table on one hand. "After the harsh treatment, this woman has suffered, for no reason other than for the enjoyment of this office. It's the right and humane thing to do for her. I will expect notification of the contents when you open the safe and filing cabinet," Kiara said.

"You will have a full report. If we find cause to talk with your client again," Brian said.

"You have my number, Charlie we're leaving," Kiara said.

They walked to the foyer where Dani joined them. As they left, she took a moment to turn and wink at Brian.

"What the hell was that?" Monique asked, upset at her actions.

"Forget it. Is Dorian at the house?"

"Yes."

He handed Monique the plastic bag. "Log it in and let's take a ride." As she left, Mark took her place. "Did you watch?"

"Until Monique upset Kiara. Interesting move bringing the toothbrush."

"The story is plausible," Brian said.

"I find it convenient, but you need to take into consideration how a jury will perceive it. An abused wife, presenting evidence of her husband's existence in Colorado thrown into jail. Why? Because she cooperated fully with the FBI and continues to do so. I do not believe that will be good press for us."

Brian rubbed his face with both hands. "No, not when you present it like that."

"It's your case, but if I were you, let it go unless there is a discovery of evidence to the contrary. I'm heading home. See you tomorrow," Mark said and left.

"Let's go," Monique said.

They took the elevator to the basement where he threw the keys to Monique. "Stop at a drive-thru, I want to pick food up for them."

"Sonic, okay?" she asked.

"Perfect."

They picked up a variety of meals, then drove to the house." Brian knocked on the front door.

Dorian opened it, smiling. "I hope you brought the combination and key."

"No. I brought something better, food, it's in the car," Brian told him.

"Guess that will have to do for now." Dorian ran upstairs, bringing two men back with him.

The bags and drinks were quickly selected with the team taking a spot on the walkway to eat.

"Thanks for bringing something to eat. We processed the cabinet, it's the same as the rest of the room, Jonathan's prints are the only ones in there," Dorian told him.

"It's going to be a long evening. Monique try to locate a locksmith that will come out now. I want the safe opened," Brian said.

"Warrant served?" Dorian asked shoving the rest of the burger in his mouth.

"Yes."

"Locksmith will be here in thirty minutes, of course, there is a night charge," Monique told them.

"When everyone is finished, head in and we'll be up once the locksmith arrives."

She took one of the sacks, opened a bacon cheeseburger, and took a couple of bites. "This isn't bad."

Brian found the sack with the cheddar peppers and leaned against the car.

She took the large Dr. Pepper and moved next to him. "Why didn't you tell Charlie and Kiara about the new life insurance policy?"

Brian finished the last pepper and wiped his hands together. "I will when it serves a purpose."

"I'd say offing your wife for that much money serves a purpose, especially if she knew about it."

"True, but how do we prove she knew?"

"We can't and as long as she looks like a doormat, he stomped his feet on, no jury would ever convict her of anything."

"You believe that?"

If I was sitting on the jury, she'd go free."

Brian stared at Monique. "You'd seriously let her go?

"I'd probably give her money, too," she answered.

"We have to find him and Lonnie Walker."

CHAPTER THIRTY-FOUR

Following The Money
The next morning Brian walked around the large conference room thinking of the continuing issues this case presented on an almost daily basis. It seemed what should have been a straightforward investigation, had turned into a nightmare of small irritating problems. When the locksmith arrived last night, they escorted him into the house presenting the safe and filing cabinet to him.

"*Good Lord, what an antique. I have a key in the truck that will open it. The safe is going to be a problem for you. Without the key card it is practically impossible to open short of blasting or drilling it,*" he told them.

Brian closed his eyes and dropped his head.

"*It has a combination,*" *Dorian told him.*

"*It's fake, a ruse for thieves. If you'll look above it, there's a small slit where a key card goes.*"

Brian walked away motioning for the man to follow him. "*What about the distributor?*"

"*I was going to tell you these safes are made in Katy. I have the information and a number in my phone.*"

Brian walked back to the closet. "*This safe is made in Katy. Dorian take down the information from this gentleman.*"

"*Are we going to need security until we can open it?*" *Monique asked.*

"*Hell no. Cut the damn thing out of the wall,*" *Brian said to them.*

It was after midnight when the safe and filing cabinet were brought to the office and logged as evidence. Brian watched Mark walk around the table studying the safe.

"What the hell does he have in here? It's long don't you agree?"

"I've never seen one like this. We cannot open it without a key card. Dorian contacted the company representative last night," Brian said.

"What are they requiring?" Mark asked.

Dorian joined them. "The woman I spoke with said normally they would require a warrant. She understands the gravity of our situation and would wave it with a simple release signature on their paperwork. Normally, there is an additional individual on a list with permission to have access to another key."

"And who is on the list, Charlie or Styles?" Mark asked.

"No one, except Jonathan, not even his father," Monique added.

"Has anyone run all this by Legal this morning?" Mark asked.

"I did," Brian answered. "Charlie is the legal resident and her name is on the mortgage paperwork. The lawyers said her permission is all we need. Her lawyer faxed the paperwork allowing us to open the safe. It seems everyone is interested in the contents."

Mark nodded. "Written permission, and a release will be difficult to question unless Jonathan shows up today and objects. Are we finished at the house?"

"We left a mess, but I think we can lock it up," Brian said.

Mark raised an eyebrow. "Any reason not to release it back to Mrs. Edwards?"

"I'd like to wait for obvious reasons," Brian said, pointing to the table.

Mark looked around the room. "I've spoken with the accountants this morning. They were unable to find anything, other than Charlie's name on their joint account, that connects her to the fraud case. The personal account, not associated with Edwards Trust, is clean. We're pushing the limits here."

"What's the hurry?" Monique asked.

"Charlie wants to leave Houston after Thanksgiving and go back to Colorado with her sister," Mark answered.

This announcement met with unhappy comments including, you've got to be kidding, coming from his team.

Brian held up a hand. "Mark, that's not a good idea. Our relationship with the sheriff isn't the best in Estes Park. It seems he wasn't happy with the tone of my inquiry when it came to Dani."

"Making friends in Colorado, are we? Charlie has agreed to check in weekly with the sheriff and come back at any point should we need her. How can I not agree? She isn't the only person who saw Jonathan alive on Sunday," Mark told Brian's team.

"It doesn't mean she doesn't know where he is," Monique said. "Maybe we should pull Dani Parks in for an interview."

Mark shook his head no. "You have no reason. She can refuse and Kiara Marshall will probably represent her, too. Whose prints are on the filing cabinet?"

"Jonathan's," Brian answered.

"Anyone else?" Mark asked.

"No. We need more time to go through these files and see what's in the safe." Brian checked his watch. "Dorian, head out to the safe company and get the card."

"On my way," he said, leaving the room.

"Kiara wants Charlie's personal account and credit card not associated with Edwards Trust released." Mark lowered his head for a moment, raising his eyes to Brian. "Unless you discover something in the filing cabinet or safe that connects her to the fraud case a judge is going to agree with her attorney."

Monique shook her head no. "This is a mistake."

"Do you believe she allowed him to beat her, then agreed to cover for his disappearance? Or are we talking about something else?" Mark asked, looking at them. "Because right now, her photograph is being passed around the district attorney's and medical examiner's, offices. She is garnering a lot of sympathy and support. We are not going to win this one, ladies and gentlemen."

"What if she is responsible for his disappearance?" Monique asked.

Mark held out his arms. "Where's your proof? You have a week to make a connection or she'll be spending Christmas in Estes Park. Call me, when Dorian returns, I want to be here when the safe is open."

Brian wanted to kick something as Mark walked away. He turned back to the team. "You heard him, we need to get busy, open the filing cabinet."

The team took photographs of its location in the room, using a key Monique opened metal filing cabinet. She removed all the folders from the first drawer, placed them on a couple of tables, and instructed them to photograph each file and its contents. Brian walked away concerned about Charlie being allowed to leave the state.

Monique walked over taking Brian by the arm. "Let's look through this, there could be something we can use to keep her from leaving."

He pointed toward an agent calling for them. "She found something."

They walked over to where the agent pointed at the photographs on the table.

"Oh my God," Monique said and turned away for a moment.

It took a moment before he could speak. "Are all of them like this?"

"I'm not sure," she answered.

"That's not all," Monique added. "I'm not sure the girls in this photograph are over sixteen."

"You may want to call Agent Woods back," another agent stated, holding up an additional file.

"Why?" Brian asked, picking it up. "Everyone stop what you are doing and back away from the tables." He made a call to Mark explaining what they found.

A moment later the door flew open as Mark entered the room. "Where are they?"

"On the tables, my people stopped and backed off," Brian told him.

Mark began looking through them. "Jesus H. Christ! What about the second drawer?"

"We're waiting until you decide on these first. This team is not set up for blackmail and child pornography. It's not just local," Brian told him.

"What a damn mess. Pull the rest of the folders and keep away from this, while I go make a call upstairs. If the files in the bottom are more of this, place them here and walk away," he said, leaving.

Brian asked Monique and one agent to remove all the folders from the bottom drawer. "Look through them for similar content, and add them to the front tables."

The door opened again with Mark and the head of Violent Crimes Against Children, Agent Darby Fisher accompanying him. Agent Fisher was a guest speaker at the academy on crimes against children. She was highly respected for the work her team accomplished.

Dorian entered shortly afterward searching the room for the team. He located Brian and Monique walking over to them. "What happened?"

Brian held up a hand. "Hang on a second." He watched Mark pick up several photographs, handing them to Darby. Her facial expression never changed looking from file to file. She removed a cell phone from a pocket and made a call.

"Did I miss something?" Dorian asked.

"Yes, you did," Monique answered him.

"What's going on?" he asked.

"The preverbal can of worms. We do not want to get involved with anything on that side of the room."

Mark walked over to Brian. "Her team is on the way to take photographs, then they'll take the files and open a case. We'll wait to open the safe until they're gone. I explained anything of a similar nature you discover will be immediately handed over to her unit. What about the ones from the bottom drawer?"

Monique motioned for them to follow her. "These files go back to the late 1800s. It appears the Edwards' shady family dealings aren't something new. I think these will all belong to our case."

"Check the most recent file for any information on a connection to Charlie," Brian said.

Mark and Brian turned as several members of the VCAC team entered the conference room moving quickly to document and remove the files. Darby walked over to them and thanked Mark for the call. Once they left, he turned to Brian.

"Open this damn thing."

Brian's team returned to the table holding the safe. Dorian opened the envelope handing the key card to Brian who slid it into the slot. The latch released, allowing gloved hands to open the door.

"Holy shit!" Dorian exclaimed.

"Photographs please," Brian said, stepping back.

Once the initial contents were documented, Dorian and Monique began removing stack after stack of hundred-dollar bills along with a small black box filled with clear stones. Three flash drives and four weapons were removed from the back of the safe.

Brian picked up the flash drives. "Dorian, find a computer and scan through them quickly. Monique, how much cash?"

"Two maybe two-hundred-fifty thousand."

"How much money did Charlie have with her?" Mark asked.

"Three hundred dollars," Brian said, and pointed to the small black box.

Mark opened the box containing the clear stones and took a pen from his upper shirt pocket moving them around. "If these are diamonds, and I assume they are or they wouldn't be locked up in a safe. There's somewhere between half to three-quarters of a million dollars here." He looked up into the faces of the agents and knew they had questions concerning his last statement. "I've had some experience in my career with diamonds, officially."

An agent checking the weapon's serial numbers spoke up. "All registered to Jonathan."

Dorian walked over handing the flash drives to Mark. "These need to go upstairs and I'll be in the bathroom washing my eyes out with bleach."

A team member handed Brian a file. "This is the most updated information you're looking for on the bank."

"Is there anything with Charlene Parks or Edwards in the file?" Mark asked.

"No, sir."

Mark looked at Brian. "I'll see if Kiara will have them as guests through Thanksgiving but after that, you'll need to call Estes Park."

"What if—"

Mark held up a hand stopping Brian. "If you find anything, I will personally go and arrest her myself. You have enough work to do on Jonathan, build your case, and find him. Your feelings or suspicions about his wife will have to wait."

Brian knew he was right. Without evidence, Charlie's involvement was just a suspicion.

Monique reached up placing a hand on his shoulder. "I know how you feel, let's get these bastards first."

Brian nodded in agreement. "Time is slipping away for us to find evidence to connect her."

"If it'll make you feel any better Lyssa is cooking for Thanksgiving," Monique told him.

Brian smiled. "Any chance there's room at the table for one more?"

"You don't even need to ask. It will be a big one on the bayou and you're expected to be there."

CHAPTER THIRTY-FIVE

Rocky Mountain Calling
Thanksgiving

The Red Oak Ranch area of Conroe is an affluent area with five-acre homes and gated drives. Kiara Marshall's four-bedroom brick home was beautiful with a homey feel. They were enjoying a pleasant Texas afternoon on the patio after a gourmet Thanksgiving meal. The sound of the small fountains in the pool was a welcome change from the noise of the county jail. There were several pathways in the backyard leading out to the corners of the property where flowers of every kind grew.

Charlie leaned back, placing both feet on the glass-top table in front of her. "This is so much better than spending my birthday in the county jail."

Dani laughed. "Agreed and less expensive than the Marriott."

"I appreciate you calling my friends," Charlie told her.

"You are fortunate to have them in your life. I couldn't stop laughing when Namisha told us the story of their meeting with Agent Woods."

"You should have heard Kiara in the interrogation room when Monique said they weren't barbaric. It was a classic tear-down. I tried not to laugh, just couldn't stop myself a couple of times. What has been really nice, is being here. No media to face, and thanks to Kiara I have money and credit cards," Charlie said.

"I am a little tired of all the bothersome phone calls about things that do not matter such as finding Jon's urine in the front seat," Dani told her.

"He's doing his job, badgering me is part of it. I'm sure he loved the video the highway department in Pueblo sent of Jon and me alive and well that night."

Dani scratched her head. "I don't understand his hesitancy to question me."

"I would imagine because he knows it will not help his case and Kiara won't allow it," Charlie said.

"At least she received the information from the file cabinet and photographs of the safe contents."

Charlie frowned. "They made quite a mess at the house. I'll let Styles deal with the damage. Did she say anything about the women in Lake Charles to you?"

"No, and if I were you, leave it alone. The infidelity, drug abuse, and embezzlement will make interesting reading in a year or two. What did Kiara say about the journal you've been keeping?"

"The same thing you did, keep it for another time," Charlie answered.

"Well, you look rested and ready to leave."

"I hope you're right about leaving."

Kiara walked out on the patio in a pair of jeans and a light-colored teal sweater. She held up a bottle of wine. "Can I fill your glasses?"

"No," Charlie answered.

"Yes," Dani said, holding out a glass.

"How can you have any room after that huge meal, sis?"

Dani smirked. "Helps with my digestion."

Kiara filled Dani's glass, then placed two small, wrapped boxes on the table before sitting down. "I have good news."

They both looked at the boxes and then at Kiara.

"What is this?" Dani asked.

Kiara smiled at them. "You didn't think I would forget what day it is."

"Thank you," Charlies said.

"I'm happy our birthday doesn't always fall on Thanksgiving, but often it does. You didn't need to do this," Dani said.

"It's nothing, open them." Kiara pointed at the boxes.

They opened the small boxes to discover gold infinity pins with three small diamonds located in one of the loops.

"I felt this represented the bond between sisters and friends," Kiara told them.

"Thank you, it's perfect," Dani said.

"Now, for the rest of your gift," Kiara said.

"Please, tell me I can leave," Charlie said.

She smiled at them. "Yes."

Dani hugged Charlie.

"The news isn't all wonderful. You can leave with the stipulations you report once a week to the sheriff."

"Luke comes for coffee at least two or three times a week," Dani said.

"They're refusing to release the house back to you. A judge agreed to allow you to get your clothes and any belongings not taken by the FBI," Kiara told her.

"Honestly, I hate the clothes Jon forces me to wear. I prefer jeans and sneakers."

"You have the option."

"Now that I think about it, there is one thing I'd like to have. Any chance they will release mother's ring to me?" Charlie asked.

Kiara reached into her jean pocket and handed Charlie a receipt. "Monique said they would take good care of it."

"What a little bitch," Dani said.

Charlie reached over, taking her sister's hand. "Dani, I will get it back, this is part of their tactics. Thinking about this now, I should have been more assertive and gone through his closet."

"The fact you didn't search, saved you. If they had found a hair, you wouldn't be sitting here drinking my wine. Dani, she's right about their tactics. Both of you stay strong and under no circumstances talk to anyone, either of you, without me," Kiara said sternly.

"Have you heard from Styles?" Charlie asked.

"Since I threatened to have him charged with assault on you? No. Linden Smyth contacted me. Styles has filed a missing person report on Jonathan."

"I'm sure he is blaming me for his disappearance."

"No. According to Linden, he believes someone kidnapped Jonathan and is holding him for ransom," Kiara said.

Charlie turned to Dani. "This is a new one."

"I do not have all the information from Linden. He did tell me in confidence Jonathan might have been kidnapped by individuals associated with Las Vegas."

"Are you talking about the mob?" Dani asked.

"What makes him believe something like that?" Charlie asked.

"He didn't go into any detail and I damn sure didn't ask. Charlie, did you know anything about trips to Las Vegas? Did he mention buying property there?" Kiara asked.

"I can't answer your questions. He made trips all the time telling me it was bank business. This is something I want no part of especially with everything else going on," Charlie answered.

"Dealing with the wrong individuals there will get you a grave in the desert," Kiara told them.

"Did Brian say anything about returning the Escalade?" Charlie asked.

Kiara shook her head no. "It isn't going anywhere, probably laying in pieces somewhere in the FBI garage."

"The Mercedes?" Charlie asked.

"Yours. I found a clear title and transferred it to your name only," Kiara told her.

"Sis, trade it in on something usable in the mountains."

"Listen to Dani, end-of-year sales start tomorrow at several dealerships. The Mercedes has a nice trade-in value. When are you going to leave for Colorado?"

"It depends on how quickly I can find something with four-wheel drive."

"Both of you are welcome here anytime." She leaned back in the chaise. "This case will be a media nightmare for months, you need to leave. Who is going to repair the house once it's released?"

"I would imagine Styles will handle it."

"You can sell it and the Escalade if you want," Kiara told her.

"I didn't know that was possible."

Kiara smiled. "It is."

"Jon is the one who made all the decisions on its construction. I've always hated it, maybe due to all the time I spent on my knees cleaning it."

Kiara glanced toward Dani. "There isn't a hurry, something for you to think about for the future."

"I'd rather just hand the keys to Styles and walk away. The FBI is holding the only item of value to me. No. I've worn the last piece of clothing bought by anyone except me or Dani."

"Think about what you're saying, give it six months maybe a year. I received a call from Namisha before Thanksgiving," Kiara said looking at Charlie.

"The county is letting me go."

Kiara nodded. "Donna couldn't convince them to keep you. They felt the publicity and your association with the bank would be detrimental to any future cases."

"I knew the chances of going back weren't in my favor."

"I'll have plenty of work for both of us in a few months," Dani told her.

"Charlie, think about what I said concerning your home. I checked the market value, it's double the price you paid. The profits would go a long way to help you start a new life. If you still feel the same in a year, I'll draw up the paperwork for you to sign."

"I'll think on it. When you have time, go by the house. In my closet there are a Hermes purse and wallet. It's yours," Charlie said, smiling.

Kiara sat up. "I may take you up on that offer, with a letter of it being a gift just to be on the legal side."

"I can never repay you for all of this."

Kiara looked at Dani and smiled. "Some debts can never be repaid." She stood up. "Ladies, we have a plan, stick to it."

"If you're heading inside, another bottle would be nice." Dani held her glass up.

"I'll get another bottle and we can enjoy the rest of the day," Kiara said leaving.

"If we can find a vehicle for you, I'd like to leave by Tuesday. There are a few items I didn't have time to take and dispose of before you called. My friends, Tim and Cletus have a welding torch which is needed to finish things up," Dani told her.

"Then I guess it's car shopping for us tomorrow. The last thing we need is an unexpected visit from Brian before we complete cleaning up loose ends."

"I need to get back, missing my Koda."

"Maybe we can go back to the lake and spend more than a couple of days this time. Kiara, you should join us. It is the most beautiful and peaceful place I've ever stayed. No one to find or bother you."

Kiara looked at Dani. "I remember, it's the sheriff's place, isn't it?"

Dani smiled. "Yes. I'll call Luke and make arrangements whenever you can find the time to leave for a few days."

CHAPTER THIRTY-SIX

Holiday Rush
December

Brian returned to his office at seven rested and feeling good after the Thanksgiving trip to Louisiana. They traveled south to a family home on the bayou for a Cajun family gathering. A new job, move and the stress of a major case faded away with the food and music of the bayou. He'd forgotten the wonderful taste of Cajun cooking, drinking, and dancing all night. Monique's partner played matchmaker bringing a friend just for him. He took her number, knowing a long-distance relationship would never work even two hours away.

The front door opened around seven-thirty with a familiar clicking of heels coming down the hallway. Brian left the office and joined Leesa in the break room.

"Wow," he said staring at six or seven containers with aluminum foil covering the tops.

"The usual Thanksgiving leftovers. My husband doesn't need them and I know they will not go to waste here," she said, starting a pot of coffee. "Did you enjoy Louisiana?"

"What can I say other than amazing, relaxing, and difficult to come back."

"You have a ten o'clock video conference with the Denver office," she reminded him.

"I'd like to think they have found something at the rental. I'm hoping someone besides the sheriff is willing to say Jonathan was actually in town."

"If I haven't told you before now, thanks for seeing the bank wasn't closed for over ten days. I know a lot of people here in the building worried it might be longer."

"You never said anything about having an account there," he said.

She laughed. "There aren't too many people in Houston who don't. I never thought about questioning their reputation until this happened. Fortunately, we have a vacation account at a credit union."

He poured a cup of coffee. "You need to run upstairs and thank the accountants when they come in today. They are a special group of individuals who made it possible to open the bank."

"They have narrowed down the accounts and computers needing a more thorough investigation. The rest are being released back to the bank in a few days," Leesa informed him.

Brian seems surprised at this information. "Guess I need to check in more with you. Please, tell Dorian and Monique about the meeting."

Leesa picked up her coffee cup and a piece of chocolate cake, leaving the break room. "Will do, have a piece, it has pecans in it."

Brian cut a small bite-size piece and ate it. A moment later, a larger piece and a coffee refill sat on his desk. He ran through emails, stopping to see his fate on the five complaints accrued before Thanksgiving. The verbal complaint from Styles had been rejected. A verbal warning by Mark on his actions with Charlie caused a written complaint from her attorney. The one filed by Namisha, Donna, and Ginger, took precedence due to their positions with Harris County. A written reprimand, for his actions, would be placed in his personnel file. He took a chance and failed, causing damage between the offices. The distrust would take time to repair.

"Good morning," Monique said, followed by Dorian carrying the pan of chocolate cake into his office.

Brian smiled at them. "I trust everyone had a nice Thanksgiving."

"It took a while for my children to call me daddy again, otherwise, everything else was great," Dorian told him.

Monique licked the chocolate off two of her fingers. "I understand Denver is calling this morning."

"Don't either of you get too excited, a lot of time has elapsed," Brian said, motioning for the cake pan.

Dorian held it back, then passed it to him. "Maybe, they have some interviews worth reading."

He continued to check emails and then stopped. "This is nice. Charlie and her sister left Houston yesterday."

"Big mistake to let her leave," Dorian said.

Brian leaned back, raising his hands. "We have nothing to hold her on."

"Call on line two from Agent Arthur Johnson," Leesa announced.

"This is not who I wanted to speak to this morning," he told them then answered the phone on speaker. "Agent Johnson, what can I do for you?"

Dorian leaned over whispering to Monique. "Arthur is the agent in charge of kidnapping cases."

Monique placed a hand to the side of her mouth towards Dorian. "I know, I know."

"I bet Styles filed a report on Jonathan," he said.

Brian motioned for them to stop talking. "Seriously, a kidnapping report to the FBI. Did you tell him the slimeball is hiding until he can slip out of the country?"

"I know Brian, nothing we can do for now except follow up. Send us what you have and we'll do the same," Arthur said disconnecting.

Brian dropped his head and took a big bite of the chocolate cake. "We need to focus on the case as if he purposely disappeared. Maybe Arthur can find out where he is hiding."

"This case has gone from embezzlement to child pornography, including certain political figures. A long family history of thieves and con men to kidnapping," Monique said.

"Don't forget domestic violence," Dorian added.

"The addition of two departments in the building having cases associated with the embezzlement means extra responsibility," Brian told them.

"We're going to need to pass on information," Monique said.

"Yes, and promptly. We cannot hold anything which may be important to their cases. If you are unsure, send it anyway and they can decide if it's pertinent," Brian said.

"What a cluster," Dorian said.

"Brian, Denver is calling to see if they can report early," Leesa interrupted over the speaker.

"Large conference room five minutes."

The three stood to leave. Mark Woods stopped by Brian's office before heading to the break room.

"Did I hear Denver is calling?"

"Yes, drop-in, I'm hoping for information and interested in what they did or didn't find," Brian said.

"I'll join you shortly," Mark said.

Brian pulled down the screen, then logged on to the computer. The Denver seal switched to an agent.

"Agent Deeds, good morning. I'm Agent Ava Gardner." She could see him trying not to smile. "Go ahead and laugh everyone else does."

"It's a lovely name," he told her.

"I appreciate that but you aren't the one who had to grow up with it."

Brian smiled. "I hope you have some information for my team this morning."

She picked up some papers and shuffled through them before looking back at her screen. "First, I wish to go on record and say interviewing the residents in Estes Park regarding this case wasn't easy or informative. I would have received more information from my daughter's first-grade class on a description of the Easter Bunny. I'm praying we never have a case there."

Monique and Dorian both bit their lips, trying not to laugh.

"Tell us what you discovered," Brian said, encouragingly.

"If you insist. I'll start with the rental company. It took some time to locate their office due to not having a specific suite number or letter. I discovered they had a small office in the building of another company. The owner of 'We Love Dirty Pipes', the local septic cleaning company, directed me to their location through the alley. Their filing system is paper, and the new secretary couldn't find any files on Danielle Parks. The copy of the receipt you sent saved me as it had been listed as being rented to a male named, Daniel Parker. The days matched and thankfully Ms. Parks paid by credit card, though the numbers were barely legible."

Brian glanced at the door as Mark entered, taking a seat next to Monique.

She leaned over to him. "Get ready."

Brian frowned at her. "Were you able to find any evidence for us?"

She started laughing, then stopped clearing her throat. "Excuse me, Agent Deeds. The rental company's less-than-accurate records say besides the group presently in the house, the house has been rented three other times since Ms. Parks' rental date. This home is enormous with multiple bedrooms each with its own bath. Against my better judgment, I drove out to the property to assess the possibility a forensics unit might find evidence. After knocking on the door for twenty minutes the occupants answered the door upset, I woke them at noon."

"Were they willing to cooperate," Brian said.

"Not really. The gentleman who answered the door pulled the I'm an attorney go get a warrant. I do have the list of occupants who have enjoyed their time in the house. On Monday, the day Mr. Edwards supposedly left the house, a family of twelve checked in that afternoon. Four days later a group of old married fraternity brothers, eight to be exact, partied for the weekend. The following Monday, a bachelorette party of fifteen arrived for six days."

"I see," Brian said.

"I don't believe you do. There have been thirty-five individuals in the house that I can verify. This doesn't count individuals who just showed up or new friends they met in town and came back for a night. They have eaten, slept, drank, and I don't wish to think of the other activities which may or may not have happened in the bedrooms."

"What about the cleaning crew? Were you able to speak with them?"

"A regular crew of four women cleans this house after each rental. I luckily found all four of them at the bowling alley on their league night. The answer to your question about complimentary items in the rental is yes. They provide toiletries for every bathroom. They informed me the septic system of the house, requires a combination of cleaners. This includes bleach, borax, and ammonia used on an alternating schedule to avoid breaking down the bacteria in the septic system. And before you ask, they used bleach after the Edwards left."

"Then I can assume—"

"The showers, toilets and every sink has been through all three cleaners since the original rental date of Ms. Parks," she told him.

"Who has the service to clean the linens?"

"I know you are hoping it might be a local company. You understand I don't enjoy disappointing you but they contract through the largest linen cleaning service in Denver. Once the linens are picked up, they go through a rigorous washing and sanitizing process for obvious reasons. This company handles thousands and thousands of linens."

Brian looked towards Mark who shook his head.

"Any chance they noticed a broken decanter?"

She looked through the notes. "Yes. A discovery in the trash, shattered, and some type of liquor inside."

"Did they notice any blood?" Brian asked.

She snickered. "No, they told me there wasn't any blood. They didn't remember anything specific other than some dirty dishes and several take-out containers from town. I'm going to fax copies of the interviews I wasted my time on. They will bring a smile to your day."

"I can't thank you enough for your time on this, agent," Brian said.

She smiled. "I'll admit it's been a few years since I've spent this much time obtaining nothing of use for a case. Good luck, Agent Deeds."

When the screen went blank Mark leaned back in the chair. "Maybe one of you should have gone."

Monique stood up. "I don't think I've ever heard of any agent or office having so much problem with a case like this one."

"I have to agree on that," Dorian said.

Brian looked around the room at the files. "Are we through photographing these?"

"I believe we have one file left," Dorian told him.

Mark stood up and walked over to Brian. "Finish this morning and get everything into evidence. We need to release five agents back to their squads by the end of the week the rest will stay on the case including Dorian and Monique."

"There is still a lot to cover here," she said.

"I understand and know you are far from finished. All of you need to remember at some point this case will go to trial." Mark left the room.

Dorian scratched his head. "You think we'll go to court?"

Brian nodded. "Yes, for now, we work the case check all leads. Eventually, you both will go back to your units leaving me to work the case with little or no help."

"You'll need our reports clear and informative," Dorian said.

"Plus, copies of all our notes," Monique added.

"Is there anything I need to be updated on?"

"Jay Hamilton is still talking to anyone who will listen. His lawyer can't shut him up," Dorian said.

"Does he have an idea where Jonathan is?" Brian asked.

"No, all he's concerned about is placing the blame on someone besides him."

"Why isn't Styles in custody?" Monique asked.

"I would imagine the CACV is going to make sure they have a clear and tight case. It will take them time to go through those files. Mark informed me the information including photographs goes back almost half a century. If you think our case is big wait until the indictments begin, especially on the politicians," Brian told her.

"The photographs were enough for me," she said.

"Styles will not be spending the rest of his life in prison alone. It appears Jonathan intended to use those files as blackmail for some future situation."

"You're thinking of a political future," Dorian said.

Brian nodded then turned to see Leesa laughing as she handed him the faxes from Agent Gardner. He gave the stack of papers to Monique.

"I can't handle any more good news this morning. You read these and see if anyone in town is worth speaking with again. Dorian run upstairs to Arthur's office and get a copy of the report Styles filed with them."

"What are you thinking?" Dorian asked.

"I'm not sure. I want to know why he believes Jonathan has been kidnapped and by whom."

Brian left the conference room, heading towards Mark's office. He knocked on the door frame before entering. "Got a minute."

"Come in."

He sat down. "How was your Thanksgiving?"

"Not bad, I understand you enjoyed some bayou food and entertainment."

"Monique's family knows how to entertain and the food, well you know how good it can be. I received your recommendations on the complaints. Honestly, I expected some time off."

Mark grinned. "This is your first case here, we all make mistakes. God knows I've made a few in my career. Anything I need to know about besides Styles filing a kidnapping report with Arthur Johnson?"

"Charlie left yesterday for Colorado."

"I suppose she'll be having coffee with the sheriff weekly," Mark said.

"I guess, without an agent there it'll be his word she's there."

"I don't believe Agent Gardner will be interested in going back and setting up surveillance for us anytime in the future."

They could hear Monique coming down the hallway laughing.

"It sounds like you have work to do," Mark said.

"Were you serious about sending someone to Colorado?" Brian asked.

Mark raised an eyebrow.

"I'll look through them with her and see if there is anything worth another interview."

"Good idea," Mark told him.

Monique met him outside Mark's doorway. "I do not know how Agent Gardner kept her composure taking these statements."

"Any of them worth contacting?" Brian asked as they entered the break room. He stopped, staring at the sight of an empty table. "Where is all the food?"

Monique sat down at the table. "Didn't people eat in Florida?"

"Yes, but not devour it so quickly."

"Welcome back to Texas. From reading the first few interviews I wouldn't be comfortable asking any of them to repeat their statements."

"Let me guess, multiple descriptions of Jonathan, no one can remember what he was wearing."

"No, actually they were exceptionally descriptive of his clothing and physical attributes. The issue I find is the multiple versions of him. Let me read you a couple of them."

"I can't wait to hear them," he told her.

"The mayor described Mr. Edwards as a well-dressed individual with a neatly trimmed beard and bald head. Agent Gardner noted the strong smell of alcohol on the mayor's breath. Then a couple of brothers Tim and Cletus Boots told her Jonathan donned a pair of overalls and waders helping them feed their eighty hogs."

"Jonathan Edwards wading in hog crap. I would believe him having a three-martini afternoon with the mayor first. Is there anyone we might want to interview again? What about Charlie, did anyone see her?"

"I have a couple of individuals who commented on how she seemed overdressed."

"In what way?" Brian inquired.

"One lady thought she seemed to flaunt her wealth in the designer clothes and flashy big diamond."

"I bet they appreciated the money she spent," he said.

"According to credit card charges, she spent money for food, gifts, liquor and at a hair salon," Monique said.

"What about the sheriff?"

"The sheriff was too busy to speak with Agent Gardner because there is real work to do in his town," she said, continuing to laugh.

"Do any of the reports have similar or exact descriptions of Jonathan?"

Monique looked through them again. "None that I can find."

"Do you know what I'm thinking?"

"That no one actually saw or spoke with him," she answered.

"Yes. A type of group psychosis."

"How is something like that possible? Someone must have seen him."

"I don't believe they did, since all the different descriptions do not match him. Charlie and Dani simply made his presence bigger than life to these people, so in their minds, they saw him."

"Why?"

"You tell me? Maybe he didn't want to be there and refused to go into town."

"Or he wasn't there, to begin with," she said.

"Are there any references to Charlie's injuries after Sunday from anyone?"

"I didn't see any, all these cover the week leading up to Sunday. No one saw her after the incident."

"Charlie Edwards will need to be put in the back of our files for now."

"You aren't convinced she isn't involved, are you?" she asked.

"As I have said before, something doesn't feel right about all of this. If she's involved, the evidence will present itself," he answered.

"What if it doesn't?"

"Then she's just another victim of her husband. Regardless, there is still a lot of work ahead of us."

CHAPTER THIRTY-SEVEN

Clean Up
Tuesday

A light dusting of snow greeted the twins as they returned to Estes Park. They spent Thanksgiving weekend shopping and driving different vehicles. Charlie decided the Land Rover would be the best vehicle for the mountains. Charlie smiled as Dani called Luke through the onboard computer system to let him know they were about an hour away. She ran a hand over the flannel shirt, happy to make decisions on the clothes she wanted to wear. As she turned into the gate of the farm, the car slowed. The sheriff's Jeep sat in front of the house.

Dani reached out touching Charlie's arm. "I promise you, everything is fine. You'll see."

The smell of fresh pine, snow, and smoke made both of them smile exiting the vehicle.

Luke walked out of Dani's front door followed by Koda who knock Dani down. "Welcome home. What can I do to help you, ladies?"

"Koda, come here boy," Charlie called and was equally greeted with jumps and wet licks.

Luke helped Dani up and gave her a friendly hug. "It's good to be home."

"Sheriff," Charlie said, sticking out her hand.

"It's Luke, and good to have you back."

"I'm really sorry about all this crap with the FBI," Dani said, pointing to the back of the Land Rover.

Luke joined them grabbing sacks and luggage. "It's not a problem. New vehicle?"

Charlie smiled at him. "A Mercedes doesn't have a lot of use in the snow."

"It looks like you two bought out a couple of stores coming home. I've got coffee brewing inside."

Dani smiled when the fire crackled as they entered. "Appreciate the warm welcome."

Luke placed the sacks on the couch. "Everybody's been asking when you were coming home."

"We had to agree to be checked on like children before I could leave the state," Charlie said, filling cups for them. She then pulled a bottle of Baileys from the cabinet, topping off her cup. "Anyone else?"

"Of course," they both said to her.

The three sat down at the kitchen table.

"I've been checking the Houston news on my computer. It sounds like you've been through quite a mess," Luke told them.

"It's nothing compared to being in the city," Dani said.

"I'm not a fan of Agent Deeds. He sent an agent from Denver up here interviewing folks and checking on the place you rented." He laughed. "I never spoke with her but heard the woman left town with a handful of nothing."

"Since you are going to be my babysitter, any particular way I should report to you?" Charlie asked.

Luke emptied his cup of coffee and leaned back in the chair. "Looks like you're reporting just fine to me. I'll send a short email weekly to him. What he doesn't know won't hurt him or us."

"Anything interesting, happen in town while I was gone?"

"We had a storm come through with an unusual amount of wind. Some stores in town were damaged, you might want to run up and check the processor."

"We'll settle in here then head up the hill," Dani said.

"I need to head back to town." He stood, picking up his coat.

The twins followed him outside. "Luke, thank you," Charlie said.

"A pleasure, Charlie. See you two later in the week. Come by the office anytime."

Dani wrapped an arm around her sister as he drove away. "See, I told you everything will be fine."

Charlie looked up at the mountains. "I'm happy to be back and might never leave."

"One day, I'll scratch off a big winner and build a new house up the hill."

"Hopefully with more than one bedroom," Charlie added.

"It's the best spot on my land. I guess we should drive up and see if the building is still standing."

"We can unpack later, let's go," Charlie said, throwing the keys to her.

Dani drove up the hill, seeing pieces of the processor scattered along the road. "This doesn't look good."

They stopped short of where the burn barrels should have been standing, both lost for words at the sight as they got out of the Land Rover. There wasn't much left of the building, three of the four walls collapsed along with the roof. Dani took a moment to look around for any equipment outside the building.

Charlie patted her on the shoulder. "The stretcher's sitting up the hill."

"Do you see the barrels?"

"I think they're under the roof," Charlie said, pointing.

This is a mess and a blessing." She moved away, turning on her cell phone. "Tim, I need some help up at the processor. Yeah, the wind tore it all to hell. Can you be here, say eight in the morning? Anything you can sell for scrap or use at the farm is yours."

Charlie stood next to her sister. "Is there much still in there?"

"I didn't have time to clear out the heavier equipment. The Boots brothers will be happy to take it all away to sell for scrap."

"I guess sleeping in tomorrow will have to wait," Charlie said.

"You'll have plenty of time to do that, this needs to be done before Brian sends someone else out here to snoop around."

• • •

Wednesday Morning

Dani layered up this morning knowing it would be cold up the hill. She filled two thermoses full of coffee to take with her, adding a little whiskey to the one for the brothers. She drove the Ford in case Tim and Cletus needed additional space for the pieces. They'd need to pick up everything on the road and in the fields. A storm like this could mean a difficult winter for the town or maybe a fluke of Mother Nature. She walked into the bedroom where Koda slept on a pillow next to Charlie. He raised his head and then laid back down. The chill in the truck was almost gone when the rattle of an animal trailer made her check the rear-view mirror.

She parked where the burn barrels once stood allowing room for their trailer to be backed closer to the building. The older model diesel truck hauler belched black smoke as Tim turned the engine off. Tim and Cletus hopped out in overalls with thermal tops and no coats. They were happy to tear down the building and take all the scrap for extra pocket money. She'd have them take any of the wood back down, placing it at the front gate. It would be used for the bonfire in a few weeks.

She stepped out of the truck handing a thermos to them. "I can't thank you two enough for helping with this."

Cletus opened the thermos and grinned. "You sure know how to start the morning out right, Dani." He took a drink and passed it to his brother.

"Damn, that wind made a mess out of this, didn't it?" Tim asked.

"Yes, it helped, too," she answered.

"Best to get this down now before another storm comes through," Cletus said, taking a sledgehammer from the trailer. He walked over moving a part of the roof away. "Anything you want outta here, Dani?"

"If you can find both the burn barrels, I'd like to save them. Save any wood for the bonfire and place it at the front gate where I can load it later," she answered.

"We'll stop by and pick it up on the way into town, adding it to ours. I hear it's going to be a big one this year," Tim told her, then put on a pair of heavy work gloves.

"Glad to know my contribution will add to the festivities."

"Did you come out and use the welder?" Tim asked.

"No. I had to leave town for a while. The invite is still open right?"

"Anytime. We moved it over in that little building by Blossom's pen," Cletus told her.

"I'll be out in a few days," Dani told them.

They worked all morning, dismantling the processor, and thankfully loaded everything on the trailer. Dani made another coffee and whiskey run keeping the men motivated. Around three p.m., Cletus and Tim loaded the freezer in the back of their truck. They intended to use it as a feed trough since it didn't have a motor.

"Dani, we appreciate your donation of this scrap. Things have been a little tight, so we appreciate the extra money," Tim admitted, slightly embarrassed.

Dani frowned at him. "Why didn't you say something? It was a good year for me, and I'm always happy to help my neighbors. I can't have you going without food."

"This will help out. We'll get a fair price up in Cheyenne," Cletus said.

"I got something in the car for the sheriff. Would you mind giving it to him?" Tim asked, grinning.

"Only if there's one for me."

After they covered and tied everything down on the trailer, Tim pulled a small box from the cab of the truck handing it to her.

"Make sure Luke gets his," Cletus told her.

Dani nodded and placed the box in her truck before walking around the empty area. One day there would be a nice home here, not too big, one comfortable for her, Koda, and maybe Charlie.

She drove back to the house, smiling at Luke's Jeep. Dani took her gloves and scarf off as she entered the house.

"The Boot's brothers helped you tear down the processor I see," he said.

"No way to save it, and I sure don't want to wait for another storm to spread it across the whole damn mountain," Dani explained, warming up at the fireplace.

"Charlie said everything up there is a mess. I hoped you might save it, and it brings a tear to my eye you won't be processing anymore." He looked across the table at Charlie. "Your sister is the best damn butcher in town."

"I've heard this from several people."

"I don't have the time and what's left of the building is stacked up at the front gate for the New Year's bonfire," Dani said.

"I understand, but it doesn't mean I still can't complain. Well, better run, wanted to make sure Charlie was all settled in." He stood, heading towards the door.

"There are a couple of items in my truck for you, on the floorboard. Leave one for me," Dani said, smiling at him.

Nodding at her. "See you two later."

"You look cold," Charlie said.

"The Boots brothers showed up without coats."

Charlie shivered. "What were they wearing, it's freezing outside?"

"Long sleeve thermal tops and overalls. They were happy to take everything with them. The wood out by the gate will be for the New Year's bonfire."

"That sounds like fun," Charlie said.

"According to them, it's going to be big this year," Dani said. She looked in the pot on the stove. "Tomato soup?"

Charlie nodded. "Thought you'd like a grilled cheese sandwich to go with it. Sorry, I didn't get up and go with you. Koda and I decided to sleep in. I found the cat food and filled the bowls in the garage, put fresh water out too."

Dani turned on the burner beneath the cast-iron skillet. "It's fine, everything is torn down and gone. Didn't need to be explaining why my clone was out there. I'll be doing a lot of that at the bonfire to people who didn't meet you the first time."

"Any plans for the rest of the day?" Charlie asked.

"I need your help to straighten up the garage. José's wife and a couple of family members will be here tomorrow to work. Playtime is over, back to work. I will be happy to have an extra hand."

"It will be nice to stay busy and keep my mind off Houston," Charlie told her.

"We need to get the online orders filled and shipped first. We'll restock the shop orders in town later. The holidays will be busy in town and I need a product for them to sell on the shelves. It appears the end of the year will be a good one for me. One more thing, we need to run to the hog farm this week."

Charlie made a sad face. "I'd love to go, unfortunately, I have an appointment that day to binge-watch a series on Netflix."

"Oh, which one?" Dani asked.

"Any of them to keep me from smelling like those pigs again," Charlie answered.

"I guess you're excused then." Dani walked over to the window and looked at the mountains. "Christmas will be here soon and a better year coming for both of us. Keep to the plan."

CHAPTER THIRTY-EIGHT

New Year's Bonfire
Charlie couldn't believe how fast the month had flown by for her. Dani's hemp business had taken most of their time since returning home. They spent Christmas with José's family enjoying the food and music at his home. It seems the town accepted her into the community as one of their own. The upcoming Wednesday night celebration for the city built to a feverish pitch. The Boots brothers picked up the lumber adding it to theirs and took it to the bonfire location.

On New Year's Eve, Dani insisted they leave early to experience the entire bonfire festival atmosphere. They drove into a huge field around six p.m., several individuals directed cars to parking spots. Koda was dressed in his harness and New Year's outfit. Charlie's eyes grew wide with excitement at the carnival sounds, including lights and music as they exited the Land Rover.

Charlie smiled looking at Dani. "I wondered why we were here so early."

"This is one of the biggest nights of the year, in Estes Park," Dani said.

"Oh my gosh, food trucks, vendors, tell me there will be liquor," Charlie said.

"There's pretty much anything you can imagine out here tonight."

They walked around speaking to people she'd come to know over the last month. Children ran over to love and pet Koda. Charlie smiled each time someone called her Dani, an issue they had dealt with since first grade. She relaxed, taking in the sights and smells of the festival, watching families and young couples enjoying the end of the year hoping for greater things to come in the new. Everyone seemed to be filled with a renewed spirit. The whole town of Estes Park and surrounding cities were there to celebrate.

Dani took her arm. "Follow me, you are about to taste the best mulled wine in Colorado." They walked over to a small truck where Dani purchased two copper cups filled with a dark steaming liquid.

They found a tree and leaned up against it. "This is wonderful," Charlie said, sipping the liquid.

Dani reached down petted Koda and gave him a treat. "I thought you might enjoy a cup or five." She took a couple of sips. "I have something to show you. Do you remember when I made the trip to the hog farm a couple of weeks ago?"

"Yes."

Dani reached into her coat pocket and pulled out a plastic bag handing it to her sister. "Look at these."

Charlie took it, opening the top to run a finger over the six items inside. She shrugged. "What are they?"

Dani looked around their location before speaking. "I thought they were diamonds until they didn't burn."

"I thought you said diamonds would burn."

"Real diamonds do, these are something else," Dani told her.

"What are they?"

"Since these shine-like diamonds I would say they are high quality cubic zirconia. They crush but do not burn. These few are all that are left, I wanted to show you first before destroying them."

Charlie raised an eyebrow. "Where are these from?"

The watch and his wedding ring."

"No, I bought his ring."

Dani sipped the wine still looking around them. "Well, at some point he replaced it."

"I wonder if my jewelry is fake?"

"If it is, you'll be hearing from Brian. One more thing, did you know Jon had more than one life insurance policy on you?"

"How many?" Charlie asked.

"Kiara said three, the premiums were substantially increased the week of his party. All with double indemnities for accidental death. It seems you were right about his plan to kill you," Dani said and finished her wine.

Charlie stepped back. "After my death he would collect the insurance and my inheritance. Did Kiara say where the information came from?"

"She wasn't willing to divulge anything further."

"What about the metal clips, any idea about them?" Charlie asked.

"I made a sketch, instead of photographing them, making note of the numbers. We'll go to the library and look through some medical books. We sure don't need to be using any internet searches on them."

"Agreed. What about the rest?"

Dani chuckled. "Everything else is unidentifiable, computer parts, his wedding band, and watch pieces, all laying at the bottom of the outhouse. I understand it was backfilled two days ago."

Charlie gagged. "I appreciate you leaving me at the house that day."

"Not a problem. How long before Jonathan can be declared dead, legally?" Dani asked.

"Seven years, according to Kiara."

"You need to remember the FBI has an investment in this and might object," Dani reminded her.

"I hadn't thought about them interfering, you could be right. I'll let Kiara handle all of it when the time comes," Charlie said.

"Did Brian ever say how much money is involved?" Dani asked.

"No. Kiara told me the information from the district attorney's office said it's hundreds of millions."

Dani nodded toward someone coming their way, ceasing the conversation.

"Happy New Year's ladies," Luke said.

"Same to you," Dani said.

Charlie turned around, smiling. "Any New Year's resolutions, Luke?"

He laughed. "No. I gave up on resolutions years ago, could never live up to them."

A deputy ran up to them. "Sheriff, we need a hand."

"The mayor?" Luke asked.

"Yes, sir."

"I keep hoping one year he will not celebrate so hard until after he makes the end-of-year speech," Luke told them.

"He was staying close to the mulled wine truck," Dani teased.

"I'm sure it isn't the only beverage truck he has visited this evening. Excuse me ladies, but duty calls."

"See you next year," Dani told him as he walked away waving at them. "How about another, sis?"

"I'll buy this time."

They strolled back to the stand, refilling their mugs.

Dani made a circling motion. "Seven years is a long time."

"I'm hoping it's long enough for the FBI to forget me and place Jon on their most wanted list."

"It's going to be tight at the house for a while. I spoke with Tim and Cletus about building an additional bedroom."

Charlie smiled. "I don't think that's necessary."

Dani gave a concerned look at her. "You're not going back to Houston, are you?"

The loudspeaker interrupted their conversation. "Good evening, everyone, gather around it's almost that time," The mayor said slurring his words slightly.

Dani, Charlie, and Koda joined the rest of the city, listening to the mayor's obligatory winter bonfire speech. It was a cold evening with a perfectly clear starry night. The town had worried for no reason that it might snow and keep people home. When the countdown began, Dani placed an arm around Charlie.

"I have a New Year's gift, something that will help with your remodeling," Charlie said, giving Dani a scratch ticket. "Who knew I'd be so lucky."

Dani looked at the large ticket win. "Damn, I should have let you scratch them off all these years. Looks like the house up the hill is going to be a reality after all."

"Maybe enough left over to buy some extra land," Charlie said.

"We'll see, remember building up here isn't like in Texas. A lot of hoops to jump through. I have something for you, too." She handed Charlie a small decorative silk sack.

She opened it allowing their mother's ring to slide into her hand. "How?"

Dani smiled. "Kiara of course."

Charlie slipped it on her right ring finger. "Best gift ever, next to being here."

"Three, two, one, Happy New Year!" The mayor yelled. A huge flame engulfed the wood and a new year officially arrived.

The twins stood with an arm around each other joining the town and singing, *Auld Lang Syne*. Koda joined in with a loud howl. They tapped the two copper mugs together, watching as smoke and embers rose above the fire. The last evidence of Jonathan Styles Edwards III ever existing drifted towards the night sky.

CHAPTER THIRTY-NINE

No Longer My Problem

Lonnie Walker walked out of the Poop Deck bar on the Seawall. He stopped at a liquor store and purchased a bottle of Johnny Walker Red leaving without the change. The last few months had been difficult ones since Jonathan disappeared leaving family and friends to suffer the embarrassment of his actions. The FBI scoured every corner, searching from Texas to Nevada for Lonnie, thinking he might have all the answers. After his friends decided he'd become a liability with the FBI and law enforcement looking for him, cheap motels and fast food became his savior. Though not his first choice, but acceptable when you're hiding and living on borrowed money.

He never thought after moving to Las Vegas he'd come back to the bad memories in Texas. His loser father spent more time in jail than at home, leaving his mother to raise a family on little money. Bad values were never easy to erase and Lonnie discovered he had a talent for gambling and began to run book. He eventually made enough money to buy a small condo and live comfortably on the outskirts of Vegas.

His association with Jonathan Edwards is what brought him to Texas and now filled him with concern and regret. When they first met, it was a non-stop party of gambling, drugs, and women. His infidelity didn't affect their friendship or business ventures. Most of their escapades were small until a casino off the strip became available to purchase. Lonnie's off-handed comment during a high rollers game to an individual who seemed to know about the sale set things in motion. A few days later he received a call to meet and discuss the terms of sale. What should have been an easy purchase ended in a problem he never wanted.

Lonnie stopped at Kempner Park, noticing the security guard leaving with a lovely young woman heading towards the Seawall. He slid the bottle through the gate before jumping the fence rewarding himself with a long pull. Usually, the security guard would be more alert of trespassers, but it was after all New Year's Eve and the party would be at the pier. Any place would be more interesting than watching for drunks cutting through the park to set off fireworks.

He walked up to the building and sat down on the steps, pulling a folded piece of paper from his shirt pocket. Lonnie smiled thinking about the twins. Charlie and Dani always treated him decent when they were kids in school, even gave him a pair of shoes once. The least he could do would be to help Charlie and take a little of the suspicion away from her in Jonathan's disappearance. He read over the letter, folded and placed it back in his pocket.

His and Jonathan's situation was dire. They owed money to the wrong person and he refused to end up buried in the desert or worse.

"There'll be no witness protection for Lonnie Walker," he said taking another drink, waiting for the liquor to stop burning. In a few moments, all these problems would no longer exist for him.

The countdown to midnight could be heard blocks away as he emptied the bottle throwing it out into the grass. As the fireworks burst in the air, the gunshot added to the festivities of those walking by the park.

"Did you hear that?" the woman asked her friend.

"Ignore it, just some kids popping firecrackers in the park. They do it every year."

• • •

FBI Office Houston
00:45 a.m.
Brian checked his watch realizing he'd missed the New Year by almost an hour and would have several missed calls from his parents and Monique. He would celebrate at home with a beer toast and a call of apology later in the morning. He walked down the hallway turning off

the office lights and locking the door before stepping into the main foyer. As Brian reached his car in the garage the phone buzzed.

"Deeds."

"Brian, this is Dorian. Are you celebrating?"

"No, heading home from the office for a late New Year's toast with a can of Guinness."

"Bummer. I have some news for you, Lonnie Walker has been located."

"Good, I'll go back inside and wait for someone to bring him in for questioning. Is he talking?"

"Not anymore, he shot himself at Kempner Park in Galveston."

Brian cursed silently. "You're sure it's a suicide?"

"According to the security guard who discovered the body."

"Where the hell was the guard?"

"I guess celebrating on the seawall with everyone else in Galveston, although he didn't admit to that when asked. When the investigator for the medical examiner's office discovered a note in his shirt pocket he called. The letter is addressed to you, Brian."

"Me? I don't know the man."

"Well, I guess he's been watching the news because your last name is on it. I thought you should know and give Mark a heads up."

"Anything else from the scene I should tell Mark when I wake him up?"

"The investigator read the note, it absolves Charlie from any involvement in the fraud and Jonathan's disappearance."

Brian rubbed his forehead and leaned against the car. "Keep that information to yourself for now. Anything written on that paper will need to be confirmed."

"Understood, I asked the investigator to do the same."

"Guess I should make that call, see you in a few days," Brian said and hung up.

He looked up at the concrete ceiling in the garage not believing the one lead who might know the location of Jonathan, is dead. The abused wife, who he still believed might be a suspect or accomplice, has received another gift. The first, retaining the best and most expensive defense attorney in Houston. Kiara will have a field day with this information and make it impossible for him to question Charlie in the future. Second, a free pass from the judge to go stay with her sister in Colorado with little or no supervision from the local sheriff.

Without knowing the full context of the note, he could see the New Year's coming events. Styles would now go full nuclear on the agents investigating Jonathan's disappearance. The possibility of organized crime involvement places this case, including the pornography case, in four different sections of the office. He knew at some point they would all be forced into one group. It would be the only way to avoid the loss or the withholding of information everyone needed. Brian knew a section chief would be in charge to run point on all cases and make the hard calls. The political schmoozing and in-house fighting will begin once the first word of a group task force is mentioned. Thankfully, upper management would make the decision and he wanted no part of the upcoming blood bath.

All this news and subjection wasn't the best way to start a new year. Brian believed the fraud case might become one of those unable to clear due to unforeseen circumstances. He knew eventually his team would be disbanded with little or insufficient leads and go cold. Was it possible Jonathan planned and succeeded with the perfect crime? Is he hiding, waiting for the right moment to fade into oblivion with his money and wife? Only time would tell. He scrolled through his contacts, found the number needed, and then pressed the call button.

"This better be important, Brian."

"It is, I have news on Lonnie Walker."

ABOUT THE AUTHOR

After a 36-year career as a high-risk labor and delivery nurse and two decades as a travel nurse, the retiree settled in Galveston Island. As a former Sergeant in a multi-city crime unit investigating homicides, the author has a passion for writing mystery-thriller novels that revolve around murder. She began writing in 2009 while working as a full-time travel nurse and has since published five full novels, including the *Look for Me* series (historical fiction) and *Archidamus and Legacy of Lies* (mystery/thriller). Her works have won multiple awards, including the Grand Prize for *Chatelaine* in the Chanticleer Book Awards for *Find Me Again*. Her novellas and flash fiction works have also gained recognition, and she was a runner-up in the Winter 2022 Fiction Contest by WOW Women on Writing.

NOTE FROM JANET K. SHAWGO

Word-of-mouth is crucial for any author to succeed. If you enjoyed *A Change in Destiny, Dark Choices*, please leave a review online—anywhere you are able. Even if it's just a sentence or two. It would make all the difference and would be very much appreciated.

Thanks!
Janet K. Shawgo

We hope you enjoyed reading this title from:

BLACK ROSE writing

www.blackrosewriting.com

Subscribe to our mailing list – *The Rosevine* – and receive **FREE** books, daily deals, and stay current with news about upcoming releases and our hottest authors.
Scan the QR code below to sign up.

Already a subscriber? Please accept a sincere thank you for being a fan of Black Rose Writing authors.

View other Black Rose Writing titles at www.blackrosewriting.com/books and use promo code **PRINT** to receive a **20% discount** when purchasing.

Printed in the USA
CPSIA information can be obtained
at www.ICGtesting.com
CBHW030342300424
7753CB00001B/11